DON'T TELL

PAUL WILLIAMS

BLOODHOUND
— BOOKS —

Print ISBN 978-1-913942-10-6

ALSO BY PAUL WILLIAMS

Twelve Days

Thanks to Crime Righters who fact-checked the Sunshine Coast police procedures in this novel.

1

SUNSHINE BEACH. SATURDAY, 4AM

He parked against the verge, backed up against the culvert, and unlatched the back of the flatbed. He had cased this place out before, so knew he was invisible to any residents who might be up this early. Satisfied he was alone, he dragged the tarpaulin off the back and dropped it on the road by the concrete drain.

To anyone watching, he looked like a typical Australian tradesman sorting out his load after a job, or preparing for one that day. And tradies were common in this ritzy area of Sunshine Beach: the residents were always needing extensions to their multi-million-dollar houses, or porches or decks or kitchens, so he would not be out of place here on this street. It might seem a little odd to any observer that he was wearing latex gloves. But no one was watching, not at this hour, not at the end of a cul-de-sac where he was screened off by thick vegetation out of the reach of surveillance cameras.

The drain was wide here, enough to squeeze a body through.

Over the grassy mound, he could hear the roar of the ocean, and smell the brine. No moon, but the stars were a splash of white across the sky. Sunrise was coming soon. A magical time.

He smiled as he read: *No dumping – drains to ocean*, the sign said. A picture of a fish.

All he had to do now was unwrap her and slip her into the drain. But he could not resist one last look. He peeled away the tarpaulin and the plastic wrap from her head and peered at her face. In the rosy pre-dawn light, he could pick out her features: blood-matted hair, pale cheeks, snub nose, full lips. She was still warm. He cupped her chin, pressed her bloodied eyelids closed – though they sprung open and her eyes stared at him.

'Goodbye, Mary,' he whispered. 'You were perfect. And so healing for me.'

He now unwrapped the rest of her body – just like a Greek statue of Venus, he observed – and rolled her off the plastic into the drain so that she did not touch the concrete. She fell into the dark opening, but her arm caught, as if she was trying to hold herself back. He had to give her a shove and she slid into the sluice, a little stiffly, and he heard her tumble down. He had done his homework. Just a week ago he had tested the drain with a log the same weight as a young woman's body and had also checked the weather. It was forecast to rain today. A good old Christmas thunderstorm was predicted, and she would be washed into the ocean, dragged out by the tide, churned and battered against the rocks surrounding Paradise Cave.

He climbed up onto the grass bank and looked over the edge of the cliff to where the storm drain opened out into the rocky bay. If she were ever found, any clues about her murderer would be gone. She would be bait for sharks, but in a way he hoped not. He wanted people to see his handiwork – what he had done to her. He wanted men to secretly admire him, envy him; those weak men who did not act on their dark wishes. His actions spoke louder than words. *Break the rules. Follow your inner desires. And always cover your trail.*

A kookaburra, which had been sleeping on the electricity

wires above him began cackling, followed by another, and another. They sounded like a bunch of madmen. 'Go ahead, laugh,' he said. Dawn was coming. '*Adios*,' he whispered to the crashing waves below. 'It was really fun, wholesome fun, wasn't it? Maybe your little sister will be next. Or your school friend. What do you reckon?'

He visualised her tumbling out to sea, snagging on the rocks by the headland and then being pulled out to deep water, the waves shredding her flesh, the fish nibbling on her until she was all bones. No trace of his fingerprints, DNA, anything. For now, his hunger was assuaged, all was at peace, and that ache in him was eased.

The sky had changed from red to pink to orange and now silver, and it was time to go. He was hungry. Noosa was a bastard of a place to be – a major tourist resort town but so environmentally correct the council had banned most fast-food chains to boost local boutiquey businesses. There was only one McDonald's here. He drove to Noosaville, ordered a bacon and egg McMuffin and coffee, ate it on the way back to the hotel.

2

ATWELL HOME, LAKE WEYBA. SUNDAY, MIDDAY

S he would never have found it if she hadn't dropped her purse. She had borrowed Steve's car to go Christmas shopping in the Plaza so she could fit the larger items in the back. But as she stepped out of the driver's seat, her bag caught on the handbrake and spilled open.

Chunky fifty-cent and one-dollar coins, credit cards and business cards scattered on the floor, under the seats, in between the gear lever and handbrake, and she scrabbled to retrieve them. She collected all her coins, credit cards, and– What was this under the driver's seat? An earring. She picked it up between two fingers and held it up to the light. It was beautiful. A gold earring for a pierced ear – a glittering disc inlaid with three different sized diamonds, or fake diamonds, she couldn't tell. She would never wear anything like this. She scrabbled under the seat to find the matching one, then stopped.

Stupid me, she thought. *Why would there be two?* Her heart beat fast. She stared at the earring again. Who had been in her husband's car recently? She thought of her friends, their acquaintances. Had any of her friends ever worn an earring like this? No. She would have noticed: it was that striking. Her hands trembled as she placed it in her purse.

She climbed out of the driver's seat, slammed the door, opened the back and collected her shopping bags. But her mind was racing. There would, of course, be some simple explanation.

She pushed open the front door, dumped the shopping in her room. 'Steve?' she called. 'Where are you?'

No answer. She hid the parcels away – presents for her sister, his parents. She wanted to get something special for him this Christmas but hadn't found anything yet besides the usual socks and underpants. He liked 'practical' gifts and was the kind of man who didn't seem to need anything or have any interests or hobbies beyond his job as a commercial building contractor and his music, which he did not share with her or talk about.

She found him by the pool poring over his laptop. He closed it quickly when she approached, brightened up and smiled. 'Good day shopping in hell?' He reached up to kiss her. She knew he hated the Plaza. But instead of kissing him, she stood in front of him and opened her purse, pulled out the earring and held it up to him between two fingers. He squinted at it. The three diamonds glinted in the sun. He smiled again. 'Nice! Is that what you got? For you? Or me?' he joked.

She did not smile back. She stared at him to see his reaction. Looking for guilt. Or some explanation – maybe she expected something like, *Oh, you found it! My secretary who got a lift with me yesterday lost one of her earrings.* But no.

'I found this in your car, Steve.'

He looked puzzled when he saw her grim mouth. Took it gingerly between two fingers, examined it. 'I've never seen it before in my life.'

She could tell that he knew nothing about it, was as bewildered as she was. Or else he was a good actor.

'Under the front seat, in your car. Any idea where it came from?'

He peered at it.

She dangled it in the light.

'Isn't it one of yours? A missing one of a pair?'

She shook her head. 'You know I don't wear earrings like this, Steve.'

He frowned. 'You sure you found it in my car? Could it have stuck to your sweater, your dress? Fallen off you, perhaps?'

She shook her head. 'Did you give some woman a lift? Take someone home from work?'

He scratched his head. 'No. Sorry. I have no idea where it came from.' That was the end of it. End of subject. 'Sorry, Carrie, I do have to get this report done by close of business. Do you mind?' He opened his laptop, and his attention slipped away.

She turned away from him and went inside to unpack the groceries and sort out the presents. Once in her bedroom she took out the earring and looked at it again. If Steve was trying to hide something, she would have seen guilt written all over his face.

Hide something? Why would she think that? What would he be trying to hide?

She placed the earring in the drawer of her bedside table.

Later, she prepared the evening meal, took a walk around the lake at sunset as usual, chatted with neighbours on the path who were walking their dogs.

Mr Johnson, the man being pulled along by two bull mastiffs, and who looked like a bulldog himself, nodded to her. He was sweating profusely. 'Hot enough for you, Carrie?'

'Sure is.'

She chatted to Marg, the neighbour who was also out for a walk. Marg was the busybody of the neighbourhood and kept her up to date with all the gossip, whether she wanted to or not:

today it was the new people who had moved into number 43 who had lit a fire in their backyard and filled the neighbourhood with smoke; those campers who had left litter all over the lake front; how she had to confront Mr Johnson who never cleans up his dog's poop and now he doesn't speak to her anymore. And... did she know that Mr Kidman has left his wife?

No, she didn't, but then she and Steve kept to themselves. She found her excuse to leave, and returned home, checked the supper simmering on the stove.

Steve was still busy on his report. He normally helped her, often made supper for her, but today he called out from his office that he was putting together a quote for some new project and had to have it by that evening.

'Okay, I got it. I have some leftover curry.'

But at suppertime he had not yet appeared. She peered into his office. His eyes looked tired. 'Shall we eat together, or...?' Steve did not look up, just grunted, so she brought him his supper and ate hers watching the 6.30 SBS news.

He startled her a while later, when he hurried into the living room, car keys and phone in hand, dressed to go out.

'Where are you going? It's Sunday night. And I thought you had a deadline.'

He held up his briefcase. 'We decided to meet tonight and discuss the new project. Boys' night out.'

She heard his car drive off and for the first time in a long while felt some sinking ache in her stomach, an old lack of self-worth kicking in. She watched the sunset on the deck, covered the pool, and then watched more TV. Tidied up her bedroom, scooped some dirty laundry into the washer.

Before bed, she opened the drawer of her bedside table and took out the earring again. She tried to imagine its owner. Some pretty young thing. Or some new secretary at work. *It's nothing,* she thought.

She had a big day the next day at work – but she did not sleep well, waiting for the sound of the front door, for the assurance that Steve had returned. A mosquito had got in through the netting and buzzed around her ear. She sat up at eleven, turned on the light, tried to find the mosquito. Eventually caught it and slammed it against the wall with the palm of her hand, leaving a bright red smear of blood.

She turned off the light, pulled the sheet over her head, but she still could not sleep.

Steve was not home yet. He had made his bedroom in the office, so as not to disturb her when he came in late at night. And he snored, so they had come to this arrangement, that she would have the bedroom to herself – some nights. Most nights, in fact.

He arrived home at around midnight and she got up and waited for him in the kitchen. She heard him tiptoeing to the stairs. Then he turned, startled to see her at the kitchen door in her dressing gown, her arms folded. 'Hi, Carrie. Sorry, did I wake you? I tried to be as quiet as I–'

'You're so late...'

'I always have to hang around until the last one goes. You know, I'm responsible for– and when Joe gets talking... but it was a good meeting. Productive. The new project is a go.'

It sounded like an excuse. As if he was guilty of something. From where she stood, she smelled the acrid synthesis of perfume and booze. The alcohol she was almost okay with, but that hint of nauseating cloying scent? She drew in her breath. 'Some perfume.'

He sniffed his sleeve. 'Is it?' He sauntered over to her and attempted to hug her, but she pulled back, looked into his eyes for signs of... what? Guilt?

'You know Sarah, she piles on the makeup, perfume, dresses to the nines.'

Yes, she knew Sarah, the middle-aged, sour-faced personal secretary who took care of Steve's appointments. 'Boys' night out, huh?'

He took her hand, but she left it limp. 'You know she always comes along for the meetings. Even if they are also socials.'

She knew. Part social, part business, the company managers insisted on having their meetings in pubs late at night. *Sure.* 'Did she stay out that late too? I thought she had children.'

'No, she left earlier. Just me and the boys stayed on, going over the new airport expansion project. Exciting project. The whole Sunshine Coast is opening up and they want a new runway pronto.'

'Where were you tonight?'

'Coolum Tavern.' He laughed, sniffed his sleeve again. 'I smell it now. It is a bit strong, isn't it? Whew. I should speak to her.'

Surely this was no different to any other night out. But finding the earring had changed things.

3

THERAPIST'S OFFICE, MOOLOOLABA.
MONDAY, MIDDAY

Carrie's long-time therapist, Julienne Van Tonder, was an auburn-haired woman whose office sat above the beach road in Mooloolaba, and Carrie liked that she could sit facing the sea, and stare at the far horizon of the Pacific Ocean as she unloaded her worries, month after month, without burdening her friends, or feeling like she'd revealed too much.

Carrie liked to be self-contained. She was the go-to person for all her friends, the adviser, confidante. She could not lean back on those who leaned on her, however. They were weak-willed, gossip-prone, and judgemental. Julienne was the sympathetic ear that Carrie needed. If anyone knew she was having suspicions about her husband, they'd pounce. Her sister and mother had never taken to Steve, and so today's appointment was timely.

Julienne was the one she could depend on. And her office was only a ten-minute drive from the university where Carrie worked, so she could come here for a lunchtime appointment, and then be back at work by two. Most of the time, these sessions delved into Carrie's past, dealing with her lack of self-worth, her invisibility, how she always let herself be pushed around by people, and Julienne had helped her learn to say no if the request wasn't an *OMG, yes!* Today she began her session by taking out the earring and showing it to Julienne, who took it, held it against the light. It looked dazzling, brightened up the grey room.

'I found it in Steve's car. Under the seat. But he says he's never seen it before.'

'It's striking.'

'That's what I thought,' Carrie said.

'What does this mean to you?'

Carrie stopped staring out at sea and looked into Julienne's eyes. 'That he's having an affair. Which seems impossible. I've never ever seen him looking at another woman. He's not the type.'

'Did he have an explanation for the earring?'

Carrie shook her head. 'He suggested it might have stuck to my clothes. That I might have unwittingly brought it into the car. And then he smelled of perfume when he came home on Sunday night. When I asked him about it, he said it was his secretary's perfume.'

Julienne placed the earring back into Carrie's hand. 'What other explanation could there be, do you think?'

Carrie shrugged and took back the earring. 'Do *you* think he's having an affair?'

'Possibly,' Julienne said.

She buried the earring back in her purse, slid it into her bag and zipped it closed. 'What do I do?'

'Tell him what's worrying you and give him the time to respond.'

'If he is having an affair, I can't imagine him just saying "Yes, Carrie, I'm having an affair". And I still can't imagine him having one. Who would he have an affair with? He's at work all day, every day.'

Julienne sighed. 'Speculation is all you have at the moment. Have the conversation if you can. Otherwise it's all conjecture at this point. Maybe the earring really was just a hanger on someone's clothes, and the perfume was nothing, but you won't know until you talk about it. Has his behaviour changed in any way?'

Carrie thought. 'Maybe. He seems to be more harassed, tired, but also dispirited. Doesn't tick any of the boxes for the behaviour of someone who's having an affair.'

She loved Julienne's discretion, the way she mirrored her own fears and feelings so gently that it felt like a poultice. Julienne nodded. 'Is he away from home much lately – more than usual?'

'Maybe. I feel bad suspecting him. I mean, aside from work he doesn't really have much of a life. He has his man cave, what he calls his "studio" at the bottom of the property, that he retreats to when he has a moment, to play his music. But he's married to his job, always working late – and yeah, away lately more than usual.'

'How are you feeling about that?'

'I don't know. Upset? Lonely? Mad sometimes? So, yep, this is all probably in my head because I'm being triggered. In fact, I'm pretty sure I'm being overly dramatic in my suspicions. I'm feeling neglected, pushed aside. On the periphery of his life. I'll talk to him; see how he reacts.'

Julienne smiled comfortingly. 'You're not being overly dramatic. Anyone in your position would feel exactly what you're feeling. Trust your instincts, intuition here, ask the questions if you can – that takes a lot of guts. Let me know how it goes.'

4

UNIVERSITY OF THE SUNSHINE COAST. MONDAY AFTERNOON

'Steve, are you having an affair? Be honest. It's better if I know than if I find out later.'

Carrie stared into the mirror of the university bathroom as she rehearsed her speech, trying not to let her voice tremble. She looked old all of a sudden. Tired. Unattractive. There had to be another explanation for his behaviour.

The bathroom door opened, and her colleague walked in. 'Hi Natasha.'

'Are you okay?'

'Why?'

'You look a bit stressed.'

'I'm fine. Just need to deal with a few things.'

Natasha put her hand on her shoulder. 'With Larry?'

Larry was the head of school at the university where she worked as a research assistant, a man who made it clear that whatever anyone did was never good enough. Her lack of a clear response was taken as an affirmative by Natasha. 'He makes everyone feel inadequate, it's not just you.'

'It's not Larry.'

'Who?'

She shook her head.

'If you need anyone to talk to, I'm here, Carrie.'

'Thanks, Tash, but I need to face this on my own.'

'I'm here, okay, if you need me. My advice, just say what's on your mind. Don't hold back.'

'I find it really hard.'

'You're always absorbing, Carrie, always taking other people's shit. It would be so good if you just stood up for yourself once and for all. I'd love to see you do that.'

'I'll try.'

They embraced.

All afternoon at work, she rehearsed her speech. *Stand up for yourself. Say what's on your mind. Don't hold back.* The advice was transferable to any situation. But when she drove home, she lost her nerve. Or rather, she decided to watch more closely for a little while – do some investigating of her own.

At home that evening, she could not sit still. She hated herself for doing it, but Steve wouldn't be back for another few hours, so she went through his things. She needed to put his clean clothes there anyway, so she opened the office door and packed them away in the clothes drawers. His office was crowded now because of the desk and computer, bedside table and closet and spare bed.

She suddenly saw how cramped his life here was, while she had the whole bedroom and *en suite* with its large French windows, king-size bed, to herself. Had she driven him out? Had he had enough of her? Was he sleeping here, not just because of his late workaholic nights, or because he snored, but because he stopped loving her? Wanted his space? Maybe, God forbid, had secrets?

Despite his absence, she had to admit she still felt his love, his attention. He was always kind to her, always considerate, just preoccupied, his work grinding him down. She opened the drawers of his desk, rummaged through all his papers. She did not know what she was looking for and was hoping not to find anything. She turned on his computer, but it asked for a log-on password, and she didn't know it. How little of his life she knew! She opened another drawer. What was this? Her heart thudded painfully. Christmas wrapping. A note. *To my dearest Carrie, the love of my life. Merry Christmas.*

She shoved it back again, felt ashamed. Tearful. He was a loving husband and she was just being paranoid. She should stop now. Give him the benefit of the doubt. He was innocent. She tidied up the drawer, so he would not see she had been here. But then, she had to, for argument's sake, keep looking. She opened the last drawer and pulled out a small paper packet labelled *London Souvenirs.*

She opened the packet and pulled out a crinkly square of plastic. A pack of three condoms –Durex Stallion. The condoms had Union Jacks on them. She stared. Was this a present? A souvenir from London from his last visit? For her? She remembered that he had been at a conference there two months ago.

A practical joke, of course. They didn't use condoms, had never used condoms. It was a sore point. They did not need to use any contraception. For years now, they had been trying to have a baby, but even if they made love at peak ovulation, nothing happened. She had been using the rhythm method for a while, but it made no difference when they made love, as she had never conceived. Pregnancy was just not going to happen, and they had decided to focus on their lives as they were, and not spoil the present by wishing for something they might never have.

Durex Stallion. For the enduring ride of your life. Steve had always said he hated condoms and was glad he didn't have to use them. Why would he give her condoms for Christmas?

Unless the condoms were not meant for her.

The obvious explanation is sometimes the right one.

Her heart felt like a stone. She placed the pack in the bag, folded it tight and stuffed it back where she had found it. She sat on the floor. Her stomach convulsed and she retched.

It could not be.

An *affair*. Such a strange word.

Julienne was right. She needed to talk to him.

She reached into the drawer again and pulled out the paper packet containing the condoms and took them with her into the living room.

She waited in a state of terror and anticipation, her fingers trembling. Texted him:

When are you coming home?

And a few moments later, he responded:

Caught up with something at the office – sorry, please don't wait for me, put supper in the oven.

Normal tone. Usually she would reply: *See you when I see you!* Sometimes she'd be already in bed when he came home, and she'd hear him creak open the door quietly, considerate not to disturb her. She shook as she texted:

What is keeping you? Can you come home? I have something I need to talk about. I'll wait up for you. Please don't be late.

She waited. His reply was slow. But then:

Sure. If I can wind up the meeting with Richard and Mark, I'll be there by eight. Love you xxx

Her heart raced. She took the packet of condoms and walked over to place it on the lounge coffee table so there was no escaping discussing this when he returned.

She made him supper, ate nothing herself, stared at the TV. The news featured Mary Stevens, the teenager missing since last week. She watched tearful parents pleading for anyone who had seen their daughter at the Sunshine Plaza where she had disappeared. She stared at the photos of the girl in the clothes she was last seen wearing.

How stupid of the parents, she thought, to let their kids go off alone. But then she felt that emptiness again. Who was she to have an opinion? She who had no children, would never have children? Steve had never been interested in adoption – and she knew she would never push for a family he didn't want.

5

ATWELL HOME. MONDAY EVENING

At nine, she heard his car in the drive. When he came in, he looked tired, dishevelled. He absentmindedly kissed her on the head, loosened his tie and sat on the couch next to her.

'I'm whacked,' he said. 'How are you? What's up?' He picked up the TV remote and searched through the channels for the news, not noticing the display of condoms and the earring she'd placed on the coffee table in front of them.

She reached over, picked up the condom pack and held it between them. 'Steve, would you look at this?'

'What?'

She took the remote and clicked off the TV. 'Look, damn it!'

Surprised at her raised voice, he turned his full attention on the condoms.

'What's this? What are these? Who are they for?'

He frowned. 'Where...'

'I found these in your office. In your drawer.'

'Why were you in my office, looking in my drawers?' He laughed. Disbelief, confusion on his face. As if she were mad.

'I was trying to find something.'

'I see.' He looked genuinely nonplussed. Or was he trying to think of some excuse? Either he was a good actor, or the condoms were as much a surprise to him as they were to her.

'With a British flag? Did you get these last time you were in London? What did you need them for there?'

His face brightened. 'Oh, my gosh, Carrie! The condoms! Now I remember. You know me. I'm an idiot. Don't tell me you were worried? It's a funny story, really.'

She folded her arms. 'Really? I can't imagine.'

He patted her leg. Got up and went to the fridge. He took out two beers, opened them, poured them into tall glasses.

'Come out here.'

She followed him outside onto the deck, still holding the condoms. 'Steve, I need an answer. There was a beautiful single earring in your car. Now I find condoms with British flags. What do you think that looks like to me?'

He sipped his beer. Frowned. 'Looks like your husband is an idiot,' he said. 'No idea about the earring, honestly. But these...'

She sipped her beer, trying to hold her hand and voice steady. 'I'm listening.'

'When I went to London recently, I asked my colleagues what they wanted me to bring back for them. I was thinking Marmite, chocolates. Tahlia came to my office – you know Tahlia – and she, little rascal, asked me to bring her back a British condom. For her collection. I said, 'You're kidding, right?' She collects condoms from all around the world. Seriously.' He looked into Carrie's eyes.

She considered. It was just the sort of thing Tahlia would do. Tahlia. Young, tattooed, without boundaries.

'But then...?' She pointed to the packet. 'I don't understand?'

He shook his head. 'I bought a few things in some tourist souvenir shop in Piccadilly Circus for my other staff, found the condoms, and before I knew it, I'd bought them. Without really thinking.'

'What?'

'Nothing,' he said. 'It was stupid. I never gave them to her, of course. I just stuffed them in the drawer.'

'Why didn't you throw them out?'

He looked at her earnestly. Put down his beer. 'I have no bloody idea. Maybe I thought I'd give them to you as a joke. I just didn't. It seems wholly unimportant.'

He seemed sincere. Vulnerable. 'Sorry Carrie, if I made you think things. I would never do anything to hurt you.'

Carrie looked again at the condoms, saw how this could have happened. It was typical Steve, always trying to please others, not thinking things through. She threw the pack onto the table. 'I'm sorry.'

'No worries.' He leaned over and slid a hand across her fingers. 'I'm sorry.'

'That was an idiot thing to do anyway,' she said.

The earring, the perfume, the condoms. Dots that didn't connect. But she could see he was telling the truth. She returned to the living room and slipped the earring into her pocket.

She heated up the supper, served him his favourite meal, roast beef and vegetables. Sat while he ate it. He smiled up at her. 'This is so good, Carrie. I love you, you know that, don't you? I appreciate you making the meals while I'm on this project.'

'I love you too, Steve.'

It was over. He turned on the TV again and they watched the ABC news. He put his arm around her. The news channel repeated the story – *Mary Stevens, last seen at the Sunshine Plaza: here is a selfie taken of her and posted on social media hours before she disappeared.* A smiling, blonde young woman wearing a denim jacket over a white dress filled the screen.

'She's a teenager,' said Steve. 'Probably taking risks or under the influence of something.'

'If my daughter...' Carrie said and trailed off. If they had been able to have children, and if they had had a daughter when they were first married, she'd be a teenager by now. 'It's terrible,' she said. 'The poor parents must be going out of their minds.'

That night they made love. She was open to him, the first time in a week, and she abandoned herself to him, burying that niggling feeling. 'I love you, Steve.'

He grunted. It bothered her that he never said it back when he made love. As if he was far away, in his own pleasurable world, and sex was a solitary act, coincidentally with her. But she pushed this aside too.

After they had made love, he went back to his own room. They had once slept entwined, in the first few years of their marriage, but he snored, and it made her grumpy and they had come to this arrangement. 'I hate thinking how I disturb you,' he'd said. 'Better if I sleep on my own.'

But on this night, she felt as though a rift had opened up between them. Even though all doubts had been put to rest, she felt alone. Cold.

She texted him before she fell asleep, *Sorry xx Love you*, but he did not text back.

MONDAY, 11PM

He made sure the door was locked, and that no one had tampered with the lock. Who knew what busybodies cleaners were, or sparkies or tradies? This was his place. He had an elaborate security system that would alert him if anyone snooped around his man cave. No one came in here, not even to clean. Men are loners and need their own space. Lone wolf predators, they hunt at night, drag their prey back into their dens, gnaw over their spoils in their private lairs. Whatever domesticated self he had to be in the day he kept very separate from the predator he was at night.

And it was no ordinary man cave. No one went in here, unless he dragged them in by the hair. He pushed his way inside, turned on the dim light, wrinkled his nose at the smell of fear and sweat, and blood. The perfume he had sprayed did not quite hide the acrid aroma.

She was in the corner, tied to the chair, staring at him from the dark, a wild animal, tamed.

He smiled. 'Hello!'

She went rigid, said nothing. But of course, she could not say anything. Her mouth was still tied tightly with her red scarf, but she could at least be polite, mumble a greeting. She stared at him with black eyes, eyes filled with a perfect blend of liquid fear, hatred, submission. It aroused him.

'Don't worry,' he said. 'No one is going to hurt you now. My intentions are pure love. You're a goddess and all I want to do is worship you.'

She moved her head stiffly to look at the altar.

'Yes,' he said. 'You've been wondering about that, haven't you?'

He checked the room, made sure everything was as he had left it. He wiped the altar, lit two candles and placed his latest memento on the stone tabletop at the centre. The ear was warm, rubbery, and cut cleanly. No jagged bloody edges this time. He propped it up against the photo he had taken of her face, when she was still living, when she smiled for the camera, and showed off her earrings. Pity about the damn earring – that was meant to be the centrepiece of this whole display – earrings were something of an obsession, he had to admit to himself, a fetish –but never mind. The ear would do...

Now he could pay attention to his latest love. She wriggled her hands, which he could see were tied a little too tight and the rope bit into her flesh. 'Sorry about that, my dear.' He loosened the ropes, retied them. He was wary as he approached – these wily foxes would try anything – but she was acquiescent, submissive, grateful even as he freed her. He kept her hands tied behind her back and her feet manacled but she was no longer tied to the chair.

She held her face as he untied the scarf. 'Don't scream. No one will hear you. And I don't like loud noises – they make me nervous.' He squeezed her throat with his free hand. 'Very nervous.'

She nodded wide-eyed as he undid the scarf. She gagged, and he wiped her mouth with his hand, then sucked on his hand. Tasted her saliva. Reached for a bottle and gave her water to sip. She drank painfully, slowly.

'Thank you,' she said, in a small voice.

'Hungry?'

'I need to go to the toilet, to clean myself up.'

He peered at her soiled dress, sniffed. 'Yes, I can clean you up, don't worry, I will do all that.' He placed a large bowl on the floor beside her. 'You go pee now if you want.'

She stared at him. 'I need my hands...'

'Okay, but this is your first test. No tricks.'

She shook her head and he untied her hands. 'No one is going to hurt you, okay?'

'I need to pee, to clean myself.'

He held up a towel.

'Pl-please... don't watch.'

'You need to pee.'

Seeing that there was no other option, no toilet or bathroom in the dark cave, and that he was not going away, she pulled down her pants, squatted over the bowl. He watched. She looked down. When she finished, he passed her the damp warm towel and she wiped herself, pulling her dress down.

'Better?'

He could see she was puzzled at his consideration, at his willingness to help her here, to know what she needed. A gentleman.

'And those clothes need a wash. Good job I have a fresh set for you.'

He passed her a simple green-and-white chequered dress that looked like a school uniform, and she undressed, her back to him, and put on the new clothes. 'Good girl.'

'Please,' she said when she was back in the chair and he had tied her hands behind her back again. He also tied her feet together in case she was a kicker, like the last one. She was shaking with fright.

'There is nothing to be afraid of.'

'Please.'

'What?'

'What am I doing here? What do you want? Please don't hurt me, I will do anything you want.'

He laughed. 'No one is going to hurt you,' he said kindly. A soft touch on her face and she winced, pulled back. 'I'm here to look after you.'

'What do you want?'

She was still puzzled, he could see, by his reverence and kindness. They all were. He was not like other men. Girls were to be revered and worshipped, not abused, not beaten up, or raped, or sliced up for no reason. 'You, Cindy, have been chosen and honoured to be the next offering to the goddess. Are you surprised? Happy? Afraid?'

Another furtive look at the altar. 'Why are you doing this?'

He smiled. 'Why?'

She had obviously thought of a strategy. This was an act to humour him, to get him off guard. These girls always tried to play him, as if he was stupid. He almost knew what her line would be... and it was exactly like the others. She spoke slowly as if to a moron. She thought he was a moron; no, she treated him as if he were a wild animal, which was better. He *was* a wild animal. 'You can have what you want,' she said. 'Take me, but please don't hurt me. I'll do anything willingly. Is that what you want?'

He laughed. 'You read my mind, baby. I think I'll rename you Scheherazade.'

She looked puzzled.

'The 1,001 Nights. Scheherazade had to tell stories to the

king to stay alive. If he lost interest in her stories, he'd behead her.'

She swallowed.

'But don't worry, my dearest, no one is going to behead you. So... talk. What is it you wanted to say?'

She stammered, stared at the ear on the altar. 'H-how many other women have you...?

He laughed. 'Quite a few. Looking for the one. Always looking for the one. Are you the one?'

'Y-you're a handsome, attractive man, I'm sure many girls would want to go out with you, would want you. You don't need to... kidnap girls. You could just ask them out. I'm sure many girls would want to go out with you. You don't have to do this. I can help you...'

She was a brave one, this. He tried to hold back his scorn. 'Would you have gone out with me if I'd have asked?'

'Yes,' she stuttered.

'Even though I'm much older than you?'

'Yes. B-better to be an old man's darling that a young man's slave, my friends tell me.'

He laughed. 'I'm an old man to you?'

'No, no. It's just a saying. Why don't we... just go out, like a date, we can do what you want... and then... I can go. You can see me when you want... I won't tell anyone – it can be our secret, a secret affair... We can...'

She was scrambling for words, for what she thought he wanted. She had thought about this – her little strategy at humouring him to let her go. But she had no idea. No fucking idea.

'Liar! As soon as I let you go, you'd go snivelling off to your mummy and the police...'

'No, no,' she said, 'I would never do that, I swear, I promise.'

Her eyes were wide, sincere, she was trying so hard. 'I don't tell my mother anything. Seriously.'

He grabbed her cheeks, looked into her eyes. She was so very beautiful when she was afraid and vulnerable, so very beautiful, better with those puffy crying eyes and the black rings under them.

'My little Scheherazade. With your little stories.'

'Please just tell me why you are doing this.'

'Because you are beautiful, the most beautiful girl I have ever seen.'

She recoiled, did not seem to appreciate the compliment, as if she had just been told she was an ugly whore. He pinched her cheek. 'I said, you're beautiful, didn't you hear me?'

'Th-thank you.'

'And you know it. Only too well. Too well. How much time do you spend looking into the mirror, posting selfies on Instagram?'

'I can give you... myself. Anything you want? Do you want me?' Her voice broke here. Yes, she had thought it through and was making a Faustian bargain. She had it all figured out: sex was better than death. And this mad man wanted sex, so all she had to do was give it to him and he'd let her go. Her bargaining tool, sex as a weapon. Like all women.

It made him angry. 'Why am I doing this? Because I've been wanting you and you're a *prima donna*, a cock teaser, prancing around the beach in skimpy clothing and thinking you can do whatever you want, and there are no consequences. Enticing men.'

'No,' she said. Wide eyes. 'I don't.'

'You are about to learn a big lesson, my dear Cindy. About how the world is. Here are the facts. How it has always been, and don't let anyone tell you differently. Women display their sexuality for the male. And men hunt women. We're predators. Animals. Cats salivate at the mouth when they stalk a bird.'

He had salivated too, at the thought of her. Wet himself at the thought of this young girl, vulnerable, the more vulnerable the better. The more fearful, the higher pitched her trembling voice, the wider the eyes, the better. It was all sound evolutionary theory. And practice. Eagles stole crying chicks out of their nests. There was no law against that in the animal kingdom. What was so different about what he was doing? He was a wolf, an eagle, a huntsman spider, a big cat. He had seen cats play with their prey, torment a mouse, pounce, release, tear off limbs, toss them in the air, bite heads off, dismember them. Keep souvenirs in their sleeping places. Or in their kitty litter. No one arrested cats for doing that. It was their nature.

He took her ear between his fingers, felt its velvet softness, drew close and bit it softly. She went rigid, stared at the severed ear on the altar. He played with her earrings. 'A bit of a fetish, I'm afraid.'

'Do you like them?' she stuttered, choking back her fear and trying to smile.

She was playing him again. So coquettish. He yanked the earring out of her ear, and her pierced ear lobe tore. She bit her lip to stop a scream of pain, staring up at him with a flash of fear and hatred and anger in her eyes – just for a second – then she calmed herself. But, good girl, she did not do anything stupid, not like the others. She just stared at him, while a drop of blood dripped off her earlobe. He sucked it, swallowed it. It tasted good.

He dangled the earring close to her eyes. 'Can I have this?'
She nodded.
'I like shiny things. Beautiful objects. Like a cat. Do you have a cat?'
She shook her head.

'I like cats. They follow their instincts. They play with their food.' He stroked her chin. 'Have you ever seen a cat catch a mouse and play with it as he tears it limb from limb, tosses it into the air, leaves you a present of a chewed off head or bum?'

Now she was crying. Her next tactic was to plead for mercy – so predictable. 'Please let me go.' She snivelled. 'I'll go out with you...'

'You think I want to go out with you?'

'I won't tell anyone; I'll do anything but just of my free will. I'll... dress up for you. Wear earrings. I have lots at home. I can... give myself to you, we can... have a relationship...'

He laughed. 'What makes you think I want a relationship? I'm a cat, you're a mouse.'

'What do you want? I can give it to you if you let me go. I can.'

He began tickling her other ear. 'You really want to know what I want?'

She nodded. Looked softly. 'Of course. Please tell me.'

'You're better than the others. I might just keep you. But of course, you don't really want to know. You're just playing a game – the game of survivor. Humouring, patronising me is your little tactic.'

'No,' she said. 'I really want to know, if I can help in any way. I'm training to be a psychologist at uni.'

He spat into her face. 'A fucking therapist?'

'A psychologist.'

'You, baby, can help in ways you cannot imagine. You are my therapy.' He wiped the spit off her face with the warm towel. 'Sorry. I just hate therapists. They think they can pigeonhole me, explain me.'

'Talk to me,' she said. 'What do you want?'

'Okay, little Miss Shrink, let me tell you what I want. You think I'm an idiot? I know more about psychology than you know in your little finger. I have an addictive compulsive urge, from my early teenagehood, when girls like you rejected me, thwarted my sexual desires. Played hard to get, teased, danced out of reach with your fancy clothes and perfume and swaying hips. So now I'm making up for all those years of sexual deprivation and denial and degradation. You understand? Why do you think you're wearing that school uniform?'

She looked down at the green-and-white chequered pattern. Looked as if she recognised it. 'Coolum State High?'

'You get brownie points! Listen, Cindy, are you addicted to anything?'

She widened her eyes. 'No. Wait. Maybe... Ch-chocolate?'

He laughed. She thought she was getting somewhere, ha-ha, cat and mouse, this game was let the mouse think it's getting away. Such fun. 'Social media, perhaps?'

She shook her head but could not help look at the floor where he had smashed the phone on her arrival.

'You're addicted to your own self-image, aren't you? How good you look in selfies you post every day on your Instagram and Snapchat and Twitter and Facebook. I know.'

'You've been stalking me? I mean, following me?'

'I make it my business to scout out my prey.'

She looked like prey just then, a timid, quivering mouse. He stroked her chin again, ran his fingers over her lips.

'And yes, they do call me sick. You're studying to be one of them. You'll understand. The psychiatrists call this a mental illness, a disease, an addiction. I've read the files on cases like mine. I follow serial killers. Learn from them. You stupid psychologists would label me a deviant, try to explain away this natural masculine urge as 'sexual sadism'. Yes, my condition is sadism. From the Marquis de Sade. Have you read any of his books?'

She shook her head.

'No, of course not. Your generation only knows Snapchat and TikTok. Maybe I should give you some reading matter while I'm away to keep you out of mischief?'

Her eyes gleamed. Hope. 'Yes, I'll read that. I would be interested in… Sad?'

'Sade.'

'Then maybe we can do some of the things you read about.' He left the room, closed the bookcase doorway and then returned with a large hardback book. '*The 120 Days of Sodom*,' he announced, thrusting the book in her face.

'How can I read with…?' She shrugged her arms.

He weighed up the possibility of releasing her. But no, once he had let a girl free in his room and she had created havoc trying to find a way out.

'Is it like bondage or S&M? Like *Fifty Shades of Grey*?'

'No.'

The pleasure was not in her compliance but her resistance, but he did not tell her that. 'Sadism, my dear mouse, is the practice of blending sex and pain – inflicting hurt, humiliation, fear, physical and mental harm on your sex victim, and deriving pleasure from it.' He had done it all – restraint, imprisonment, deprivation, slicing of body parts, exquisite torture. 'All men, if they admit it to themselves, are sexual sadists, for that is what sex is, hunting, with the aim of killing your prey, playing with it, hurting, making someone else suffer, making women cry out as you thrust into them, but most men are weak cowards, denying their manhood. Not me.'

She stared at him. 'Whatever you want.' She closed her eyes, trembled. Like the mouse going slack in the jaws of the cat.

7

ATWELL HOME. TUESDAY MORNING

He brought Carrie tea in the morning, kissed her, and told her he would be back late that night. 'I'll keep away from Sarah's perfume, I promise,' he said. 'And Tahlia – I haven't spoken to her in months... She doesn't work in my section anymore.'

He blew her a kiss as he marched through the front door. All was back to normal. But when he left, she could not help but take out the earring again and stare at it. She had to figure this out. Earring. Condoms. Perfume. She could still smell that sickly scent on the work clothes he had discarded in the laundry basket. She emptied out his pockets, took the laundry basket down to the garage where they had the laundry room. Threw his clothes in the washing machine. Fetched some more laundry powder from the back of the garage.

Behind the garage, overgrown in the forest end of the property, was his studio, his 'man cave', a large storeroom he had converted, soundproofed and heavy-doored with no windows. She had been in there only once and had commented on its stink and dirty mugs and piled up musical equipment. So he had banned her ever since. He would still retreat there sometimes, late at night, hot Sunday afternoons, to pursue his hobbies. He had bought himself a Fender Stratocaster, a guitar amp, some recording equipment, guitar pedals, and had quite openly told her that his 'studio' was off limits, reserved for his mid-life crisis.

She tried the door handle, but it was locked.

Why lock it? she wondered. What was so precious in there, or what was it that he didn't want her to see? He had told her before – valuable equipment, worth thousands of dollars. That shaky feeling came over her again and she hunted in his office drawers for keys. She found a bunch, an odd one she had never seen before, and took them, tried them all in the lock. But none fitted.

She had to work on a research project for her professor that afternoon and evening, and that distracted her. She had been commissioned to find out all the animal references in Dickens's novels, so that her professor could write a paper on animal treatment in the novels. It felt silly, frivolous, but this is how academics made their living somehow.

She called her therapist as soon as the office opened. 'Do you have a slot this morning? I need to talk.'

'We can fit you in at 10am,' said the receptionist. 'That okay?'

8

MOOLOOLABA. TUESDAY MORNING, 10AM

'About the earring,' she said, looking at Julienne and then out at the ocean.

'Yes, did you have a chat?'

'He swears he has no idea how it got in his car. I believe him. Believed him. Believe him. He wouldn't lie. I mean, if he wanted to lie, he could easily say that he picked up a hiker with earrings, or... gave his secretary a ride to a meeting, or something. But he was honest. Defenceless.'

'But?'

'I'm unsettled.' At the park next to the beach, a group of young women in the skimpiest bikinis she had ever seen strutted past the young men hanging around the skate park. 'I found condoms in his clothes drawer. We never use condoms. He had a perfectly good explanation for those too. Which, when he told me, made sense.'

'What was it?'

'They were a joke gift for a colleague at work. He never gave them to her. I felt stupid.'

'Do you believe him?'

'Yes, of course.'

'Well, then, that lays that to rest.'

'I just don't know,' Carrie said. 'I feel distrustful still. Is it a coincidence? An earring in his car? Perfume after a late night? Condoms? Maybe I'm in denial. From the outside, does it look like something is going on here?'

Julienne looked at Carrie. 'To me? As I said, maybe.'

'Could he be having an affair?'

'He could.'

'I didn't want you to say that. He's not the type.'

'Can you just ask him?'

'He just said he'd never do anything to hurt me.'

Julienne looked her in the eye. 'Men being unfaithful, having affairs, is the most common thing I have to deal with.'

'I can't imagine Steve having an affair. We have a good sex life and though he's withdrawn, it's okay. More or less.'

'More or less?'

'He's so closed. He's never opened up to me about anything. He was in the military, and I know he has some heavy things he's carrying, will never talk about it.'

'The military. That's interesting. Do you think he has some sort of trauma?'

'He mentions it now and then. But always changes the subject.'

'Look, if you want the relationship to work, to grow, this is an opportunity to have an honest discussion with him. Otherwise the distrust will grow and you two will drift apart. Ask him straight up if he's having an affair. Get him to talk. Open up. Is that possible?'

'I'll try.' Carrie felt her mouth dry up again as doubts returned.

'I think it's the best way.'

9

NOOSA WATERS. TUESDAY, EARLY MORNING

He had planned it all carefully beforehand. After his work, there was always the body to dispose of. Luck would have it, or rather, good forward planning, when he had bought this acreage property backing onto bushland with a dirt road at the back. Here he could load the remains of his recent lustful adventure onto the back of the ute, wrapped up in black plastic sheeting and then covered with the tools of his trade, as if he was on his way to a job. Murderer at work – do not disturb.

This one had proved most exciting, and challenging. He had to punish her for her cunning, devious lying, the way she tried to humour and belittle him, and all she represented. She said she would do anything, and he had pushed her to the limit.

Early morning was the best time. This time he had covered the black tarp with wood chips and drove her to the canals near Noosa Waters, the posh suburb where everyone lived on the water and moored a boat or a yacht on their own private dock. He despised this pristine area, with its immaculate, architecturally-designed glass houses, built for show rather than for privacy. So artificial. Even the canals had been carved into straight lines, the water levels regulated by a lock system to make sure those precious fertilised and trimmed lawns would not get flooded in a spring tide.

On a recent trip here he had spotted at the end of one canal a dead-end screened off from the housing estate so that the unsightly sluice waters and drainage pipes could not spoil anyone's view. The body might drift out to sea, but this time he wanted it to be found. Here. It would be swept like a mermaid along these clear blue Noosa Waters and was sure to be spotted by a fisherman bobbing along in their tinny, or by tourists sipping cocktails on the Noosa ferry, an open-mouthed, open-eyed corpse naked as the day she was born; cut, disfigured, mutilated; a sacrificial lamb pierced and marked and worthy of anything the Marquis de Sade could have done.

The media would be buzzing. People would talk: another strike by the girl killer! He wished he could write the news, maybe even write some new commentary on this serial killer, say how sick he was, call him *The Mutilator*, or even *Jack the Australian Ripper*. That would be good.

The usual emptiness settled over him as he wished her farewell and pushed her over the concrete edge into the sluice drain, to float and drift until she slowly succumbed to the currents and tides of the river and battered against the canal walls, maybe mooring at one of those fancy houses. That would be nice.

He drove slowly – he was hungry again – and fancied his usual quick stop at Macca's, but he had to get back to his respectable life, to his workplace and his grey self. He felt exhausted. It had been a long night, but the ache was diminishing in his soul. He was a young man again. He had discovered the fountain of youth.

Blake the Romantic poet had written in his *Proverbs of Hell*,

'Sooner murder an infant in its cradle than nurse unacted desires' and so he had followed his desires to the full. 'Expect poison from the standing water', Blake had also said, and he had got his waters flowing again. Flow, flow, act, be. Do. He felt alive.

10

ATWELL HOME. TUESDAY EVENING

W hen Carrie heard his car in the driveway, she tensed. He was ages coming. She heard the thudding bass of his radio as he was listening to a song, probably waiting till it finished before he came inside. But it annoyed her, as if he was deliberately postponing this moment. Then he turned off the radio, slammed the car door and whistled as he headed to the house.

He was surprised to see her in the hallway. 'Hi there. Boy, what a day at work.'

'Steve, are you having an affair?'

That stopped him.

'What?'

She watched him closely.

His first reaction was guilt. Then fear. Then laughter. Then incredulity. He looked at her as if she was saying something insane. Then the reproachful look. 'Carrie? Are you crazy? What are you talking about? Let me at least get inside and take off my jacket and tie...'

He marched past her, into his office where he dumped his

briefcase with what seemed like excessive force. She stood in the kitchen, hovered by the stove where the meal was warming up. He was stalling for time. Probably wanted to run. But he walked back into the kitchen, minus the jacket and tie and briefcase, and opened his arms for a hug. 'Carrie.'

She folded her arms.

'What bad movies have you been watching?'

'Just tell me the truth.'

'The truth is, Carrie, I love you, I would never– Why would you think I'm having an affair? Who have you been talking to?'

'It's been eating away at me. Like some bad sitcom or detective story. The mystery of the one earring. The mystery of the perfume. The mystery of the British condoms.'

'Don't be silly, Carrie. There's no mystery here. I've told you everything.'

'Then what can I think then? Put yourself in my shoes. If you found a... cufflink, I don't know, a tie in my... purse, and I smelled of aftershave after a late night out, and...'

He swigged his gin and tonic, and then refilled his glass. 'Is that what you think, Carrie? I'm having an affair? Is that how little you regard me? You don't trust me, believe me?'

'Steve, I'm merely asking a question. A simple answer – yes, or no – is all I ask.'

'I've told you, no. No, I'm not having an affair. I work hard all day, late at night, for what? For you, for us...' His voice rose with each statement. 'Who do you think I am?'

'It's just all confusing, Steve.'

He looked at her warmly. 'Carrie, let me tell you straight: you're the only woman in my life. Stop creating links between things that are not links.' He seemed genuine. Concerned. Open.

'I was talking to my therapist–'

He shook his head. 'Is that who put you up to this? I was wondering what had gotten into you.'

'Don't blame her, Steve. She was just reflecting back my own paranoia, my fears.' This time she let him hug her.

11

ATWELL HOME. WEDNESDAY MORNING

W hen Carrie woke in the morning, Steve was in the shower. When she got up to make tea she found he had left a note for her in the kitchen.

In case you have forgotten, I love you. Xxx.

She looked forward to letting Julienne know about how she had managed to confront him and resolve the issue. Case closed.

The Daily News feed came in Carrie's inbox every morning and she read it on her phone, in bed, scrolling past the politics and sport to more interesting personal interest stories. She scrolled down to a breaking story about another missing girl. Two of them now. Cindy Liptrot had not come home after a night out at the Junction. Her friends had seen her leave in an Uber shortly before midnight, but no Uber driver reported picking her up. Although the police had not made any statement linking the two missing teenagers, the media was having a field day. First, Mary Stevens, now Cindy Liptrot. Were their disappearances related?

The media reports highlighted their similarities: same age –

nineteen – blonde hair, thin (emaciated, Carrie would have said), each with that Barbie doll, wide-eyed, plump-lipped look. She sipped her tea and flicked through news item after news item. Steve was still in the shower – he always spent a long time in the shower.

A new close-up picture of Mary Stevens had been posted, a head and shoulders of her last seen pic, in low-cut dress, no denim jacket this time, her hair swirled back over her bare, tanned shoulder. She was beautiful. It took Carrie a while to realise what was making her heart jolt – in the picture, Mary was wearing a pair of earrings, dangling gold discs, each with three diamonds embedded in them, glinting in the sunlight. The photo was in full colour, so Carrie could see them in detail. In shock, she zoomed in and the photo became grainy and pixilated, but there was no mistake – the earrings looked exactly like the one she had in her bedside drawer. Her heart beating, she listened to make sure Steve was still in the shower and pulled out the single earring. She held it to the screen.

It was a match. As far as she could tell.

She looked again at the photo, zoomed out, scrolled down for other pictures of the girl, and sure enough, in three pictures she was wearing these exact earrings.

Maybe this was a common earring, the latest fashion, maybe any market stall sold them, maybe... She jumped as Steve opened the bedroom door dressed for work. 'You okay?'

He adjusted his tie, leaned over to see what she was looking at on her phone. She quickly snapped her phone closed. 'Just reading the news. It's so depressing.'

Steve gave her a peck on the cheek. 'I don't bother. Always some disaster after another. And I don't want to know what antics our pathetic politicians are up to next.'

'You have time for breakfast?' She kept her voice steady, tried not to shake. But her heart was racing. *The same earring?* A voice in her head kept telling her. *The exact same earring you found in his car?*

'Sorry, love, I have to dash. Early start, late finish today. Don't wait up for me this time.'

'Steve... I thought we were going to spend more time together.'

'I know, Carrie, but... What are you doing today?'

'It's Wednesday. Going to the Eumundi Markets to pick up a few things.'

He gave her another kiss on the cheek. 'I love you, Carrie.'

She pulled him closer. 'Kiss me properly. You're always rushing off.'

'Sorry.' He sat on the bed, took her hand, kissed her for a long five seconds. 'Better?'

'Yes.'

'You're trembling.'

'Am I?' She breathed out, held herself still. Smiled. And felt again a terrible guilt as she looked into his concerned, sincere, clear blue eyes. She was surely paranoid. But demon thoughts tumbled into her head again, one after the other. Maybe Steve did give a ride to a hitchhiker, forgot about it. And the hiker had dropped an earring. And they were common earrings, just a coincidence.

Nothing to do with the missing girl.

Steve stood to go, adjusted his tie in the mirror. 'Have a good day!'

'You sure you didn't give anyone a ride?'

He turned back to her and she could feel his impatience, and that rising anger and frustration. 'What?'

'Just allow me this, okay? I understand all the other things, but the earring in your car. It just doesn't make sense.'

'At least you admit it's paranoia.' He held her under her chin, looked into her eyes. 'Carrie, I don't give people rides. You know

44

that. For all I know it could have been in the car since I bought the thing.'

'Sure,' she said, feeling ridiculous. 'Call me later.'

'Love you.' He blew her a kiss and marched out of the house as if he were in a hurry to get away from her.

She watched him drive away, and then picked up the earring again. Was she going mad? What was she thinking? On the one hand she could see it was all paranoia, all a chimera. On the other hand, her gnawing conscience was telling her that something was wrong here. Should she go to the police? Call the missing person hotline? *Any information is welcome.* If she had found the earring similar to that of the missing girl, then surely it was her duty to report it. She had to do something. She looked up the Crime Stoppers site, scrolled down to the phone number.

'Call us if you have any information. Any piece of information could help solve or prevent a crime. Report anonymously. Tell us what you know, not who you are.'

She could be anonymous. She could just send a photo of the earring; say she had found it. But what was she thinking? How could this be anonymous? As soon as she reported the earring, she would be implicating her husband in something outrageous. She would be questioned; he would be questioned. He would know she had gone to the police behind his back. She would have to tell him if she did this. So she closed the page.

Another idea: she googled images of gold disc earrings with three diamond stars to see if she could find one like it. She scrolled down hundreds of images. But she found nothing like this earring. It was one – no, two – of a kind.

Her next idea – it was market day and there were many jewellery stalls, locally-crafted earrings. She could browse and even ask jewellery makers about the earring. Who knows? She might find these exact earrings. Maybe she would find every young woman at the market was wearing a pair like this.

12

EUMUNDI MARKETS. WEDNESDAY, LATE MORNING

A few hours later, she went to the market, found parking not too far away, but was still sweating in the thirty-degree morning heat and high humidity by the time she had trudged along Main Street to the craft area. She meandered through the clothing stalls, pretended to be interested in the jewellery. But she found no earrings like it at the first stall, nor the second or third.

'Can I help you?' A hippy girl in long blue dress and braided hair smiled. She was wearing every conceivable ornament – a line of studded earrings, nose ring, toe rings.

'I'm looking for earrings for my young niece for Christmas. She's blonde, eighteen years old. Do you have anything like this one?'

She looked around, made sure no one was watching, and then pulled out the earring from her pocket. Could she trust this young woman?

The girl took the earring, laid it on her open palm like a sacred heirloom. 'Wow. Pretty cool.' She held it up to the light. 'This is handcrafted. Look, there are initials here... JM.'

Carrie took back the earring and squinted at the initials. She hadn't even seen them scratched by hand in uneven tiny letters on the back. 'JM? Handcrafted? Is it local, d'you think?'

'Don't know,' the hippy woman said.

'Do you have anything like it?'

'Nope. Reckon that's one of a kind.'

She stole a look at the young girl. Was she suspicious at all? Had she seen the missing girl? No one looked too closely at details, except maybe an earring seller at a market.

'Can I see that again?' the hippie girl asked.

Carrie handed the earring back.

'Are they real diamonds?' Carrie asked.

'Could be. It's pretty unique. Handcrafted, as I said.'

'One of a kind?' Carrie said. 'You sure?'

'Two of a kind,' smiled the girl.

'How... how could I find a "JM Jewellery"?'

The girl shook her head. Then she brightened, turned to her computer and typed in the letters – JM jewellery. 'I would stock these,' she explained, 'if I could contact the person who made them. But if they're real diamonds, they're way out of my league.' She frowned as she scrolled down. Shook her head. 'No luck. Can't find it.'

'Thanks, anyway.'

The girl tapped her lips with her fingers. 'You know, I swear I might've seen this somewhere. I've an eye for earrings, and something feels familiar. Oh well. Leave me your number and if anything comes to mind, I'll call you.'

Carrie gave the girl her mobile number and buried the earring in her pocket, leaving the stall.

No other jewellery stalls had anything remotely like the earring in her pocket. She did not bring it out after that first time, did not speak to any of the jewellers.

13

THERAPIST'S OFFICE, MOOLOOLABA.
WEDNESDAY AFTERNOON

S he was fortunate that her therapist was flexible with appointments and would be able to see her that same day.

'Our sessions are confidential, right? I don't want you to go running to the police.'

Julienne smiled. 'We do have an obligation if anyone has committed a crime, or there is child abuse, a little like the new law pertaining to Catholic priests in a confessional. But no... don't worry, this is a safe space. Anything you say here won't go outside the room unless you want it to, unless I have your permission. So, tell me, what happened? Your last email was so positive. You said you'd resolved everything and felt so much better asserting yourself, and he'd come clean. What did he say?'

'I'm so tangled. I don't know what to think.'

'What's happened now?'

'Not much. In a way. He's been so nice to me, so kind.'

'And?'

Carrie sighed. 'Okay, let me say it. I didn't want to tell you this because it just feels outrageous and paranoid. The earring. It feels, I don't know, associated with some terrible thing.' She took the earring out of her pocket and looked at it. 'Something happened this morning and I feel stupid even telling you.'

'Go on.'

'You know that missing girl, Mary Stevens?'

'Yes.'

'I saw a photo of her this morning in the news – a photo of her just before she vanished, and she was wearing earrings.'

'Yes?'

'Earrings like this. Exactly like this one.' She took out the earring. Dangled it against the light so that it sparkled.

Julienne said nothing.

Carrie was trembling and cold. 'Probably plenty of girls wear earrings like this. I googled it, couldn't find anything like it, went to the Eumundi markets and there was nothing like it at all. And the police are asking for evidence, anything that would help with the missing girl, and this would definitely be something. Maybe she – Mary – hitched a ride with Steve and he can't remember. Maybe... maybe... he does remember and won't tell me. I don't know. What should I do?'

Julienne sighed. 'This is a big deal. You should go to the police.'

'But do you know what that means? They'll want to question Steve. Maybe put him through a horrible investigation. I can't.'

'But what if Steve had something to do with her disappearance?'

Carrie felt all the blood drain from her face. 'No. No. It's not possible.'

'You could hold a key to a crime, Carrie.'

'Or not,' she said. 'Could be coincidence. Involving the police would be devastating.'

'What are your options?'

'Investigate further. I need more information.'

'Like?'

'The earring is unique. Handcrafted. Uncommon. Maybe one of a kind. And it has what I think are the maker's initials scratched on it... here.' She showed Julienne the tiny letters JM at the bottom of the earring.

'The owner or the jewellery maker?'

'Must be the maker. It would be hard for someone without jewellery tools to do this.'

'And if you find out where it came from, how does that help you?'

'I'll find out who made it, where it was sold.'

The therapist shook her head. 'You're not a criminal investigator. Why not leave that to the police? Give them the earring and let them do that.'

'I've already found out a lot. And it's not good. From a logical point of view, if I were an investigator, here are the facts: if the earring is one of a kind; it's hers, the missing girl's, I'm sure of it. And if it is, then... at some point Steve must have had contact with her.'

'Maybe he gave her a ride without knowing it was her. Maybe he didn't want to tell you for the same reason – the police would start investigating and questioning.'

'That would make sense.' But Carrie felt she was clutching at straws here. Any explanation would do, anything but the one she felt deep inside her but could not admit.

'But he said no. Adamantly. Believably. He would remember that... and if he thought he had given a lift to the missing girl, he would have told me, I'm sure, or reacted when we saw her on TV. "That's the girl I gave a ride to the other day", he would have said. "Let's go to the police!" But he genuinely looked like someone who had no idea.'

'Listen, Carrie, I have a suggestion. Get him in here. A joint session might help. You can't take this all on yourself. And if he has some trauma from his military past, it would be a good idea to see a therapist anyway.'

'He hates therapists, but I'll ask.'

14

ATWELL HOME. WEDNESDAY EVENING

After the session with Julienne she drove home, waited for him. Dialled his mobile.

'Hi. Everything all right?'

'Where are you, Steve?'

'Conference dinner at the Sheraton, sorry, didn't I tell you? I did. Hope you didn't make supper tonight?'

'It was your turn tonight.'

'Jesus. Sorry.'

'Who are you with?'

Silence. Then, with slight impatience: 'A client. Can I call you back?'

'When will you be home?'

'Don't wait up. Listen, I have to go. I'm in the middle of a meeting. Love you.'

She held the phone to her ear long after he hung up. Pushed down the fear, the paranoia, the nausea in her gut. She had to be rational, cool, a detective here, not the emotional wreck she felt herself becoming.

She looked up the Sheraton, Noosa Heads. Dialled reception. 'Is there a Mr Atwell having a dinner in one of your conference rooms?'

The answer was swift. 'We have no conferences on at the moment, ma'am. We have several Christmas parties, but no business conferences.'

'You sure? Is he in the restaurant, by any chance?'

'I don't know, ma'am. Do you want me to page him? Who shall I say is asking for him?'

'Never mind. I may have the wrong Sheraton.'

She looked up all the Sheratons on the Sunshine Coast. Called them all and got the same negative answer.

Be the detective here, not the emotional, paranoid wife, Carrie, she told herself. She spent the evening calming herself. She searched JM jewellery, found nothing. She suspected that whoever made these did not have a business advertised on the internet, that it was maybe a one-off design. And how would it help if she found who made them? Who sold them? How would that take her closer to the truth? She was being methodical, and there was nowhere else to start.

She examined the condoms, noted the expiry date. This month. So, it was likely he had bought these in London on his last visit. That story seemed true. But what if it were only... half true?

The perfume. If she could check what perfume the secretary wore that would be simple, and if they did not match, she would know he was lying. But how could she do this? She would have to go to the office and get into a casual conversation with Sarah. Women could ask such things. *Such divine perfume? What is it?*

But for now, she had a more immediate problem. Was Steve lying to her about where he was?

She felt sick to her bones.

If her husband was not where he said he was, where was he and why had he lied to her?

She opened his office door and pulled open the filing cabinet under the desk, leafed through his files where he kept his bills. But there were no car bills. She suspected he kept those in the cubbyhole of his ute. She would have to go through the logbook when he was home. The ute was still under warranty and he made sure the services were recorded faithfully, so that should be no problem, if she could do it without him knowing. She needed to find the mechanic who had serviced the car, but there were no business cards or any record of that here either.

She would save him from suspicion by proving him innocent. If she were a lawyer, she would take on his case.

She waited up for him: 11pm; 11.30pm; 11.45pm. Still no Steve. She resisted the urge to call him again, to text him. He had sounded so annoyed, and it would look obsessive if she kept calling. He hated her to be possessive. 'Clingy,' he called it. So, she sat and browsed the internet, looking for every detail she could find about the missing girl, Mary. She had left home at 7pm as usual to waitress at a bar in Coolum Beach, but never arrived. Her car was parked on the esplanade, and there were no signs of a struggle or anything out of the ordinary. Had she run away with a secret boyfriend? Had she been murdered, kidnapped, or had she simply gone off to the Gold Coast without telling her parents?

Mary Stevens was slight, waiflike, and pale-skinned, almost translucent. Her hair was wispy blonde, and her eyes pale blue. Her ears pierced, and in every picture of her she wore earrings. Other exotic types of earrings, as well as the ones she was wearing when she disappeared.

Carrie could not sleep. She was listening out for every car that drove by, waiting to confront Steve. But the later it got, the more she resolved rather to talk to him in the morning, if she could get up early enough to catch him.

15

MOOLOOLABA ESPLANADE. WEDNESDAY NIGHT

The dark was his element, like water, a viscous fluid, and he belonged in it, his skin melting into the night as if he were one with it. He liked the gleaming wet pavements and reflected street lights, the twinkling Christmas lights in the distance, the Mooloolaba lighthouse flashing every fifteen seconds as it rotated. He liked the throbbing pounding of music from the nightclubs that simulated sex, the clumps of drunken people swaying past him bursting out of pubs, the late strollers on the boardwalk, the loners, like him... and the women. Always the women. In gaggles, or in gangs, or loners clicking their high heels as they walked to their cars, mobiles pressed to their ears.

He prowled the dark streets like a big cat on the hunt. No one could understand the ache in him. It compelled him like a black hole – it sucked and sucked at his being and his meaning. Until it attracted some shiny object into its vortex. But he was not a spider who sat patiently at the centre of his web – he had to go after, hunt, track down and corner his trembling prey. He followed a few women, passed them, smiled at them, and they – stupid fools – smiled back at him, only seeing his mask, thinking he was like them, a respectable human being.

And then he spotted her. A stupid girl parking her car in the back lot, in the dark against the gleam of the purple night sky. Her silhouette like a goddess of the night. Waiflike. Blonde. Young. Most important, she wore long dangling earrings that danced in the moonlight. She walked steadily on the pier towards the food court. But he knew she would never reach it. She was perfect in this light, in the crescendo of the waves, and his senses were full, his adrenaline pumping, his heart rate high. His senses tuned for the chase, the hunt, the encounter, the capture. The lighthouse beaming its approval every fifteen seconds.

He crouched by her back tyre, took out the knife, did his work.

She was not too far away. He rushed to her, breathless, polite, non-threatening. 'Excuse me, ma'am.'

He stood in her path. She looked up from her phone.

'Sorry,' he said, 'but do you know your back tyre is flat? Looks like you have a puncture, I saw it when you were parking.'

'Really?' She did not look afraid, just startled. Her eyes gleamed. She was staring at his sweatshirt, which was unusual, distinctive, a baggy cream hoodie with the McDonald's logo in bright yellow, a picture of a Big Mac, and underneath, the words McDonald's University.

The incongruity of it made her smile. 'Is that a real place or is it a joke?'

He looked down, pulled his sweater so he could read the words. 'A real place, believe it or not. It's where they train franchise managers...'

A sparkle in her eye, as if she enjoyed being chatted up. Her earrings were gold feathers in a disc. He had to have her. He tried not to show the quivering lust in his eyes, his mouth twitching like a cat about to pounce on a mouse. 'I know it's none of my business, but you don't want to be coming back late at night to a flat tyre.'

Now she looked a little disturbed, but he reassured her. 'It's okay. Do you have RACQ? They can come and fix it while you're at work or wherever you're going.'

'I don't.'

'Or I can be the Good Samaritan that I am and fix it for you. I can do that for you...'

'What's a Good Samaritan?'

She's dumb, he thought, *so much the better. Oh sir, what big teeth you have. All the better to eat you with, my dear.*

She did not quite believe him. She wanted to walk on, erase him from her little bubble, and she looked in that moment so deliciously vulnerable, doubtful, her voice quavery. 'How do you know my tyre's flat?'

'Didn't you notice as you were driving? Feel the car unstable? I saw it a mile off. A nail or something? Have you been driving on dirt roads?'

'No.' The briny sea whipped its wind around her, and the cloak of psychological darkness he swirled around her was inky black too. He was in charge of these elements, a dark avenger, an evil Batman.

She stopped. Turned around and he pointed out the tyre he had just slashed to shreds with his knife.

'Jesus,' she mumbled. 'I'm late for work too.' She pointed at the food court.

'I can help.'

She stared at him critically, but she could not see much in the light, just a nice smile. He followed her back to her car, and she fumbled with the keys. He leaned over her and popped the boot. 'Listen, I can do this, and you can go to work. Just let me get the spare tyre out, you lock up the car and I can change it. No problem.'

'Really? I can always call my dad.' She raised her phone.

'It's no problem, ma'am. I do this all the time.'

She was naturally suspicious. In this isolated car park, just the two of them and the dark wind swirling around them like a cape.

'When you get back it'll be done.'

'You'd really do that?'

'I wouldn't want my daughter stranded late at night with a broken-down car.'

That relaxed her. 'Who are you? Mr McDonald's University Man?'

He reached out his hand. 'John Grimes. You?'

'Tara Cruickshank.'

He shook a cold, limp hand.

Now was the moment. A quick slip of the wrist and she'd be on the ground. But he wanted to play her a little more. So he turned away, pulled the spare tyre out, grabbed the tools, slammed the boot. 'Lock the car. And just leave me to it, okay?'

She beeped the key and the car flashed its orange lights three times. Locked.

'Listen, thank you...' She was still in doubt.

'Go to work, you're late.'

'You sure? Thank you so much, John, I really appreciate it.'

'And just one thing...'

She turned.

'You shouldn't wear such skimpy clothing at night. If you were my daughter, I would not be happy for her to be dressed like that.'

'What?' she said, shocked. She stepped back, tried to look into his face but he had deliberately stood in silhouette with the city lights of Mooloolaba behind him. Not that it mattered. She had seen him anyway and so she would not live to tell the tale.

But to her credit, she fought back. 'Really, that is not... an appropriate thing to say...'

'I'm just concerned as a father would be.'

'I think I'd better go now. Please don't fix my tyre, I can call my dad. I'm calling him now.' She lifted her phone again, as if it were a weapon.

He raised his hands as if surrendering. 'I'm trying to show a little kindness, concern. For your safety. There are some weird people out there.'

'I have to go,' she said. She stared at the tyre on the ground. She could not very well ask him to put it back into the boot. 'Please just leave it. My dad will sort it out.'

She pushed past him, and he called after her. 'If I were your father, I wouldn't let you out dressed like that.'

She walked faster, clutching her phone, not looking back.

'Wearing that whore-red lipstick and nail polish. You know what that does to a guy, what message it sends?'

She was walking so fast now she was almost running. He felt that adrenaline kick in. He could easily rugby tackle her and bring her down, and he savoured the thrill of the chase. He paced after her, calling out, 'You see, men are turned on by looks. You're saying "rape me, I'm here for you, I'm an object of desire". By dressing like that you know that you want to tease men, but then you complain when they actually do come after you.'

She started running, her fuck-me high heels clattering on the pavement. A huge spray of water splashed up and drenched her and she stumbled, tottered and fell.

He caught up with her, reached out his hand. 'Are you all right?'

The look of a cornered rat. 'Please...' She was begging already.

PAUL WILLIAMS

'I'm so sorry. I didn't mean to scare you. Here, let me help you up.'

She took his hand and he hoisted her up.

There were two possibilities here. He could just snatch her right here, take what he wanted, make her watch in terror as he tore off those whore-red nails and ripped the whore-red skin off her lips and ripped out her earrings. But it was too public. Anyone might walk by. He revelled in the thrill of her fear.

'I'm sorry to frighten you, ma'am, I'm just concerned and wanted to help. You see, I have a young daughter of my own, and she was attacked once, wearing clothes like yours. I'm sorry. Please just take care, okay?'

She caught her breath, gave him a wary glance. 'Okay, but really that is not on...'

Easy meat, he used to say in his teen years, when he'd prowl the streets and catch silly girls like this, dope and rape them. But now he had to be careful. And he had to be home soon. Just a quick souvenir perhaps this time.

But he had dawdled too much. A group of young men and women appeared on the pathway, walking in a long line. They were heading for the car park.

'I can still fix your tyre. No trouble. Shall I?'

'That would be very kind.'

He desperately wanted to rip out her left earring, take a souvenir, but instead he bowed theatrically. The group passed them, talking loudly, and made for the car park.

'Have a good evening.' And he watched her go, walking fast, not looking back, her body tense. He was trying not to laugh. He still had the urge to jump her. But not with a crowd watching. And he had to go. When she had gone, he looked out at the black sea, breathed in the briny air. He felt so alive now. So alive. And he felt so magnanimous letting her go. It showed his power, his self-control. He could take who he wanted. He was a god. He had spared her, and when she returned to her car, she would find the tyre all fixed, and a note to call him for a meeting, just a quick coffee, and then he would take her.

16

ATWELL HOME. WEDNESDAY, MIDNIGHT

A t midnight, she heard his car roaring down the road then slowing down and easing into the driveway. He did not smell of perfume when he walked in the door, but oozed guilt, or was it just surprise that she was up so late? He looked frustrated, tired, disappointed for some reason.

'So sorry, Carrie, you really didn't have to wait up for me.'

She blocked his way with arms folded. 'There was no conference.'

'I'm tired, Carrie.' He tried to kiss her, but she pushed him away. 'Honey, what are you talking about?' He held up his briefcase. 'We got a great deal signed tonight. US firm.'

She shook her head. 'The Sheraton? The Sheraton? You think I'm stupid?'

He frowned. 'Did I say the Sheraton? We were at the Prickly Piñata in Maroochydore. The Sheraton was fully booked so Sarah organised a last-minute change of plans.'

Carrie was not letting him get away with this one. 'So which lie do you want me to believe? That you told me the wrong restaurant by mistake or that the restaurant was switched at the last moment?' She stared into his eyes, but it was too dark to see his expression.

'Carrie, it was both. No, not both lies. No lies. I mean Sarah organised it all. I thought it was the Sheraton when I spoke to you.'

'Was Sarah there?

'Of course. I had a word with her.... About the perfume.' He sniffed his shirt. 'See? Now can I come in? I should have told you that we switched restaurants. But I didn't think it was important. Why is it important?'

In the hallway he looked so bewilderingly tired and hurt and innocent. She sighed. 'I'm sorry, I'm going mad.' She let him through and when he had dumped his briefcase and taken off his jacket and tie, fell into his arms. 'You spend too much time away and the thoughts go around and around. Can we talk?'

He smelled of ocean and brine. 'Across from the Prickly Piñata is the river estuary. Beautiful walkway. We all took a stroll.' He held her tight, but with a quizzical, condescending look: he was humouring her, treating her as if she was indeed mad. And maybe she was.

'Steve, I need to talk with you. I need– I want us both to go to therapy.'

He frowned. 'Are you still going to that shrink? What are you telling her about me?'

'Oh, just earrings and condoms and perfume and late nights...'

'Jesus. That woman is perverse! And you air all our dirty laundry in front of her?'

'Then you admit it's dirty?'

'It's an expression, Carrie.'

'Can we go to therapy together? She suggested that would help a lot.'

She could feel him tense. 'No.'

'Steve...?'

'What have you told her about me?'

'Nothing, nothing.'

He pulled back, sat on the edge of her bed. 'Christ! You told her about the earring, didn't you?'

She nodded. 'And the perfume. And the condoms.'

'Did you tell her the reason for these... things...? No wonder she thinks I'm having an affair. Did she convince you I'm having an affair?'

'No, Steve.'

He raked his fingers through his hair. 'You know how I feel about therapists. They look for something in your childhood, some Freudian claptrap. Why should I go to her?'

'We could go together. It'd make me feel better if you came along.'

He was quiet for a long time, then sighed. 'I'll think about it.'

'Thanks, Steve.'

'You know how I feel about those people, Carrie. I'm prepared to go if it makes you feel better but really, they're quacks, the lot of them.'

'Last session she told me she thought it might be when you took your car for a service. The mechanic might have dropped his wife's earring.'

He crinkled his eyes, thinking of this possibility. 'Why are you obsessed with that earring?'

'Or maybe you gave someone a ride and forgot?'

'Carrie, this is really obsession. Are you sure you're all right?'

'No, I'm not all right,' she said, letting tears run down her cheeks. 'What am I supposed to think? You're at the Sheraton, then you're not. I called them and they said you–'

'You called them? Carrie, this is borderline insanity. Really–'

'I need help. Please Steve, think of it from my point of view.'

He sat her down, smoothed her hair. Kissed her. 'Sorry Carrie, I just didn't think– I'm so preoccupied with work. Such pressure just before Christmas. Who is this therapist, anyway?'

She reached for the card in her purse, passed it to him: Julienne Van Tonder, Mooloolaba. 'I can make us an appointment.'

He read the card, turned it over, pocketed it. 'I'll think about it.'

Here she should have told him that this was the same earring the missing girl was wearing. Here she should have told him she was going to the police.

'I'm sorry.' He held her tight, squeezed her head tight against him. 'I'm emotionally numb, I know that. I'll come to the therapist, okay? I didn't realise what a state you were in.'

He wanted to make love that night, late as it was, but she pushed him gently away. 'I'm not in the right mood. Just hold me.'

He held her, as you would a frightened dog, and told her he loved her. Told her that he had neglected her and would try to do better. He realised how he had been distant.

When he left at around one o'clock, she watched him go, as if he was glad to get away from this mad woman, and she listened to her heart beating painfully fast. She saw how cleverly he avoided the so-called 'conference' meeting at the Sheraton. A last-minute switch? That sounded so suspicious. But it might have been true. She could check with Sarah the next day. If she was a good detective, that was what she had to do, without trying to be nosey, just fact-checking. So important these days when the truth slipped into grey areas the whole time. It seemed that Steve too had slipped into this realm of grey truth. Nothing was to be believed anymore. Could be. Her whole past began to unravel.

She fell asleep with the image of the earring in her mind. She dreamed that a young blonde woman came up to her, at the market, wearing the matching earring, smiling at her. 'Where did you find my earring? I've been looking all over for it!'

17

ATWELL HOME. THURSDAY MORNING

I n the morning she had pulled herself together. No sense in being emotional or spilling out all her fears and paranoia to Steve. If she was to be detective, she must be calm and rational, logical. So she sat with him for breakfast. He made her tea as usual, and even served her breakfast. It was a kind of penance, she could tell.

'To what do I owe this treat?' she said as he laid out grape-fruit halves, a smoothie, and toast.

'I love you,' he said simply, and kissed her. 'You need some more attention. You need to be looked after.'

Poor Steve, even though she could see he was trying to be attentive and loving, it was still an act he put on, a conscious, calculated act. She 'needed' it. And she could not help feeling he was humouring her, as if she was some hospitalised patient he had to dance around and talk down to so she would not go psycho on him.

'I've been so preoccupied at work. But I'll make up for it, I promise. We'll have some time.'

'And see the therapist?'

He hesitated a little too long. 'Sure.'

While he was in the shower, she took his car keys and located the logbook in the front cubbyhole of his ute, paged through and found the service date and stamp. The garage was Checkered Flag Motors, Eumundi. She noted the phone number. It was the same mechanic who serviced her car. This service had been done a few weeks ago.

She made sure he was still in the shower and searched the car again. She scrabbled under the seat where she had found the earring. Perhaps there was more to find here? More 'evidence'? She noted exactly where she had found the earring and speculated how it could have fallen here. It could not be from the front passenger seat, but more likely from the driver's side. A passenger would not have lost her earring this way, unless she was leaning over the driver. But then it could have rolled. Or not. She enacted the scene. Took the earring and dropped it from various places until it landed under the driver's seat.

If she was to be a detective, she needed forensics here. But she had handled the earring too much, she feared, even given it to Steve to hold, to Julienne, and that jeweller at the market. But what other clues might she find in his ute that would help solve this puzzle? She checked the seat pockets, the old ashtray, found nothing. She scratched the floor mat to see if any embedded long blonde hairs came up, but she found nothing.

She climbed out of the car to find Steve standing on the pathway, doing up his tie. 'What on earth are you doing, Carrie?'

There was something about his stance that was menacing, in a way she had never felt before. Threatening. Her answer was quick, and it was a lie. 'When I went shopping in your car, I dropped the receipt for something I want to return. I thought I left it in your car.'

'What was it?' His frown showed that he did not believe her.

'Oh... a Christmas present for you.' She swallowed. 'Surprise.'

Now she was as bad as he was. Two of them lying to each other. She should fess up, tell him her fears, that they should go to the police. But his manner seemed hostile.

'Socks and underwear again?'

She shook her head.

'I have a surprise Christmas present for you too, Carrie.'

She forced a smile. 'Soap and shampoo?'

For years they had given each other 'practical' presents for Christmas. She had always hoped for something more thoughtful, something more romantic and from his heart but had long resigned herself to the fact that he was not a 'romantic' person.

He broke into a smile and that menacing Steve was gone. 'This year, something special.' He kissed her, held her tight. Warmly. Looked her in the eye. You'll be okay today, Carrie? You working?'

She nodded. 'From home. Some stats for the mad professor.'

'Love you!'

Then he was off.

She watched him drive away, steadied her fast-beating heart. He had oozed menace and anger when he had caught her, but then quickly became the Steve she knew. Was it her imagination or her fear of being caught that had created this impression, or had she seen a glimpse of another Steve, a different personality that had suddenly reared its monstrous head?

No, she reassured herself, he was just concerned to see her snooping in his vehicle, searching ashtrays and cubbyholes. But if he had any secrets to hide then he would be alarmed. Or was he alarmed to see her behaving so weirdly and obsessively? That must be it.

She went inside, made tea and began working on her report for the professor. She needed to print something, so she sent the job from her laptop to the printer in Steve's office. But when she walked down the corridor, she found his office door not only closed, but locked.

Mm. A statement, definitely a statement. What was he saying to her? *I need my space? Don't go psycho on me and hunt for things that are not there.* Or: *I have something to hide?* Or maybe he had absent-mindedly locked it without thinking.

She was making excuses for him now, anything to deny the reality that was forming in her mind – Steve had a secret life, had something to hide, was not telling her the truth, was having an affair, or worse, was mixed up somehow with the missing girl.

She called her therapist who was busy with a client but called her back on her coffee break. 'How are you, Carrie?'

'I got Steve to agree to come to therapy,' she said. 'So, can we make an appointment?'

'That's wonderful, Carrie, well done. Did you tell him your suspicions about the earring?'

'No, I couldn't. He thinks I'm mad as it is.'

'Probably sensible not to confront him at this stage.'

'Will you bring it up?'

'Don't worry. I'll be very careful not to confront him. I just want him to see things from your point of view.'

'Thanks, Julienne.'

'Hang in there.'

Next, she looked up the name of her mechanic at Checkered Flag Motors, Eumundi and called him.

'Dave? I'm Carrie Atwell, you service our cars. You remember me?'

'Hi, Carrie, of course I remember you. The metallic blue 2016 Honda Jazz, right?'

'I think it's time for my car to get a service,' she said. 'And didn't Steve just have his done?'

'Let me check... Hold on.'

She caught herself biting her nails, a habit she thought she had stopped years ago.

'Three weeks ago. And yours, yes, is due for a service at 60,000 ks.'

'Can I ask you something, Dave, did anyone else drive Steve's car while you had it? Or anyone sit in it?'

A silence. 'Why?'

She had to think quickly. Why did private investigation involve so much lying and subterfuge? 'I just left a personal item in his car and it's gone. Did you see an earring... er... a pair of earrings in the car when you serviced it?'

She was hoping to hear, 'That's funny – my wife lost an earring and we took your car for a test drive and she was with me.' But no. 'Sorry, Carrie, I didn't see anything in the car. Was it in the glove compartment?'

'No. Never mind. I might have misplaced it somewhere else.'

'No problem.'

'How are your wife and kids, by the way?'

He was silent. 'Didn't you know? Jo passed away two years ago... and George is at uni in Melbourne.'

'Oh, I'm so sorry,' she said. 'I thought I saw you with someone last time we brought the car in...'

His tone was cold. 'No.'

'An apprentice mechanic, maybe?' *Maybe a young man who dropped his girlfriend's earring?*

'I work alone.'

She felt bad about prying into his personal life, but she was determined to leave no stone unturned. Private investigators, she also suddenly realised, had to have no shame.

'Thanks so much then... I'll bring my car in next week. Monday okay?'

What would a detective do next? Perhaps find out if the missing girl was actually wearing the earrings when she disappeared. Where had she been last seen? Was it by any chance on a route her husband might have been?

The information was readily available. The media had sucked every juicy detail they could out of the police, and from interviews reporters had conducted. Mary Stevens had left home at 7pm on Friday 5 December to waitress at a bar in Coolum Beach, but never arrived. Where was Steve that night? On his way back from work, he could have used the Coolum Beach route. Or had Mary lost the earring days earlier? Did she hitch rides? In this day and age of Ubers, it seemed unlikely. Though if she was working as a waitress, Ubers might be too expensive to take, and the buses did not run frequently at night. Did she not have a boyfriend or parent to help her with transport?

All this the police would be onto, of course, Maybe Carrie's best course of action was to talk to the police. But they wouldn't disclose any information to her, she was sure.

She had to get down to work, a different kind of investigation, but she was too distracted to plough through all those academic databases and Google Scholar citations, so she kept investigating earrings, Mary Stevens and the other missing girl. Strangely enough, she was happy to take some sort of action, and she was sure that whatever she found out would dispel her fears and the foreboding, that sick feeling in her gut. All that was needed was a little rationalism, logic and clarity.

She wanted first and foremost to prove her husband was not having an affair. And secondly, she wanted to prove that he had nothing to do with the disappearance of the missing girl. What a strange detective she was, trying to prove someone's innocence, not guilt, looking for clues to exonerate, not trap him. But maddeningly, she could find no explanation for the earring in his vehicle.

She was convinced that some simple explanation would turn up, if she kept looking. Either he was having an affair; or not. Either the earring was nothing or was a glimpse into another parallel world, one in which her husband was lying and deceitful.

18

ATWELL HOME. THURSDAY EVENING

C arrie sat paralysed as she watched the headlines on the TV news that evening – 'Young Woman's Body Found at Noosa Heads'. The view was a cul-de-sac, a storm drain, and treacherous rocks. A reporter pointed over the chasm and had to yell to be heard over the sound of the crashing waves. 'Homicide detectives say a woman whose body was dumped in this storm drain and washed out to sea was found on the rocks near Paradise Caves early this morning. No details are available as to her identity except that she had died a "gruesome death".'

As the story ended, she flipped channels to find out more. Every news channel carried the same story. Details emerged slowly over the hour.

The police spokesperson would not say anything, but the reporter for Channel 7 News allowed herself some speculation. 'The body is thought to be that of nineteen-year-old Mary Stevens who has been missing for over a week. Investigations are ongoing but because the body has been badly decomposed it will be difficult for the forensic pathologist to confirm identity, or even cause of death. Foul play is strongly suspected.'

Later that evening, the officer in charge of Sunshine Coast

Criminal Investigation Bureau – a Detective Senior Sergeant Shelby – stood before the microphones set up outside the neighbouring town Maroochydore's police station to make her official statement to the media. She said that it could not be confirmed that the body of the deceased female was Mary Stevens, and that it was unclear when or where she had died, but that it appeared that she had sustained significant injuries, including mutilation, not likely to have been caused by an accidental fall off the cliff.

When questioned on the word "mutilation", she would not elaborate, but she pointed to her ear and made a gesture of cutting. 'The deceased female died a gruesome death, that's all I can reveal at the moment,' she said. 'Police are urging anyone with information to come forward.' She indicated the officer behind her, a man with striking blond hair and blue eyes. 'Detective Sergeant Summers will be very interested to hear from members of the public with regards to any information you might have.'

Detective Sergeant Summers nodded and stared directly at the camera, and into Carrie's eyes. She stared at his image and the number scrolling at the bottom of the screen. Crime Stoppers.

She could not stop watching. The local ABC Sunshine Coast was giving extensive coverage, so she changed over to ABC and watched the same report again. Her tea sat on the coffee table, cold. She smelled the supper on the stove burning and had to take it off. But she came back to the TV and watched an interview with the man who had found the body. The TV reporters had seized on the detective senior sergeant's word "gruesome" and wanted the details. And if the detective was not forthcoming, then here was someone who was: a fisherman had found her body in the early hours of the morning while fishing off the rocks near Paradise Caves. He looked scraggly with wispy hair, lined face, a tooth missing. 'The body was waterlogged and ragged, naked, bashed by the rocks, torn, and... one ear was missing.'

The reporter asked him to repeat the revelations. 'An ear missing? Could the body have been attacked by sharks?'

He shook his head. 'The ear had been cleanly sliced off, not eaten by sharks or fish, but like with a knife.' He made the same gesture as the detective had made, slicing his finger through the air.

Carrie stiffened. Her heart was already pounding and her hands shaking. She tried to calm herself. The poor girl.

The camera then swept over the bushland again, and the voice-over concluded the report. 'A crime scene has been established, and the area cordoned off as emergency services are searching for clues to reveal what may have happened. The police are treating the death as suspicious.'

She kept flicking from channel to channel, hungry for more details, but there was no more new information. There had been no CCTV footage as the incident had occurred in bush bordering on the National Park. But on the ABC, after a tour of other news, the news anchor returned to the main story. 'We're going live now to Noosa where the detective senior sergeant in charge of the case is taking questions...'

'Anyone with information should contact Crime Stoppers.' The detective senior sergeant in charge of the investigation was the same mature woman who had spoken earlier, with a wide-eyed determination in her expression, her jaw set and grim. And behind her that same handsome baby-faced man – Detective Sergeant Summers, Carrie remembered – who was investigating the case, and looked no older than thirty, stared at the camera, again directly, it seemed, at her. She wondered why such a man with an innocent face would take up such awful crime work. He must have seen some things in his time, and his face was stoic as the detective senior sergeant again described the body as 'grue-somely mutilated'.

'What are your next steps?' asked a reporter of Detective Summers.

'We will do all in our power to arrest the offender and bring him – or her – to justice,' he said to the camera, right into her living room with his corn-blue eyes directed – it seemed – at Carrie personally. 'And if anyone has any information, come forward. Call me.'

'What is the condition of the body?' asked another reporter.

He shook his head. 'We are not going to go into details now. But it was a brutal act.'

Read between the lines. Rape, torture, disfigurement, mutilation, dismemberment.

'Is this related to the other missing woman, detective?'

'We cannot say at this stage.'

She switched off the TV, rushed to the bathroom and threw up. She took the earring from her bedside table drawer, matched it again to the image of Mary Stevens. Last seen in these clothes. Wearing these earrings.

On impulse, she picked up her mobile, tapped in the Crime Stoppers number 1800 333 000, but did not press call. She stared at the number, tried to form what she was going to say. 'I found what looks like the dead girl's one earring. In my husband's car. He claims he has no idea how it got there.'

No.

Maybe she should just mail the earring to them. 'Where can I send you some evidence?'

No.

She cancelled the call and instead found her therapist's mobile number and dialled that. It was late, but she would not sleep that night, and the therapist told her she could call her personal number if there was an emergency. This was an emergency.

'Julienne, so sorry to call you at home in the evening. It's Carrie?'

'Are you all right, Carrie?'

'Have you seen the news? About the girl Mary – they found her body – the missing girl with the earring that matches... They said her ear was sliced off.'

'I saw... you have to go to the police, Carrie.'

'But it's my husband I'm accusing if I do.'

'No, you're just giving information. Let them piece it together. For all you know it may have nothing to do with your husband. But they have to follow leads, Carrie. Don't you want this killer to be caught?'

'But if my husband had something to do with it... then I'd be... like dobbing him in. I'm frightened, Julienne. He can't possibly have anything to do with this.'

'Then talk to him, Carrie. Tell him everything. Don't accuse him of anything. Just show him the earring and the picture of the missing – sorry, dead – woman. Tell him how you should both report this.'

'I can't do that.'

'I can understand how you feel, Carrie. But keeping it to yourself is not a good thing to do, for the case, and for your own mental health. If you can't tell all this to Steve, then the best thing to do is to talk to the police. If you think he's innocent. But do you feel he's innocent? Or do you think he's lying to you?'

'I don't know. I don't know. It's self-preservation, Julienne, can I tell you my niggling horrible thoughts? If he was involved somehow with that girl – I don't know how – I can't imagine how – but then if he's trying to cover it up, lying to me, then the worst thing I can do is tell him that I know. If he's involved, I need to keep quiet.'

'Do you really think he's involved? How?'

'I can't even begin to imagine. I can't believe he has anything to do with the disappearance and brutal murder of a young girl. Or girls...'

'You won't believe it. But Carrie, the police will need every clue they can and if somehow her earring ended up in your husband's ute, then they need to know. I think underneath you have this dread that he's involved – whatever involved means – that he's lying to you.'

'He will never forgive me for doing something behind his back.'

'He knows you have the earring. If he is somehow involved and I'm not sure – I can't believe he would be from what you say about him – then I think you should tell the police. Maybe let's interrogate that word "involved".'

'Involved? Well, I don't think he... murdered her. Kidnapped her? No. Of course not. But maybe he knows something. I don't know, I don't know.'

'The best way to deal with this is to let them have the earring. Let them do DNA testing, see if it matches the one she was presumably wearing when she was abducted and murdered.'

Carrie sighed. 'You're right. I'm so sorry to call you – are you in the middle of supper?'

'No, it's fine, Carrie.'

'Bill me for this session.'

'No, I'm talking to you as a friend here.'

'What shall I do? He's coming home tonight. I won't be able to face him.'

'Behave as normal. You don't sleep in the same room, do you, if I remember? Just go to sleep and come see me in the morning.'

'Wait, he's here. He's home early... I can hear his car. I have to go.'

19

ATWELL HOME. THURSDAY NIGHT

S he must not arouse suspicion. Carrie hid her trembling. Brought out his supper, greeted him with a smile and a kiss. 'Sorry, I burnt the potatoes.'

He did not look happy.

'Did everything go well at the office?'

'Fine, fine.'

Something was bothering him.

'You're a sight for sore eyes.' He kissed her, held her hand. 'No, nothing at the office. You've been bothering me. The things you said. The way you've been acting lately.'

She steeled herself. 'Tell me.'

'I've really been shit to you, haven't I? No wonder you thought I was having an affair. I've been neglecting you, always late from the office, and you were crying out for help, using all these things... to get my attention.'

She stared at him.

'I'll come to therapy if that will help things. Have you made an appointment?'

She tried to sound strong. 'Sounds like you've been to therapy already.'

'Let's start again, shall we?'

It was hard not to believe him. But then as they sat outside on the deck to eat, he stared at her, his eyebrows knitted in a fierce frown.

'Why are you staring at me, Steve?'

'Can we forget the earring? I know you've been obsessing about it. You keep it in your drawer. Give it to me.'

'You know me well,' she managed to say. Why was he bringing up the earring now? Was this all just an act so he could get back the... evidence?

'I'm so sorry.'

'I'll find it, but it's late. Let's eat.'

He reached for the bottle of wine and poured her a generous amount, and clinked glasses with hers.

'What are we celebrating?'

'An awakening,' he said. 'I'm going to change, Carrie. I'm not going to let work consume me. I'll take some time off, and we must have some quality time together, to repair our relationship.' He reached across the table and squeezed her hand.

She responded. She leaned over and kissed him. And felt awful. 'I'd love that.'

They sat through the rest of the meal in silence and she threw furtive glances at him. Looking at him now, this sincere, apologetic, soft-hearted man, she could not imagine how she thought all those things about him. Her intuition would tell her. She looked at him, trying to detect signs of another life. And saw nothing.

'Now why are *you* staring at me?'

She wiped away a tear.

She could not imagine him doing anything like that.

She was going mad.

'I love you, Steve.'

'I love you, too.'

She wanted to bring up the news story of the murdered girl. It would normally have been easy – *did you see that awful thing on the news, they found the missing girl and she had been... mutilated... and tossed in the ocean right near here. Can you imagine?*

And he would have shaken his head – *terrible, just terrible.*

Surely though, he would have heard the news while at work: it must be the talk in every office and workplace up and down the coast. He would also normally bring up something as striking as this. So to realise that throughout the whole meal nothing was said made her begin to doubt again. Why wasn't he mentioning it? And why had he, now of all moments, asked her for the earring?

But he said nothing. She was on the verge of bringing up the subject to see his reaction, but her self-consciousness was so heightened now that she could not do it. Maybe she would wait for him to turn on the TV and then sit next to him and they could watch the news together.

But he did not turn the TV on that night. That struck her as suspicious as well. He always watched the news after supper. Why not tonight? Did he know already that every channel would be blasting out the news of the murder and he did not want the subject to come up? 'Sorry, Carrie, I know I just said we should spend more time together, but I have to finish up these reports for tomorrow morning. I'll be done by nine or ten. Is that too late for you? Could we spend a little time together then?'

'Sure.'

It was long after ten that he emerged from his office. He did not come to her room where she was waiting for him but headed outside and took a dip in the pool. The water was over thirty degrees and was like a hot bath, and he often took dips after working, just to get some exercise. She heard him doing his lengths, and then he splashed onto the deck, dried himself, put on his pyjamas and tinkered about in the kitchen. He knocked on her bedroom door, walked into the room, all smiles. 'Here – hot chocolate?'

'No, thanks. I'm falling asleep. You were ages.'

'Sorry.'

He wanted to make love, but that was the last thing she wanted. She wanted to talk. To be reassured, for him to be normal, and not have all these fears multiplying. But he was pressing, urgent and she let him undress her and play, while she lay passive, steeled against her own fears. She felt lonelier than ever that night, going through the motions, pretending to echo his brief ecstasy. After he came, as usual, he stumbled off to his room, leaving her bereft, vacillating between love and doubt. As she sat on the toilet and let his sperm drip out of her, she wept.

Pull yourself together, she told herself. A detective must be impartial. The question she had to ask was: would a guilty man behave like this? And the answer was yes, yes, yes.

20

ATWELL HOME. FRIDAY MORNING

The next morning, Steve brought Carrie tea in bed and sat with her. This was their daily ritual since they were married, and it had always endeared him to her. He was always full of sweet gestures like this, even though he could not show too much affection to her. This was his way of doing it.

'What happened to your hand?' she said.

He showed her the finger on his right hand, which he had bandaged.

'Oh, just a cut. I was opening a can of tuna for lunch at work and cut myself on the lid. Stupid me. I spent the next hour licking my finger, it bled so much, all over my clothes. And the steering wheel as I drove home. I bandaged it so it wouldn't keep opening. But I've messed my new shirt. How do you get blood-stains off cotton?'

She took his hand and examined it. She saw where the blood had seeped through the white bandage already.

How come I didn't notice this when he came home last night? she thought. 'Leave the shirt with me,' she said. 'I'll wash it today.'

'You're an angel,' he said, kissing her forehead.

'And did you see the news about the missing girl?' he said as he sipped his tea. 'I just saw it this morning. Terrible stuff.'

She tensed up. Could not look him in the eye. Was he testing, sounding her out, to see if she suspected him? 'I watched it on the news last night,' she said, sipping her tea and staring out of the window at the glittering lake across the road. 'Yes, it's horrible. I could hardly watch.'

The silence that followed told her nothing. She could not tell anything from his response to the murder, except that it was delayed. Surely he had heard about it the day before?

That morning, he made his own breakfast and ate it on the run – and while she was in the shower, she heard him drive off to work. He had left a note and the stained shirt on her pillow. *Love you!*

He had also made her breakfast and left it on the table – a fruit plate with yoghurt, and freshly squeezed orange juice.

She soaked his new shirt in cold water. The key was to use cold water, not hot, as hot water binds the protein to the fabric. *A lot of blood for a small cut,* she thought. And another thought unwelcome, unbidden – maybe she shouldn't wash the blood off, but have it tested. Who knows whose blood this was? *Should I be taking this to police forensics to see whose blood it is? No, I'm being stupid again: he would not give me the shirt if it were stained with a dead girl's blood.*

His conversation about the dead girl was nothing unusual: he normally commented on the news, but as she scrubbed the stains out of his garment, she had a wild thought: maybe she should go to the detective privately, see if she could talk to him without having to give evidence.

She thought of her husband's conversation last night: he had resolved to fix their relationship, but he had gone right back to his routine of working late into the night then making love to her as if she were not there. Something was not right. And he had talked with such smooth ease about the victims.

She reached into her bedside drawer for the earring but could not find it. She was sure she had put it back in its usual place last night.

Where had she put it?

She searched in likely places, her handbag, her car, even her jewellery box, but it was nowhere.

Had he taken it? Or had she misplaced it?

Fear, up to now a prowling wolf in the distance, stalked closer. Her heart was pounding. She should listen to her intuition. Her instinct told her something was very wrong here, with his overly kind smile, his patronising gestures. Even his kisses. And last night, her body recoiled at his making love. She had to trust her body on this one. She had withdrawn into herself. Could not give herself to him.

What had he said? *Can we forget the earring? I know you've been obsessing about it. You keep it in your drawer. Give it to me.*

Now she couldn't find it anywhere.

Why now would he say that? Damn. He had taken it, she was sure, snooped into her drawers and taken it without telling her.

She checked her news feed to see if there were any more developments about the case. Any more information? No.

Steve, she texted, *did you take the earring?*

A text came through immediately in response.

Hi Carrie, I should have told you, yes, I took the earring. I think it belongs to the mechanic's daughter so I'm popping around there after work.

Her skin goosed up. Two parallel worlds: one, he was just doing what she suggested, and stopping her obsessing about a no-big-deal earring; or two, he was lying, gaslighting her... he must know perfectly well that the mechanic did not have a wife or daughter, and that this earring was incriminating evidence that could be used against him, and so he had got it out of her hands in case she went to the police.

Which reality?

She called her therapist, but the receptionist told her she was sorry, she was in a session with a client and was booked up for the day.

'She told me to come see her in the morning.'

'Sorry, Mrs Atwell, I can fit you in tomorrow, as Dr Van Tonder works every second Saturday, but if there's a cancellation, I'll call you right away. Is this an emergency?'

'No, no, it's fine. Thank you.'

She scrolled down to the number she dialled last night. Crime Stoppers. Pressed dial. But again, before anyone could answer, she hung up.

A few minutes later, the phone rang. She brightened. A cancellation already?

'Crime stoppers, you called us a few minutes back.'

'No, sorry it was a... wrong number. Misdial. Sorry.'

'You sure? If you have any information, don't worry – this is an anonymous call. You can tell us anything.'

'No, sorry, it really was a misdial.'

'Sure?'

'Sure.'

The sun was baking down outside, so she was sure the washing was dry. She pulled off the shirts and dresses and bed sheets and looked to see if she had got all the blood off his shirt. Yes, all gone. She felt stupid now – she should have scraped it off with a knife before washing it, placed the speck into a plastic sandwich bag and sent it to the police for testing.

She had to go to the police. That man on TV had looked directly into her eyes and appealed to her to come forward. To him personally. Something had clicked here – a kinship, a kindred spirit. She was never wrong about these things. If she could talk to him, maybe... she needed to speak to him and him only, in private.

The police station at Maroochydore was on her way to work, and she could simply drop by and talk to him. She had to do something. But she did not want to dob on her husband. She would just go and find out some information, if she could, without incriminating him.

She felt better now. She was not going to tell them anything. She would continue her role as investigator. It was the only way through. Self-preservation. Self-empowerment.

Next minute, before she could think too much about what she was doing, she was in the car and driving south on the Sunshine Motorway, her Waze app directing her in a sexy male Scottish accent to take the Maroochydore exit and to go left for about a kilometre to the police station.

21

MAROOCHYDORE. FRIDAY, MID-MORNING

S he was met by a woman at the front counter of the Maroochydore Police Station who introduced herself as the client service officer. 'I need to speak with Detective Summers, regarding the Mary Stevens case.'

It was a long shot. Maybe he was not even in the station. But the woman asked her to wait in the front area. She waited for half an hour, and just when she decided that this all was a big mistake and that she was ready to walk out and never come back, the man himself, Detective Summers clomped down the steps, came up to the counter, and asked her to follow him upstairs.

Without speaking, he ushered her into a CIB office interview room. He held the door open for her to go in, hesitated, and then closed the door behind him. She sat at the desk, looking around at the stark walls. Detective Summers sat opposite her, pulled out a laptop, and a large camera. He grinned. 'Have to decide whether to go with a typewritten statement or an interview statement, on camera.'

She shook her head. 'No cameras, please. If possible.'

He nodded.

'I'm so glad I caught you,' she said. 'Thanks for taking the time to speak to me. I thought you'd be out... investigating.'

'My job is mostly a desk job, ma'am.' He leaned forward on the table. He was as handsome as he looked on TV, with those startling blue eyes, but was older than she had first thought. His face was a little sun-ravaged, he was clean-shaven, his blond hair and his teeth looked too perfect, like a Hollywood movie star, all implants. He smelled good, a hint of some aftershave, and he looked fit – bodybuilder fit – the muscles rippling under the tight uniform, which strained to contain him. She liked his energy. He was restless, urgent, and his eyes were sharp on her. He would not miss a trick. She suddenly felt inadequate, nervous to think she could negotiate her way here.

She had dressed up for the occasion. She did not want to come across as a crazy dishevelled housewife and had learned that men respect you more if you dress for the part. She wore her black mini skirt, tight body-hugging blouse, high heels, had applied makeup – red lipstick – and styled her hair in a long brown swirl. It always worked and it was working now. Men opened doors for you, smiled, listened to you. Amazing how easy they could be manipulated. She consoled herself – she was in control here. *Use it. Use it.* His eyes gleamed as he stared into hers. *Such blue eyes,* she thought.

'So,' he said, 'you have some information about the case you'd like to share?'

She shook her head. Held herself together. 'No, I didn't say that. I told the woman downstairs that I needed to talk to you about the murder case.'

He gave her a critical look. 'Would you like some coffee?'

She shook her head.

'Mrs...?'

'Atwell. Carrie. Please call me Carrie.'

'I don't have time for people who just come for information

instead of giving it. If you want all the gory details, read the media. They sure are making the most of it and misquoting me most of the time.' He smiled, and his eyes crinkled.

'I'm not interested in "the gory details", as you put it, and I won't waste your time, detective. But I need to know some information about the case first and maybe I will be able to help. I'm not sure if what I have is worth sharing.'

His smile was patronising. 'Let me be the judge of that. Just tell us what you know.'

'Us?' Was that a one-way mirror in this room and others were listening in and watching her demeanour, like they did in the movies? She looked up to see a camera mounted on the wall. But his manner was soothing, and she felt she could trust him. But not if others were listening in. So she kept to her script. Still she was wary of a camera. Of what she said that could be used against her. Or her husband. *Take control.*

'First, I need your full name, date of birth, address and contact phone number.' He took out a large blue detective's diary. Good sign. No laptop or phone. Old fashioned pen and paper.

'I told you my name already. Carrie Atwell.'

She recited her date of birth, address, mobile phone number.

'Are you married?'

'That's a strange question,' she said. 'A rather personal question.'

He showed his perfect teeth in a wide smile. 'Sorry. Just paperwork. Routine.'

She nodded. 'Married. No kids.'

'What information do you have for us, Mrs Atwell?'

She critically evaluated him. Her intuition told her she could trust him – there was warmth between them, a connection. He was a strong presence, had an iron will, and she liked that energy in a person. He exuded power. Authority. Self-confidence. Intelligence. Yet she felt she could wrap him around her finger if she wanted and this sense of her own power was good. She was definitely in control here. 'I have been following the Mary Stevens case since she disappeared and before I say anything, I need to know something.'

He looked bemused, and she felt his eyes sweeping over her, assessing her. 'Yes?'

'Is it possible to see the evidence, I mean the photos, you must have photos of the... er... dead body? Mary. Something has been bothering me about this case and I need to know.'

He leaned his head closer to her over the table and forced her to lean closer too. She looked for a bulge in his pocket that could be a digital audio recorder, but saw nothing.

'Are you a private investigator?'

She hid the alarm in her eyes. Was it that obvious? 'No.'

'Journalist?'

'No.'

'Then what business is it of yours? Why do you want to know anything about this case?'

'It's just I may be able to help... but I don't know unless you give me some information.'

His eyes crinkled again. He laughed. 'So you have said three times already. This sounds like extortion. You want me to give you something before you give me information?'

'No, not at all. I have nothing to gain here, and everything to lose.'

Now he was interested. He stared a little too long into her eyes. She refused to look away. 'So why do you want to see the photos? Maybe I was right. You have a gruesome fascination with dismemberment and mutilation?'

'Not at all. I don't want to see any bad stuff.'

'They are, I warn you, not for anyone without a strong stomach.'

'I don't want to see any horrible details. Just her face.'

He nodded. 'Interesting. If this is not just morbid curiosity, what is it?'

'I just need to see something then I can tell you.'

He laughed, leaned back. 'That is completely out of the question. This is a police homicide investigation and to reveal any such information to the general public would be a serious breach of QPS policy and procedure. And confidentiality.'

'I need to know.'

He folded his arms, and frowned at her, still with a sardonic amusement on his face. 'You're not a journalist, not a private investigator. What are you? Who are you?'

She smiled. 'I just want a second. Just her face... just her...' She was about to say 'other ear' but stopped herself.

He shook his head. 'Out of the question.'

His eyes wandered, and she felt him scrutinising her lips, her burning red cheeks. She decided to put her cards on the table. 'Can you at least tell me if she was wearing earrings?'

His eyes lit up again. Corn blue. Deep sky blue. 'Now we are getting somewhere. Earrings!' He licked his lips. But she could see that he was playing a power game of his own. He leaned back, folded his arms. 'I'm afraid that information is confidential.'

'Nonsense,' she said. 'It's a simple question. Yes or no.'

'You're a PI, aren't you, a private investigator. I knew it.'

'I'm nothing of the sort. Check out my profile. I'm a research assistant at the University of the Sunshine Coast. But this has nothing to do with my job. This is a private, personal matter. So yes, or no?'

'No comment. Ma'am, let us do the sleuthing. If you do not have any information for us, then I'm afraid you're wasting our time. You know how many false tips, leads, red herrings we get every day on this case?'

She sensed he was shutting down. She was not going to play his game. And she had gone too far. She should never have said anything about earrings or that she had everything to lose. She stood up. 'Well, good day then, Detective Summers.'

He looked surprised, disappointed. But he did not stop her. He opened the door for her to walk out and escorted her downstairs. At the doorway to the station, he said nothing. She knew he was watching her, and she wanted him to call her back and say 'Okay, okay, let's talk,' but to her disappointment he didn't. She had miscalculated. She was not used to playing this game.

The heat was dazzling bright as she stepped out of the station and onto the pavement to the car park. She dug in her bag for her keys, clicked the open car door button and slumped into the driver's seat. It was so hot she couldn't even touch the steering wheel. She turned the engine on, blasted AC full onto her face and caught her breath, steadied her heartbeat.

Well, that didn't go well, did it?

Only when she put the gear into reverse did she turn and see him walking out of the building holding up one hand.

Or maybe it did.

She opened the driver's seat window and he leaned into the car. Spoke in a low voice. She could smell his sweet chocolate coffee breath. He also smelt strongly of aftershave. He looked her in the eye, then made a quick 360-degree surveillance as if he did not want anyone to see or hear this interaction. 'Listen. I can meet you for lunch. Are you free this afternoon?'

She laughed. 'Pardon?'

He shook his head, pointed back at the window of the room they were in. 'It sounds like you have information that may be useful, but you can't talk in there.'

'Very perceptive, mister detective sergeant.'

'Perhaps we can talk more freely somewhere else.'

'Can you show me the photos?'

He looked furtive. Licked his lips. 'I'll bring what you want. It's not procedure. But... if it will help the case in any way, I'll listen to what you have to say.'

'Thank you.' She gave him her best smile.

'Shall we meet at My Place?'

'What?'

'My Place – a restaurant in Coolum. Just up from the main beach. On the beachfront.'

'Oh... sure.'

'At 1pm?'

She smiled. 'One o'clock it is.'

He stood back and watched her drive off. She felt his eyes following her. *Well he's a cop, surveillance is his job,* she thought. She drove up the Sunshine Motorway, stopped in at Coolum to do some shopping and then headed for My Place.

22

COOLUM BEACH. FRIDAY LUNCHTIME

C arrie found the restaurant overlooking beautiful Coolum Beach, parked across the road and sat in her car watching the joggers go past, the crowds on the beach, surfers in the far distance catching waves. Wouldn't be a good look to arrive early. At one o'clock exactly she saw him arrive and talk to a waitress who escorted him to a table with a prime view of the ocean. He was not in uniform but she still recognised him instantly. He was wearing a long-sleeved shirt and tie, black trousers, and what looked like RM Williams boots. He caressed a glass of wine, and when he saw her get out of her car and cross the road, he stood and signalled to her. She waved back, climbed the steps and told the waitress she was with 'that gentleman.' He pulled out her seat and offered her a glass.

'I don't drink,' she said.

'You should.'

'You shouldn't. Aren't you on duty?' She stared at his tie, which had a 'Sunshine Coast Detectives' monogram on it too.

'No.'

She ordered prawn risotto, he the steak. The waitress hovered around him and bantered with him. He sent her away.

'They can pick me as a detective from a mile away, even if I'm not in uniform,' he said. 'For some reason, ladies like detectives.'

'Well?' Carrie said.

'Well, what?'

'Let's see the photos. I hope you have them. I didn't come all this way to waste my time.' She said all this with a smile on her face. He smiled back, sipping his wine. 'All this way? It's 12ks from here to your house, but you didn't go home: you went shopping at Coles in Coolum, didn't you?'

'What, you're stalking me now? Did you put a GPS on my car when you saw me off?'

'No, my dear. Just some elementary deduction here.' He pointed to her car. 'Your hatchback is stuffed with full Coles shopping bags. The nearest Coles is down the street. And you would not have had time to go all the way home first.'

'You know where I live.'

He laughed. 'You told me your address. And it would have been derelict of me to not look at your details to make sure you were not a journo or a PI.'

'And...?'

'You're legit.'

'Well, thank you. At least that proves you are a good detective. But now, photos.'

'You mean business, don't you? No beating around the bush, no small talk, I like that in a woman.'

'Afterwards we can small talk if you need to. I don't want to waste my time. Or yours.'

'Right then.' He pulled a large envelope from under his chair. 'I don't normally do this. It's against all the rules, but if it will lead to any breakthrough with the case, then... I'll do anything. Follow any leads, especially when they come from unexpected sources.'

He placed the envelope on the table but when she reached

for it, he stayed her hand. Held her wrist. 'You sure you want to see these?'

She nodded, sipping the wine she said she was not going to drink. *What the hell.* She took a large gulp.

'They're not pretty. And I will get into a shitload of trouble if anyone knows. Just between us, okay? And when no curious waitresses are hovering.'

He had picked a spot where she was wedged in the corner with a high glass wall behind her so when she opened the envelope, no one could see.

'Trust me.'

'I'm a maverick,' he said. 'I watch too many movies perhaps. The rogue cop who solves the case when the others go by the book. Did you see that doco on TV last night about the case in the UK – *To Catch a Serial Killer*, I think it was?'

She shook her head, tried to pull her hand away but he was holding it on the envelope.

'Where the cop was charged with wrongful procedure and the killer got away with it, because he didn't go by the book? He coerced the killer to reveal where he'd buried the bodies of the young girls he killed, but because he didn't read him his rights or charge him at the station, it was inadmissible as evidence and couldn't be used in court. Fuck!' He held her hand tighter as she tried to pull away. 'Sorry to swear, it's just that the legal system defeats us every time.'

'Are you going to let me see the photos?'

He let her hand go, and she slid the photos out of the envelope. He sat back, watched for her reaction. She was already red in the face, and she made sure no one was seeing what she could see. The waitress did try to hover, to fill up their water glasses, but he sent her away again.

She braced herself but was still shocked at what she saw.

And he seemed to gloat at her shock. 'You see. Did you really want to see these?'

The first photo of the girl's face was taken from the side. Her ear had been cleanly sliced off, her eyes were disturbingly wide open, surrounded by bruises, and her mouth was a bloody mess. Carrie turned it over.

'Look at the next one. That's the one you're after.'

How did he know what she was after?

Frontal view of her head and shoulders. Marks around her neck. Her left ear was visible. From it dangled an earring, a gold earring with three diamonds. Carrie closed her eyes. Took a deep breath.

The exact earring.

'Too much. I know, I'm sorry. But you insisted.'

She shook her head. Looked at him. He tried to take her hand and she pulled away. She felt sick, not at the photo but at the man who could do this to this poor woman. *Who would do this?* She thought too of her loving husband who she believed would never do any harm in the world to any living being.

'This earring...' She pointed to the photo.

He looked at her sharply. 'Yes?'

'Do you have it?'

'No, we don't interfere with a corpse, we leave that to the criminals.'

'So, the earring is still on the body in the morgue?'

'No, it has been logged and stored as evidence. What is this fascination with an earring?'

'Where is it? The sliced-off ear. Is it with the corpse? Did you find that too?

He looked nervous. 'Why are you asking about the ear? Do you know something we don't know?'

She shook her head. 'Of course not.'

He leaned over to whisper, but she could hardly hear, the

roar of the ocean was so loud. 'We did look but it had been removed… before death, we think, by the killer. If we find the ear, we find the killer.'

'So, we can assume there was the matching earring on the ear.'

He smiled drily. 'We can't assume anything, Mrs Atwell. Some women wear one earring. Some women wear unmatched earrings. But yes, it might be a reasonable assumption to make.'

'In the photo of Mary when she was last seen, she was wearing two earrings, so I can assume reasonably that she was wearing the same two matching earrings when she… died.'

He scrutinised her. 'My, you are a detective!'

'Don't patronise me, Mr Summers.'

'It's admiration, not patronising.'

She picked up the photo again and stared at the dead woman's face. How she must have suffered! The earring was exactly the one she found in her husband's car. Exactly. She pushed the photo away. She was shaking. She hoped he did not see, but he picked up everything – he was a detective, after all. 'You okay?'

'It's sick, ghastly, hideous.'

'I did warn you.'

She slid the photos back in the envelope and passed them to him just in time. The waitress arrived with the meals, smiled and placed them down. 'Enjoy!'

Carrie looked at the steaming pile of rice and seafood. 'I don't think I can eat after seeing those photos.'

'I'm sorry,' he said. 'We should have eaten before.'

He took the envelope and slid it back into his laptop bag. 'Is that all you wanted to see? There are others…'

She stood, as surprised at her impulsive action as he was.

'You're leaving? Again? We haven't eaten yet. And you haven't fulfilled your part of the bargain.'

'Bargain? There was no bargain. I need to go for a walk.'

'Sure. But come back. Your food is waiting. You feeling a little queasy maybe?'

'I'll call you,' she said.

'Don't go.' He looked disappointed. 'I might be able to help you if you tell me what you want–'

'I do feel a little... weird.' *Not because of the photos,* she wanted to say, *but because of the connection to my husband, because the earring is a match, because I can't tell you what I know.*

'I'll wait here. I'm going to eat my lunch. Only have to be back at the CIB office at two thirty.' He passed her his business card.

She strode across the road and onto the path to the beach, took off her shoes and left them at the entrance. The sand was hot, the wind strong, the sun baking, and the smell of the ocean tangy in her nostrils. She was sweating and wiped her brow. She ran into the shallows to stop her feet burning on the sand. That was better. She was surprised at how cool the ocean felt. She let the waves froth at her feet, bent over and splashed her face with seawater. She would take a swim if she had her bathing suit: she needed to wash away this terrible feeling in her gut, to get away from these terrible thoughts. But she couldn't.

She thought of the body – cold, naked, bruised, mutilated – and tried to imagine the man who did this to the girl. She could not. Her husband? Not in a million years.

The earring was a perfect match. No doubt about that. But what did that mean?

She pulled out her phone and called her therapist. Her office was just down the road – in Mooloolaba. She could just get in her car and drive there now.

'Hello?'

'Julienne, it's me, Carrie.'

'So sorry I could not fit you in this morning. I'm free tomorrow morning though. I'm at work on Saturday this week.'

'I just need a quick word.'

'Okay. But I'm about to start a session now with a client, Carrie. What's happened? Are you okay?'

'Fine, fine. I'm meeting a policeman at the My Place restaurant in Coolum and I need your advice.'

'Great! You contacted the police?'

'I haven't told him anything yet. But the earring is a match. The one I found in Steve's car is exactly like the one Mary was wearing when she was murdered... He showed me the photograph.'

'Great. Let him take care of everything? You can let it all go now, Carrie.'

'I didn't tell him anything, this policeman. Should I? Can I trust him...? I was about to, and I had to go for a walk, he's waiting for me. I just want to go home.'

'You have to tell him, Carrie. Isn't it a criminal offence, or at least a moral offence, to withhold evidence? Go back and tell him.'

'I can't.'

'I have to go, Carrie. Go back there and tell him everything. You'll feel better. You can't carry this burden. Well done for approaching the police. Now go tell him. And I'll see you tomorrow.'

She slipped the phone back into her purse. Steadied her heart. The therapist was right. She had to be logical about this. Could Steve be a serial killer? Could he do this to this poor young woman, and to others? That was what was impossible for her to imagine. Could he be a split personality? She tried to understand how a person could have two completely opposite personalities.

Not impossible. As she waded through the shallows, she

googled 'schizophrenia'. It was the wrong word; she typed in 'split personality', and it corrected her, offered her 'dissociative identity disorder'. Could be more than two, she read. A person could split into thousands of different personalities.

How was that possible? Could Steve suffer from dissociative identity disorder, be a wonderful husband at home who brought her tea in the morning, and then went out and murdered and mutilated young women at night? This disorder, she read, was often the result of childhood trauma or abuse. But what trauma had Steve experienced as a child?

She realised now that she knew very little about him – he did not talk much about his past. He had been in the military – she knew that much, signed up for the army after school, and was sent to some country in the Middle East. That had to be traumatic. But she had never asked him, and he had told her that he didn't ever want to talk about it. He needed therapy – she was right, but now she feared the worst, that he was beyond hope of therapy.

But why the worst? Maybe he had simply given the girl a ride and didn't want to tell his wife about it. Maybe his secret lover had a set of earrings just the same and it was all coincidence. She had bought the pair at the same market stall as Mary. And feared she would discover his secret affair. Even an affair was better than where her fears were taking her now.

She could not let that cop suspect anything. She should not have mentioned the damn earring. Now he'd be sniffing around trying to find out why she was so interested in it. She had to go back and stop his suspicions.

But first, she did something impulsive. She tossed her phone and keys and purse onto the sand, and threw herself into the waves, clothes and all. Drenched herself completely. Dived under the waves and came up feeling much better. Her skirt and top clung to her skin and her hair was a ragged tangle, but who cared. She swept her hair back, pulled the clinging cotton off her skin, collected her belongings and walked back through the sand to the road. An outdoor shower by the path beckoned her. She stood under it for a few minutes, enjoying the fine needles of water as they invigorated her skin, as she pulled her fingers through her hair, and straightened her clothing, digging sand out of her pockets and underwear. She must look a sight. But this was the beach, and everyone looked like this. Some women wore shorts and bras, some lay topless on the sand by the far rocks. She found her shoes and picked her way across the road to the restaurant.

'You're back!' He stood up when he saw her. 'And looks like you had a quick dip in the ocean.'

She slid back into her chair. 'I'm not normally like this, I just had to.'

'I understand,' he said. 'It's such a muggy day.'

She moved her chair into the sun and began to dry off. She saw that he had eaten his steak, but her meal was covered with a plate. 'The waitress was going to box it up, but I told her to wait. I had an inkling you'd be back.'

She took off the covering plate and began to eat. The risotto was still warm, and she was hungry now. Maybe the food would stop the trembling in her stomach. 'Sorry, those photos affected me. How can you stand to do your job? Don't you get nightmares?'

'No, I get angry. It's my job to catch the man who did these things to that girl. That's what drives me. That's why I'm here. Anything to get the man who did this before he does it again to someone else.'

She ate her food in silence.

'You have to tell me what you know. You have some information. The earring, is it? Why are you so interested in her earring?'

She continued eating.

'Well?'

'Nothing. Women just notice things like earrings. I'm sorry, I was just being curious. I'm wasting your time.'

He leaned back. 'Not at all. I needed to take a lunch break. Detective work is a twenty-four seven job.'

'You have family, Mr Summers?'

'I'm divorced. Why?'

She shook her head.

'Now,' he said, 'I'm ordering dessert, and coffee.'

'I really have to get home and out of these wet clothes.'

He called the waitress, and ordered two coffees, and a fudge brownie to share.

'I said–'

But he smiled. 'It's on me. I really need to talk to you about that earring. If you leave, I may have to require you to come down to the police station to make a statement.'

She scrutinised him to see if he was joking or threatening her. Then she gave him a skew smile. 'And if you do, I'll have to tell them how you went against police procedure and showed me confidential photos.'

He laughed. '*Touché!* Okay, okay. But I know you have something to tell me. Otherwise you would not have come to the station in the first place or agreed to meet me here.'

The risotto stuck in her throat and she had to sip down a glass of water.

'You all right?'

She banged her chest. 'Risotto is a little dry.'

He was eyeing her closely now. With intense interest. Could he read her thoughts, sense her fear? She considered what to say, whether to tell him more. The coffee and brownie arrived, and she sipped the coffee, but did not touch the brown doughy mess, which he divided in two and passed over to her.

'Trust me,' he said. 'Whatever you say will not go further than this table. It can't anyway. As you rightly deduced, Ms Amateur Detective, because I am not following procedure, have not obtained your statement or recorded any of our conversations, nothing you say here can properly be used as evidence in court. So, tell me what's on your mind. You look very stressed.'

She looked at him critically. He could be lying, and she suspected that he could use anything she said, but she had to trust her intuition, and her intuition said that he was all right – and she needed to tell him.

She waited and in the long silence she wagered that she was safe telling him, as he had already broken police protocol. He sat, patient, considerate. But she was still careful.

'I just want to ask you something, that's all. Advice. Suppose... just suppose someone found an earring, and it was the matching, missing earring. What should they do?'

His eyes lit up. 'They should turn it over as evidence and tell me where they obtained it.'

'And if they no longer had it in their possession?'

'Then how would I believe them? We get many crank calls.'

She took out her phone. 'You promise this does not go further than here, because I will deny it if you try to make me give an official statement.'

'I swear on a stack of Bibles this high.' He held his hand a metre off the ground.

She scrolled down, found the photo and showed him. 'This earring.'

He squinted at the small screen. Took it so he could see it without the reflection of the sun. Zoomed out with a deft movement of his two fingers. Then he placed the phone on the table and slid out the photo from the envelope again to compare the two. Whistled. 'That certainly looks like a match. But there are many earrings similar to this.'

'No, I've checked. It's one of a kind.'

He looked into her eyes. 'Where did you get this photo?'

She sighed. 'That's the problem. I can't tell you.'

He cut up the remainder of the fudge brownie, offered it to her, and when she shook her head, stuffed half of it into his mouth. 'This is so good. Really have some.'

She took the remaining quarter and nibbled it.

'You can tell me. You can trust me. I'll treat this as an anonymous tip-off. You won't be questioned or get into any trouble.'

'I found it in a car.'

'The photo?'

'The earring.'

'Whose car?'

'My husband's.'

'Shit.'

'He didn't do it, he's not a murderer, he doesn't even know where it came from. But I don't want him to get into trouble. Or to know I dobbed him in. I just don't know what to do.'

'So, he knows that you found this earring in his car?'

She nodded, wiped away a tear with her free hand.

'How did he react when you told him?'

'Bewilderment. Denial. I thought he was having an affair, that this belonged to his mistress, that I had caught him out, poor man, then I saw the missing girl photo, saw the earrings matched... and now this.' She pointed to the photo of the girl which was still on the table. 'I don't know what to think.'

He leaned forward, looked into her eyes. She looked away. Wiped a tear. She suddenly had the feeling that someone was watching her, so she looked around, saw – or almost saw – a figure turning his head and disappearing behind the high-rise next to the restaurant. She leaned back in her chair. Without thinking, she picked up the crumbs of the remaining brownie and ate it.

Now he became the investigator firing questions at her, one after the other, but still in a soft, kind voice. 'Does he know you connect the earring to the victim?'

She shook her head. 'He doesn't know that I think it's the matching earring on the dead girl. I don't know what he knows, actually.'

'How is he acting towards you?'

'He's kind. But it feels like he's... humouring me, as if he thinks I'm paranoid, mad. Maybe I am.'

'But what explanation does he give for having a woman's earring in his car?'

'He was just as bewildered as me. He has no idea how it got there.'

The detective laughed. 'Or he's a good actor.'

'Or he's right – maybe the mechanic did drop it there by mistake. Or someone he gave a ride to at work.' *Or he's a cold-blooded killer and is deliberately gaslighting me. Or has a personality disorder.* But she did not tell the detective this.

'Where is the earring? You said you didn't have it anymore.'

'He took it.'

He pursed his lips. 'You gave it to him? Why?'

'He went through my things and found it.'

He whistled. 'That's not good, Carrie.'

'No.'

'Now this is very important – have you told anyone else about this?'

She shook her head. 'No, because I thought he was having an affair. My family would judge me, my friends would pity me. No.'

'You sure? Because if – and only if – he is involved, if he knew you had told someone else, their lives would be in danger.'

Her chest constricted. 'Danger? Why?'

'Think about it from a killer's point of view. You find the evidence of his crime; he has to cover up that evidence.'

Carrie frowned. 'He's not a murderer.'

'Did you tell anyone, anyone at all?'

Carrie felt her face go white. 'My therapist.'

'Yes?'

'I told her everything. She helped me get through this. In fact, she's the one who urged me to come to you.'

'She knows everything?'

She nodded. 'Even this photo – I called her on the beach just now. That's why I'm talking to you now. She made me do it.'

'That's good. But...'

'She won't say anything. It's all in confidence... she told me it's their professional code of conduct, she won't divulge any of her clients' conversations.'

'It's not that I'm worried about,' he said. 'I know about client confidentiality – only it does not apply when there is a serious crime involved... like murder, or if someone's life is in danger. She has an obligation to go to the police herself.'

'But we didn't know for sure, I still don't think he could be capable of... this.' She pointed to the photos again.

The detective sergeant looked worried. 'It's not that I'm concerned about. Does your husband know that you told your therapist about the earring?'

'Yes. Well, I don't know. He knows I'm in therapy. I wanted him to come to therapy too, and he agreed.'

'Hmmm.'

'Yes. What is it, detective? You're scaring me.'

'He knows who your therapist is?'

'Yes. Julienne Van Tonder. I gave him her card... made an appointment for us both to see her. Here...' She fished another of her therapist's cards out of her purse.

He took it, read it, gave it back to her. 'Shit. Not a good move.'

'Really, this is making a mountain out of a molehill, Detective Sergeant Summers. He's not a murderer... he wouldn't do anything like this, and this is why I didn't want to go to the police. You understand he's not the killer. He... I don't know.'

'Where is she?'

'Who? The therapist? Here.' Carrie pointed down the beach where the high-rises of Mooloolaba were hazy on the horizon. 'Do you really think she's in danger?'

He nodded. 'Listen, Carrie, I don't know your husband. But from what you've just told me, and the way he's behaving, I think we have a very serious matter on our hands.'

'He's... there is an explanation for it. It could all be coincidence.'

'Coincidence is what we look for – joining seemingly unrelated dots. No, Carrie, don't be alarmed, I'm not making any judgements or assumptions. Thanks for telling me. I'm just looking at hypotheticals, what ifs... it's how I work.'

'What shall I do?'

'Carrie, listen to me, you need to come to my CIB office and make a statement.'

She stared at him in terror. 'But you just said this is just between us.'

'Carrie, someone's life may be in danger. And I don't want anything to happen to you.'

'Me?'

'I don't want to scare you... but did it occur to you that if this is what I think it is, then you're the first on the hit list. If you know something about the crime...?'

'You think he did it, don't you?'

'I'm not saying anything. It's just how a policeman thinks. I need to get things in motion – seize the car and examine it for prints, DNA testing, definitely bring him in for questioning... And for that I need you to make a statement.'

'I can't. You promised. I mean you said...'

'Can't? So why did you tell me all of this? What did you think I would want to do with this information?'

'I don't know. I didn't know what to do. I was hoping to clear it up, hoping that the earring was not the same... that this would all go away.'

'The only way to sort this out is for you to give me your statement; we bring him in for questioning and look at the evidence. If he's innocent, that's how we exclude him as a suspect.'

'But he'll know I dobbed him in.'

'No. We'll keep you out of it.'

She thought of Steve, his innocent, hurt look. She knew what he would say: *Why didn't you just ask me? I could have told you I'm innocent.* He would be angry that she had even thought he could be involved. *What me, a killer? Carrie, seriously?* 'No. I'm sorry. I can't do this. Forget it. I'm not making a statement.'

'For your own safety even?'

'Isn't there another way? You said so yourself. We don't have to go by police procedure, by the book. You're a... maverick, you said, you're subverting police procedure now...'

He nodded. Took in the sweep of blue ocean, the waitress who had come to collect the plate and cups and watched her every movement. She turned back, smiled at him. 'Anything else you need, sir?'

'No thanks.' He handed her a credit card and waited until she walked back to the till before speaking again.

'Okay. If we play it your way, the best thing to do is to act normal. Don't say anything, don't bring up the subject to him again, pretend it's completely out of your mind. Don't ask for the earring, and for God's sake, don't talk to anyone else. Maybe stop seeing the therapist for a while so he doesn't get anxious about what you're sharing with him.'

'She. Her. Julienne Van Tonder.'

'She.'

'I can do that.'

He stared at her until she grew uncomfortable.

'What?'

'Can I confide in you?'

'I'm confiding in you. Of course.'

He leaned forward. 'What I should do in this situation is swiftly move in with a search warrant and arrest your husband for interview and investigation.'

'No! I trusted you. You said you wouldn't do that.'

'If I don't, I'm at a grave risk of losing the most important piece of evidence. You understand that.'

'Yes, of course... But I can get it back for you. I can bring it to you. Don't go after him. Please.'

'You can get it back?'

'If he has it still. If you go after him, he'll just get rid of it. Deny it. Then you have nothing. I can help you.'

He frowned. 'You want to play detective...'

'Yes.'

He shook his head. 'I don't want to put you in danger. No. I'm just going to arrest him. Then we can seize his ute, search the premises.'

She reached forward and clutched his hand. 'Please don't.'

He squeezed her hand, looked into her eyes. Smiled.

'What?'

'I have a plan. We need the earring. So, is there is any way you can find out if it is still in his possession, without any risk to yourself?'

'If he still has it, I think I know where it would be.'

'I hope he hasn't disposed of the evidence. But I have a feeling that if he is the person we're looking for, he would keep it.'

'Why?'

'As a souvenir... a memento of the crime he committed.'

She went pale. 'No.'

'On the other hand, if you could find it, it would help clear him, if he's innocent.'

'That's what I want. I'll try.'

'But I want you to be safe. Don't arouse any suspicions, okay? And for God's sake if you find it, don't touch it with your fingers at all.'

'I have already touched it.'

'First rule of detection. Failed.' But he had a gleam in his eye. 'But if you can get the earring, I'll forgive you.'

'Thank you, detective. I promise I'll get it back if he has it.'

'I'm doing this for you. I could get into a lot of trouble for this. I'm not playing by the rules, but' – he sat back – 'when have I ever played by the rules?'

'Yes, you told me you're a maverick.'

He smiled. 'I'm just worried about you. You shouldn't be involved.'

'I'll be fine.'

'Give me your phone so I can give you my mobile number.' She unlocked her phone, found her address book and passed it to him. 'Stay in touch. You did a good thing, coming to me and telling me all this. And don't worry.' He zipped his mouth shut with his fingers.

She took his hand this time and when they both stood, she embraced him lightly. 'Thank you so much.'

23

COOLUM BEACH. FRIDAY, LATE
AFTERNOON

He had had a good afternoon's hunting. He was, he admitted, obsessed. And why not? Did other men feel this way? Of course. But they chose to live grey, sexless, defeatist lives. Girls were his drug, and he was addicted. He walked down the street at Coolum Beach, and wanted to take every pretty girl who passed him. This want, this ache, burned in his soul. And it was never enough.

As a teenager his friends had joked and called him a sex maniac. Did he have more testosterone than other men? More sex drive? Sure. It was a river of fire running through him. *I want, I want, I want.*

He walked onto the beach, made sure he passed by those three women lying in bikinis and eyed them shamelessly. One opened her eyes and looked up at him, smiled. He gave her the appreciative gesture, mouthed, 'you're beautiful,' and placed his hand over his heart as if he were in love. If only she knew what he was really thinking. They bought it every time. She smiled back, blushed, and nudged her friend who was lying with a book over her face. She looked up too: 'What?'

But he had moved on. He liked loners, vulnerable women,

not these cocky, confident gaggle of women with narcissistic tendencies. Well, he liked them too, but only to punish them. Itched to cut out their vanity, one fingernail at a time. Those who were too self-assured needed to be taught a lesson. And no point in letting them think he was after them. Play hard to get. Be above them. He could have this one, he was sure. Chat her up, take her back to his place and then start to hurt her. He loved that bewildered look in their eyes when they realised who he really was. But by then it was too late.

He was blessed. He was fit, young, handsome, and somehow looked bright, innocent, attractive. Women smiled at him on the street. He fantasised about what he would do to them, which body part he would carve out of them while they watched. Sex was about pain. Making them scream, hurting them.

He was not one to keep a girl for long. In the past he had tried to keep a few but they had become a nuisance and had to be dumped. Now he discarded them as soon as he had got what he wanted. What was the point of keeping a whining, teary, hysterical girl alive? No, girls were rags you wiped yourself on. He knew how clingy women were. He knew how necessary it was to have his Clark Kent life. Paid the bills. But in his Superman life – his real life – it had to be a new girl every time. You? Yes, you smiling at me, waddling your ass on display as if you want to be caught and tied up and torn open, like a roast chicken.

Was she the next one? That one on her own, frowning at her mobile phone? But he was meeting a special one here today. She brightened when she saw him.

'Hello, Mr McDonald's University Man.'

'Hello, Miss Tara Cruickshank.'

He eyed her up and down. She was wearing a top that was buttoned up at the neck, and a longish flowing skirt. Ha. So she had listened to his advice after all. Most important, she was wearing those earrings again, the ones that had attracted him in the first place, dangling from her ears like talismans.

'Hmm, you remembered my name, I'm impressed.'

'Thanks for agreeing to meet me for an early supper.'

'It's the least I could do for a knight who rescued me.'

'Jump in.' He opened the car door for her.

'Where are we going?' She looked a little concerned. 'I have to be at work by seven so I thought we could just get something around here?'

'None of the restaurants around here are any good. I want to treat you to something really special. And don't you worry, I'll have you back here way before seven.'

He would cut off those plump lips while he ravaged her senseless. *Smile for me, babe!* Maybe bite off those soft earlobes.

She ticked the boxes, this one. In the light, now he could see her properly, he knew he had hit the jackpot. Blonde, skinny, tan lines, must be in her early twenties, looked as if she lacked self-confidence, needed affirmation. Perfect.

She smiled. 'Okay, but only if you promise to get me back on time.'

She pointed with those beautiful red painted nails of hers to the fast-food restaurant she worked at, and he watched her delicate fingers.

'Better an old man's darling than a young man's slave,' he said and winked. 'Let's go then, I'm starving.'

24

ATWELL HOME. FRIDAY EVENING

How could she face Steve again? Weirdly, Carrie felt guilty, as if she was doing something wrong, and was being unfaithful. If anyone saw her and the policeman at the café, it would look like she was the one having the affair. She pulled into the long driveway and was relieved to find he was not at home. She took the detective's card out of her bag and tore it up, worried that Steve would rummage through her stuff again. If he found this, he'd know she'd been to the police. She had his number in her phone if she needed to call him.

She texted her husband as soon as she was home.

When are you home tonight? Want supper?

A few minutes later he replied:

On a project in Brisbane. Sorry, will be back late again. I'll grab a bite here. Don't worry Love you xx

And a few moments later he texted again:

You okay?

She replied:

Great! Love you!

And the response came back:

Love you!

She wanted to do this straight away before she lost her nerve. And if he was in Brisbane, she had plenty of time. It was a two-hour drive home. Still, she locked the front door so that if he did come home unexpectedly, she would hear the car, and the key turn in the lock.

His office door was locked again, but she had a spare set of house keys in the kitchen drawer. She tried each in turn, the second last key fitted, and she clicked open the door, entered, looked around, deliberated where she thought he would hide the earring. Here? No. Not in the drawer – too obvious. Behind his clothes? Where she had found the condoms? No, he was wise to that now. He must now do things with the knowledge that she was a stickybeak rummaging through his clothes all the time. No wonder he had locked the door.

She went through the drawers, his filing cabinets, his wardrobe. She found nothing. Then she looked in what could be hiding places – behind the drawers, under files, under his bed even, under his pillow, and in his clothes. Still nothing. He might have simply thrown it away. She searched the rubbish bin in his room, went to the bins outside. Nothing. Or he might have it on him, kept it safe, or... if Detective Summers was correct, if he had something to do with the murder, for a souvenir.

No, this was not Steve. Could not be.

If he had not thrown it away, and if he did not have it with him in the car (and why would he if this was incriminating evidence he had to dispose of?), then there was only one place it could be. But this room was locked. Bolted. Forbidden. She doubted any of these keys would fit his studio.

And though she was conducting this search methodically, calmly, as a detective would, her heart was racing and her mind tumbling over thoughts and fears. How well did she know her husband? *How well do you know anyone?* She thought she knew Steve well, but she realised now, not at all. He was a private person who never shared, who always guarded his emotions, if he had any buried in that stone heart of his. And he never shared his past. Or present for that matter. She didn't know his friends, what he did all day at work, what he did at the conferences when he was away so much of the time. He was closed emotionally, but then she thought this was just him, and all men she had known. Nothing unusual there. But was there a vast dark side to him that she has been unaware of? She had to find out.

The studio was positioned away from the house, at the bottom of the two-acre property, in the forest, behind the double garage he built. He would go down there for hours at a time, sometimes nights, and she was not allowed to go in, or she would 'tidy up'. He gave other reasons that she took at face value like, 'A man has got to have a room of his own'.

Her women friends in the neighbourhood had the same issue: *Let your husband tinker in his workshop; he needs space.* Steve did tinker down there with his guitar and mini recording studio, but she had never seen anything come out of that shed. What projects did he busy himself with? When she asked him to play any of the music he had recorded, he had laughed and told her 'it was not for the public ear'.

With heart racing, she waded through the overgrown grass

to the garage, tried the door to the studio, and sure enough, it was locked. She fiddled with the keys she had brought with her one by one, twice in case she had missed one, but no, none of them opened this lock. She could see it was a newish lock, and this bunch of keys was at least a few years old, inherited when they had bought the house, and never used, as no one locked their doors in this neighbourhood.

She had seen a number of keys on his car key ring, but she had never paid attention to them. But even so, she was sure he had a spare. And this would be in his office. She searched again, found nothing. Then she began to think like a detective. *If I wanted to hide a key from someone who was looking for it, where would I put it? I would tape it to the inside of a drawer, or at the back of a drawer.* She pulled out the drawers. Still nothing.

She locked his office, left it as she had found it, and went down to the shed again. Maybe something so obvious you would not think of it. Maybe, just maybe, he had left a key hidden somewhere. It was his usual practice. A house key was hidden under the BBQ in case one of them was locked out. She hunted for likely places. The mat. Large stones near the doorway. She peered in the one window, but it was too dark to see inside. Then she spotted it. Taped to the inside lip of the fly screen to the window was a key.

That was easy. Too easy.

It fitted the lock, which clicked open effortlessly. The door squeaked as she pushed it open and she was overwhelmed by the smell of mould and stale air. Ants had made piles of dirt along the edge of the doorway, and huntsman spiders scuttled away; a gecko ran up the wall.

Who was this man she had married? She feared stumbling into a dark abyss, a bottomless pit – who knows how far he had gone into another self? As a child she had been haunted by the story of Bluebeard – what a frightening story to tell kids – about a monster man who married women who one by one mysteriously disappeared. And how his latest wife was forbidden to go into his man cave, his secret room, but curiosity consumed her and inside she found the dead bodies of all these women he had killed. The moral of the fairy tale was, she had been told, curiosity killed the cat. Women's curiosity will get the better of you. *Absurd,* she thought now. *The moral should have been: don't murder your wives! Don't have a secret room where you keep your wives' dead bodies.*

Don't go in! a voice in her head told her. *You don't want to know his secret life.*

But she was now an investigator, and she had been sanctioned by a real detective. Now she was on this path to truth, she had to go on. She had to find out what was here, who her husband really was.

She found a light switch by the door, and the room flooded with ugly neon brightness. She closed the door behind her, nervous about transgressing one of their marriage's unspoken codes. And she stared in wonder. Steve was a slob in the house, leaving his clothes everywhere, dishes in the sink, teacups by his bed to grow mould if she did not collect them. But this room was spotless, neat, orderly, everything in its place. A tidy desk, with a recording system, an amplifier, headphones. A keyboard. An electric guitar on a stand in the corner. On the wall, she found a series of medals, certificates, a map of some military site, a hook with dog tags, photos of Steve as a younger man standing with a rifle in uniform with buddies next to a rocket launcher in a desert somewhere. Iraq? Iran? Afghanistan?

This was the life he never talked about. On the desk, on display, a few photo frames. She peered at the old, grainy photos, and saw that some of the people in them were scribbled over with a pencil, and a date written underneath. *Deceased.* In one photo, Steve was the only one without the scribble. A group of five men, boys then, dead. Here was one of a man at a makeshift pub in the desert somewhere, a beer in one hand, standing on what looked like a soccer ball at his feet. Behind him a skull and crossbones design on the crumbling wall.

Another photo of two men who she did not know standing over what looked like the body of a naked man, his hands tied behind his back, his eyes blindfolded.

Another photo of a grinning man, bare-chested, wearing a necklace. But no ordinary necklace. A black fist clenched around a rope hanging around his neck, what looked like a real dried fist. But shrunken, like a monkey's paw.

She shuddered, turned away. Who were these men? Friends of Steve's? This was a side of Steve she did not know. He had once had a very different life without her and seemed to be a very different man in these pictures. What life had he lived in the military? Only now she realised how traumatising it must have been. He had buried this past life so well, glazed over it every time she asked him about it. A damaged self he had hidden from her. And if he had another self back then, could he still have another hidden self she did not know about now? If he was a different person to the one he was with her, and clearly he was, then it was likely he had a dark self also hidden from her. He could easily be having an affair. He could easily be doing terrible things to young women and she would not have a clue. If he had dissociative personality disorder, she would not know it because he kept his separate selves so watertight, even he did not know them.

He had a few times hinted at atrocities, at unspeakable acts the soldiers did. And once she overheard him talking to his old army mates a year ago about an incident they had heard about of soldiers playing soccer with the severed head of a terrorist, or mad joe who sliced off body parts of enemy combatants to keep as souvenirs, or who notched up their kills literally on the wooden butts of their rifles.

But when she had asked him about it afterwards, he dismissed it all as bravado and bullshit. 'Did you ever see anything like that when you were over there?' And he had shaken his head. He didn't want to talk about it. But now those stories came alive with new horror. Souvenirs. Body parts. Notching up kills.

He had lied to her. Kept that part of his life so well hidden.

She looked again at that first photo of the man with his foot on a soccer ball. But she saw now it was no soccer ball. It looked like a severed head. And the man was grinning, posing for the photo, proud, chest out, a mad gleam in his eyes.

Why would he keep such a hideous photo?

It was unlikely her husband had DPD. What trauma had he suffered in his past? PTSD maybe.

Now she knew. There were dark spaces in his soul. And he kept them in this room. She was married to a man who had witnessed... and maybe even committed... war atrocities. And kept mementoes of them in his secret room. Here was evidence indeed, not direct evidence, but proof that he had witnessed atrocities, been complicit in them even, maybe even committed them himself. He was capable of things she could not imagine. She felt sick. But she had to remain focused. She was not here to unbury his military past. She was here for one thing only. The earring. A detective had to be single-minded, not tremble and get overwhelmed with emotions.

Where would it be?

She looked in the most obvious places first. This was his private place, so he had no need to conceal anything. The earring would be on the desk, or on a hook on the wall. But she could not find it at all.

She began looking methodically through the drawers.

Neatly ordered, his past life – military trophies, awards, certificates.

But no earring.

Wait. Here was a shoebox file labelled 'Souvenirs' on a shelf.

She pulled it down. It was sealed with tape. She hesitated. He would know if she opened this. But she spied a roll of the same tape on his workbench. She could always reseal it. She carefully pulled off the tape and it came off easily. She took off the lid of the box.

She thought of the Ancient Greek myth of Pandora's box, where all the secrets of the world were kept, and once it was opened, there was no going back to innocence. She knew if she opened this box, her life would change.

But like Eve, like Pandora, like Bluebeard's wife, she had to do it.

She expected more war mementoes. Who knows? Body parts? More clenched fists? But maybe an earring?

She took a breath as she slid the lid off.

No earring. But an envelope.

The envelope was labelled 'Mandy'.

She stiffened. What was this?

She shook as she opened the unsealed envelope and pulled out a lock of golden hair, bound with pink ribbon.

Her hands were trembling so much she had to place it down and take deep breaths.

Mandy?

The hair was straight, blonde, white gold and had been cut cleanly with a pair of scissors. The lock was a centimetre thick, and about 30 centimetres long, a lot of hair, and she thought how if this was cut from someone's head, it would leave a gap. She smelled it and detected a faint whiff of perfume. Was it the same perfume she had smelled on Steve recently? She could not tell. She placed it back in the envelope, then as an afterthought, pulled out a few strands from the lock. She did not know much about DNA testing but had heard you could tell exactly who a person was from a few scraped cells of hair or skin. She placed it carefully in her top pocket and buttoned it. If she was a real detective, she would have thought to carry Ziploc plastic bags with her for evidence. And wear gloves. She was leaving her prints all over this place. But she had been secretly hoping not to find evidence.

And evidence of what? Murder?

She would rather have found him cheating, with a mistress, as many mistresses as he wanted, anything rather than think he had abducted, raped, tortured, dismembered and then murdered an innocent young girl and tossed her into a storm drain to be battered by waves, eaten by sharks. And kept a lock of her hair.

But the murdered girl was Mary, not Mandy.

Her husband was a man who filed photos of grinning men standing on severed heads, standing over a tied-up prisoner, maybe even a corpse, a severed hand necklace, and a man who could do this was capable of anything. Steve was not who she knew him to be. Who was he?

She would take these strands of hair to Mike for DNA testing. Even if she did not find the earring, this would be good enough.

Was this a 'souvenir'? The word chilled her. That is what Mike had said about the earring, that the killer had kept Mary's ear as a souvenir. Would she find perhaps an envelope labelled Mary, and inside would be her sliced ear, with the earring reattached?

But there was no envelope labelled 'Mary'.

At the back of the room, a pile of empty boxes, and a small door beyond. Another storeroom perhaps or a back entrance? She did not want to go there – it was dark and cobwebby, and guarded by huge spiders. She wanted to leave now. *Get out! Get out!* the voice in her head told her. But she had to find the damn earring.

She heard a noise behind her, not coming from the doorway, but behind the boxes at the back of the room. Or was it coming from the entrance? If so, it could not be Steve – he could not possibly be home yet. The wind?

She looked at the entrance but saw nothing. She slid the envelope back into the box. She had better get out of here.

In an instant, the lights went out and she was in the dark, and before she knew it, she was in a neck hold and a strong arm was tightening around her windpipe. Her left arm was forced behind her back and she was pushed to the ground and made to kneel. She could not breathe. An excruciating pain as her arm was snapped up behind her back.

A terrible voice hissed in her ear. 'Who the hell are you and what the fuck are you doing?'

'Please... I can't breathe...'

'What the fuck?'

The stranglehold loosened and she coughed, took a large gulp of stale air. She knew that voice. 'Steve?'

He let her arm go and it fell limply to her side. The man pulled her around to face him. In the dim light, she saw his angry face. It was Steve. 'Carrie? What the fuck are you doing?'

The voice was cold, hard, unlike any voice she had heard before. Steve let her go, helped her up. Her arm felt like fire.

'Shit, Steve, you dislocated my arm.'

'I did?' He felt it gently. It was excruciatingly painful when he twisted and turned it.

'Ow. Shit. Steve–'

'No, not broken, probably bruised, that's all. Sorry, Carrie, what the hell? I thought you were a... thief, a burglar? I saw the door open, and saw this figure snooping around in my stuff. I didn't think... I jumped the burglar. Old instincts. Are you okay?'

'No.' She held her throat. Her throat was raw. Her windpipe was damaged, she was sure. 'Steve you scared me... I can't speak...'

He sat her in a chair, pulled out a plastic water bottle from the bar fridge on the countertop. 'Here, sip slowly. Damn, I'm so sorry.'

He felt her arm. It was okay, just twisted, he said, but it felt like it was on fire. He walked back to switch on the light. And he saw – the opened envelope, the shoebox, the dishevelled desk. 'So sorry, did I hurt you? I saw the door open, the shadow by my desk, I thought...' His glance swept across the envelope and her terrified hands.

How am I going to explain this?

No, she thought, *how was* he *going to explain this?* She eyed the door behind him and debated whether she could make a run for it. For the first time in her life she was afraid of her husband, this man before her who was nothing like he had ever been to her. No violence, ever, no raised voice. Until now.

His eyes softened. 'Carrie, what are you doing here?'

She could not speak, and even if she could, she would not know what to say. She reached for her mobile and thought if she could just speed-dial the detective's number. *The game's up, Steve, I've called the police. You'd better just sit back; don't do anything stupid, the cops are coming.*

He stayed her hand, held it tight. He followed her eyes to the envelope marked 'Mandy'.

'Oh, is that what's bothering you? Carrie, Carrie, what did you think? Do you still think I'm having an affair? Is that what this is? Is that why you're snooping through my things? Come... I can explain everything. But first, let's get that arm tended to.'

She had to confess. 'I was looking for the... earring.'

He massaged her arm gently. 'We'll get some arnica to stop the bruising, shall we? And maybe a painkiller. Whisky is best for the throat. Here...'

He pulled a bottle of whisky from behind a curtain under the desk. 'Take a swig.'

She felt the fire burning down her throat, then a sweet numbness. Another swig and her muscles began to relax. But the pain returned, both her arm and her throat throbbing.

'Did you think... I get it now. You thought– the earring– an affair...?' He did not look dangerous or threatening anymore, but vulnerable, the Steve she knew.

She could not relax. Her throat felt as if she had a knife in it every time she spoke in spite of the whisky. 'Wh-who is... Mandy?'

He laughed. 'Oh Carrie, Carrie, Carrie. I can explain. I should have told you.' He usually laughed when he was embarrassed. Or ashamed. He touched her throat. 'A little bruising there too, I should imagine. Let's go to the house and I can sort it out, okay?'

'You sure know what to do if a burglar breaks in.'

'Military training never leaves you. I thought someone was stealing my stuff.' He pointed to the guitar and amp propped up against the wall.

'I'm okay,' she said, pulling her arm away. She rubbed her neck and was still tense.

'It's not what you think.'

He was lying. She could tell.

That noise again behind the empty boxes made her jump. She looked at him, wide-eyed.

'Probably some rats a little disturbed by all the activity. Let's get back to the house. This is not a good place to talk, is it?'

She was only too glad to get out of the man cave with its

photographs, its secret life. And Steve seemed in a hurry to get her out of there too.

'Okay.'

She walked first, wary, the absurd thought in her head that he would attack her again, but he put his arms around her gently, guided her out, locked the door, and gave her a quizzical look.

'I found the key on the windowsill. A little obvious, for a burglar, you think?'

He turned the kettle on, sat her down on the sofa in the living room and brought an array of ointments, arnica, some painkillers and a cup of warm, sweet tea. 'Drink, for the shock.' He massaged her arm gently and dabbed her throat. 'Sorry, it's a move I learned in the military.'

She knew now that he could hurt her if he wanted, easily. This military man who collected photos of war atrocities. *Who are you, Steve?*

But she felt better when she sipped the sweet tea and felt his soft hands massaging her arm.

'Okay, Carrie, talk to me. What were you doing in my room? You know we made an agreement that you wouldn't go snooping in my private spaces.'

'The earring.'

He shook his head. 'Why would I put the earring in there? I told you I took it to the mechanic. Listen, just ask me if you want to go in my room. Here...' He dangled the key. 'I'll leave this in the kitchen if you want. You don't have to sneak around behind my back. Just be straight with me.'

'Steven,' she said, 'just be straight with me too, okay? Really, tell me the truth here. Mandy? A lock of her hair?'

His expression was pained. 'Oh, dear Carrie, you still think I'm having an affair?'

I wish. I think much worse things. She sipped her tea, waiting for his explanation.

He was silent for a long time. Then he took her hand. 'Mandy was my high-school sweetheart. You've heard me talk about her.'

She did remember vaguely something he said once, his first love, big crush, never got over her.

'When we broke up, I asked her for a lock of hair to remember her. That's what that is. All those years ago. You thought...?'

Now she doubted herself. 'An old g-girlfriend?'

He nodded. 'Mandy. Married, lives in the US. We don't keep in touch. But I kept her... lock of hair. And all her letters. Is that weird or what?'

'As a... memento?' She cringed to use the word and took her hand away.

He nodded. 'Carrie, I am not having an affair with anyone, not Mandy, not anyone. I know you thought that... And I know it must seem bad to you, but I promise I'm not. What did you think?' He reached for her hand again and she let him take it and massage it. 'I get it. The perfume, the earring, the condoms, I get it. You're right – anyone would think, would add it all up and conclude – an affair – but it's not true. I'm telling you the truth here, Carrie. I'm not having an affair. I would never do that to you.' He stared into her eyes. 'You can see that. Believe me. Trust me.'

'I was looking for the earring.' She decided to play the 'affair' game here. It was safer and would explain her behaviour better. Put him off guard, if he needed to be put off guard. 'I was obsessed, couldn't stop thinking about it. Whether you were having an affair.'

He pulled the earring out of his pocket. Dangled it in front of her face. 'Is this what you were looking for? I took it to the mechanic, but it turned out, his daughter doesn't wear earrings. Or his wife.'

Her stomach knotted. 'He doesn't have a wife or a daughter.'

He looked puzzled. 'George?'

'John at Checkered Flag Motors where you took your car for a service.'

'Oh no, I meant George at Tyre Busters. I had the tyres changed last week and his daughter was in the office, so I thought it must be hers.'

She stared at him. Was he lying again? His face was all deadpan innocence.

She took the earring, looked at it, and shuddered at the memory of the photo she had seen of the dead girl's face, one ear severed, the other with this very earring dangling from it. If he was lying, he was bloody good at it. Or was she going completely mad? She placed it in her pocket, with the strand of hair. If he was innocent, Mike would determine that very easily with a DNA test.

'And how come you're home so early anyway?'

'Meeting ended early. I raced back to be with you.'

Her heart was still beating too fast. But as a detective she had what she wanted, the earring and the strand of hair. More than what she wanted. But as a wife, as Steve's companion, she was destroyed. No matter what explanation he came up with, it still didn't add up. And that violent attack in his studio? She had been attacked, literally attacked and he could have killed her. She knew that. He was trying to choke her. Would have broken her arm. She had been attacked by a man she did not know.

He poured her a drink. Scrutinised her in silence. She hoped he could not see the terror in her eyes, hear the thudding heart.

PAUL WILLIAMS

She tried to smile. Tried to make the world the place it was before she opened Pandora's box. 'Tell me about Mandy.'

'Sure.'

He talked fast, and she could not make out if he was covering something up. It might have been that he still had feelings for this woman or was still hurt. That was okay. Better that than...

Mandy was his first love at university, and they had gone out for a year or two. Very intense emotional relationship, like Heathcliff and Cathy in *Wuthering Heights,* he said. They had played music together in a rock band, she the lead singer, he the lead guitarist. She wanted to marry him, but he was too young, and she was going away anyway to the USA to study. They exchanged love tokens. She cut a lock of his hair, he cut hers. He remembered how cross she was because he cut so much of hers that it left a gap in her beautiful hairstyle and took months to grow out.

Wait a minute, didn't he just say in the studio that he had asked her for her hair when they broke up? 'What happened? Did you stay in contact?'

'She went to the States, and we corresponded for a while, then it became less frequent and then she told me she had found someone else, a musician, a better musician than me, which hurt a lot, and then later I received a wedding invitation. She was getting married; she was over me. It was gesture of reconciliation.'

'Did you go?'

'No, of course not. I was still hurt. Some things you never get over.'

She was surprised at that. He was so stoic, so unemotional, and never let anything hurt him. 'You still... have feelings for her?'

'No, Carrie, not feelings. Scar tissue. Don't you have any scar tissue from people who have hurt you in the past?'

'My wounds are still open,' she said.

'Carrie...'

'...from you.'

'Oh, Carrie, I'm hurting you? How?'

'All the time. You're so... closed off.'

'Carrie, how can I stop hurting you?'

The million-dollar question. By loving her, by not having a secret room, by telling her everything. But it was too late. She had steeled her heart. 'Did you still keep in contact after then?'

'No.'

'Why keep her hair?'

He looked at her, and she saw pain in his eyes. 'Some things you never get over. I mean I'm over it, but it always leaves scars.'

'Why didn't you tell me about her? I told you about my past loves and crushes and heartbreaks.'

'I thought you'd be jealous.' He looked cagey. 'You are jealous.'

She shook her head. 'Not at all. I don't mind that. It's dishonesty that hurts. Tell me everything, Steve.'

'I will. I do. I will try.' He looked relieved.

'What's her last name?'

'Wilson. Mandy Wilson. Why?'

'I grew up on the Sunshine Coast. I might have known her.'

'I don't really want to bring her up again. It took long enough to get over her.'

'So why do you keep her hair?'

'I honestly didn't even remember that hair was there.'

'Really? Like the condoms?'

'Come.' He led her to the bedroom. 'I want to make love to you.'

She tensed up when he tried to undress her. She folded her arms. 'Steve, I'm a little... in shock... and sore. You nearly broke my arm, remember?'

'I'm sorry.' He was gentle, loving, apologetic. 'Carrie... I am so sorry. For neglecting you... for being so busy at work that you thought I was having an affair. Work has taken over. Listen, I'll even go to the therapist with you, try to repair the damage done.'

'Steve, do you love me?'

He frowned. 'Of course.'

'Then why don't you say it? I tell you I love you all the time, but you never say it.'

'I know I'm emotionally like a wall,' he said. 'Maybe therapy would be good.'

He made a move towards her, but she pushed him away 'My arm hurts like hell, my throat is full of razors and you want to make love?'

'Sorry. It's just that I'm away for the weekend at that Gold Coast conference. I want to spend some time with you before I go.'

'Good night, Steve.'

She waited for him to close the door and shuffle to his office and creak onto his bed. She opened her laptop and searched for Mandy Wilson. She found a host of pictures. Same age as Steve, from the Sunshine Coast, went to school in Coolum Beach, but now living in Florida with her American husband. A singer in a band. She had kept her maiden name. She flipped through photo after photo on Google images, staring at the woman who had captured her husband's heart.

But there was one thing wrong here. This was Mandy. But Mandy Wilson was not blonde.

Maybe she dyed her hair recently. Carrie scrolled through pictures of her when she was younger, at high school. But no, Mandy Wilson was a brunette with long, straight, dark-brown hair. She had always been a brunette.

Was this all a lie, one big elaborate lie?

She got up, walked to the door, and locked it. She wanted to call her therapist but it was too late at night. The detective? No way. She had no one to turn to.

She did not sleep much that night. Her arm throbbed, her throat kept closing up, and the world had shifted. Her husband was a military man, had attacked her, kept photos of dead body parts in his man cave. Had committed – or at least glorified – war atrocities. Was she in some bubble, what her therapist called gaslighting? All those lies, or were they lies?

She tossed and turned and fell into a series of nightmares, waking to seeing the door opening, and Steve rushing at her with a knife, smothering her with a pillow. Another nightmare where a severed black fist clawed at her throat. She woke, drenched in sweat, and checked to make sure the door was locked, and he could not get in. When she pressed her ear to the wall, she could hear his faint snores from the office.

25

ATWELL HOME. SATURDAY MORNING

T he next morning, Carrie woke not knowing how to face Steve. Should she confront him with these brunette images of Mandy? Would he have another lie handy to cover up his previous lie?

But she did not have to. She unlocked the door and walked into the kitchen. Looked out the window. His car was gone. The kettle was still warm – the early riser, he normally brought her tea in bed in the morning, but today he had left already. Then she remembered his two-day retreat at the Gold Coast. She checked her phone, and sure enough, he had left her a text.

Sorry, Carrie. Had to leave early. Hope I didn't wake you. The conference is such bad timing. I was hoping to spend more time with you. Make it up next weekend okay? I'll call tonight. Love you xxx Steve

PS so sorry for all the pain I caused – am causing. Please forgive me. I'll try to be a better husband, lover, person. No secrets, okay. I'll tell you everything. Take arnica tablets for the bruising.

She was relieved.

She had breakfast out on the deck, and watched some black clouds roll in over the ocean. Thunderstorms were predicted for today. She loved Australian summer days at the coast, with the moody skies and warm ocean breezes. The birds were screeching in the trees and she soon saw why. A python slithered across the lawn and curled up on the stone outside the laundry door. She was used to seeing this python. It lived in her roof. Most Australian rural properties have a snake. A carpet python was a good snake – ate all the rats and smaller poisonous snakes, so she tolerated it, even admired its savage beauty. But today it had annoyed the lorikeets and butcherbirds who were screeching and swooping on it. And she saw its middle was swollen with something it had just eaten – a bird's egg or even a chick. It preyed on the vulnerable, the weak, the young. She sipped her tea and contemplated the brutality of nature.

And here was the Sunshine Coast, plagued by a serial killer, who also snatched the young and vulnerable.

And here too was her husband, a man she didn't know, a man who kept a blonde lock of hair, who kept photos of war atrocities, who could have killed her if she had not identified herself. Or perhaps he knew it was her. What had the detective said? *Carrie, someone's life may be in danger. And I don't want anything to happen to you.* A man she didn't know who looked more and more like the killer Detective Sergeant Summers was looking for. She should call that detective. She had the earring. She had played it well. Got what she wanted. He would be proud of her.

But instead she took out photos of their honeymoon and flicked though them. Steve was such a good man. His constant attention, those small gestures such as bringing her tea in the morning, doing the laundry, emptying the trash every week. He loved her, she was sure of it, but didn't know how to show it. Like many men, he was emotionally stunted. That was all. He had

had a rough, brutalising military past, and it had damaged him. Yet he was kind. She thought of the care with which he made her breakfast.

She knew what her mother would say: *Of course men have another life – don't even go there. Be grateful for the life they have with you. Look on the positive.*

But her father had affairs, and this was her mother's only way of coping with them. She didn't want to leave him, or divorce him, so she turned a blind eye to his 'other side' as she called it. Carrie couldn't do that. But she should. If Steve had a secret life, she should ignore it, believe in him. Stop unstitching things. And if he didn't have another life, then she was foolish. Close Pandora's box.

On impulse she texted him:

Steve, I love you!

Love you too, Carrie. Can't wait to see you again.

Sorry about all my foolish prying.

Totally understandable. Things will get better between us! I will make it happen.

Xxx

~

It was his favourite part of the whole experience. He had left her to stew for a while in the dark, and now made his grand appearance. She would be pleased to see him, he was sure, and willing to do anything to make him happy. He had promised to let her go if she was good. Stupid girl, she had seen his face. If she thought logically, she would know he could never let her go, no matter what wild promises she made to keep it a secret... to be a good girl. She was tied up, her mouth bound but her eyes were wide, staring at him, following him like a cat. He smiled at her. She wriggled, shook her head.

'You want me to take off the mouth gag?'

She nodded violently.

'And you promise to be quiet? Not to scream?'

She nodded.

'Okay, but I want to show you something first.'

Her eyes widened as he approached and fondled her ear. 'Hmm, nice earring but no pierced ear. Would you like a pierced ear?'

She shook her head.

He fondled her blonde hair, stroked her head. 'So soft, so soft.'

She pulled back and his brows knitted. 'You don't like me touching your hair? I thought you said you were going to be good.'

She nodded.

He picked up a souvenir from the altar and brought it close so she could inspect it. She jerked back.

'You know what this is?'

She shook her head.

'Each girl who gives herself to the goddess sacrifices a favourite part for her pleasure. I keep that for my collection. If you give me a part, then I will let you go. Which part, Tara?'

She shook her head. He frowned. 'It is Tara, isn't it?'

She nodded.

'So here is my riddle. Which body part of yours do you think will give me the most pleasure?'

He returned the item to the altar, showed her another body

part. 'Which body part is your favourite, Tara? If you were in my position, which would you choose?'

She shook her head. Closed her eyes.

'Eyelids?'

She stared, terrified.

'Oh, of course, you can't speak, can you? Cat got your tongue?' He smiled. 'Let me see.'

He removed the gag and forced open her mouth with his fingers. She bit down on his hand and he pulled back. Smiled. 'Oh, teeth is it?'

She spat at him. 'You fucking monster, let me go. You'll never get away with this. They know I'm here. My father will track you down.'

'Hmm, your tongue seems to be the issue here, Tara. You should be grateful to me. After all, I'm the one who spotted you had a flat tyre. And I, chivalrous gentleman that I am, offered to fix it for you that night. You didn't seem very grateful, did you? And you didn't take my advice either, did you? Dress provocatively and you attract mad men who read your message. *Fuck me, rape me,* that's your message. I'm only doing your bidding here, Tara. You asked for it. Literally.'

He pulled her jaw open so wide she yelled out in pain. He may have broken it, but no, she tried to bite down on him again. He grabbed the slippery tongue out as far as he could. 'Quite a tongue you have there, Tara. I think this will be the item to remember you by when you're gone.'

She thrashed against him and he let it go.

'No time like the present.' He turned, selected a knife from the tray under the altar, and held it against her cheek. 'How about it, eh, Tara? Anything more to say before we perform the sacred deed?'

'You fucking bastard.' She tossed her head back and forth. He stood back; watched, amused.

'I would have thought you would have chosen some more fitting last words. How about... Please Mr McDonald's University Man, I'll do anything for you, anything if you don't cut out my tongue?'

She swallowed. Stared at him. Reassessed her situation. Caught her breath.

Here goes, he thought, the next phase where they try to humour him as if he's stupid.

She spoke in a small voice. 'I'll do anything, Mr McDonald's University Man, anything... I'm sorry, I'm scared and when I'm scared, I... swear.'

'Nothing to be scared of, Tara. Nothing. Just do as I say, and everything will be all right. Now give me one good reason why I should not cut out your tongue.'

'I... I'll be quiet. I won't scream... I'll do anything you want me to... And I didn't dress provocatively.'

'But you agreed to meet a strange man you didn't know and get into his car. How stupid!'

'Fuck off.'

'Do you have any other special talents with that tongue of yours, besides swearing? Any ideas...?'

'Fucking bastard.'

He held the knife to her throat. 'Show me.'

26

MOOLOOLABA. SATURDAY MORNING

The view of the blue Pacific Ocean stretching out for thousands of kilometres calmed Carrie as she drove along Marine Parade into Mooloolaba. In the glistening morning of a perfect Sunshine Coast summer's day, her nightmares receded. But she felt she was in shock, that her body knew something she didn't, and was keeping her flight or fight defences at their optimum.

'I'm so glad you could see me on a Saturday,' she said as she sank into the armchair in the therapist's office and stared out at the sea.

Julienne poured her a glass of water. 'So many of my clients can't make it during the week, I take a weekday off and work every alternate Saturday. And you're my number-one priority.'

'I have no one else to turn to.'

'I am concerned about you, Carrie. Sorry I couldn't see you yesterday. You managing? Tell me what has happened. Are you coping?'

'I can do this. I found a way. Instead of being a helpless victim, I'm taking charge of the investigation.'

'What?'

'I mean, I've decided to be the detective, to find out exactly where the earring came from.'

'You told me you went to the police?'

'I did. And Mike is a nice man. He understood and wants me to work with him.'

'You told this policeman everything?'

'Yes. We won't file a report yet, but I'm helping him with the investigation.'

'That sounds... highly irregular. I don't understand.'

'Instead of me giving over to him, I work with him, and we won't make a report yet.'

'Carrie, this sounds very... weird. The police should not have asked you to do their dangerous work for them. Who is this officer?'

'Detective Sergeant Summers. He's a sweet guy. He asked me if I could find the earring and I did.'

'I thought you had the earring?'

Carrie passed the plastic sandwich bag to her and she took it in two fingers, held it up to the light. 'Steve snooped in my things to get it, so I snooped in his studio to get it back.'

'And you found it there?'

'It's a long story.' She loosened the scarf around her neck to show the bruise that was already blackening on her throat.

'He... did that?'

'He didn't mean to. He thought I was a burglar.'

'Carrie, what did he do?'

She showed Julienne her arm too, which was purple all the way down.

'You've got to get out of there. Does this detective know the danger he put you in to get the earring back?'

'I haven't called him yet. Well, I have but he's busy, as you can imagine, with the case. But Steve gave me back the earring, was very sorry, wants to make up.'

'How do you feel about him? Do you trust him?'

She shook her head. 'I found some disturbing things in his studio while I was looking for the earring. Some... gruesome photos of the war he was in.'

'Such as?'

'His friends posing with a severed head. Some prisoner tied up. A man wearing what looks like a man's hand cut off at the wrist.'

'Carrie, that does sound disturbing.'

'And then there's this. Look what's also in the bag. I found it in a box in his studio, labelled 'Mandy'.'

'Blonde hair. What does that mean?'

'Wasn't the murdered girl blonde?'

'Carrie!'

'That's exactly what I first thought. But then Steve – that's when he caught me – told me it was his ex-girlfriend.'

'And is it true?'

'Mandy is a brunette.'

'Carrie, he's gaslighting you. Put all those "explanations" together and they don't add up. The Sheraton, the blonde ex-girlfriend, the condoms. The taking of the earring. Then he beats you up "by mistake"? Come on. Too many of these lies... that is exactly what gaslighting is. You're not safe there, Carrie.'

Carrie dabbed her eyes. 'That's exactly what the detective told me, too.'

'He's hiding something. If he took the earring, he doesn't want you finding out what he's up to.'

'He gave it back.'

'Perhaps after he wiped it clean of anything that may incriminate him.'

She had not thought of that. 'What do I do?'

'I think you had better get out of there as soon as possible.

Stay with family for a few days. Who is this policeman? Can you trust him? Does he have a plan?'

'Mike. He understands my predicament. He's gentle. Kind. Intelligent. And he can handle this properly. He sees me, knows exactly how to–'

'Play you. He got you to find the evidence at a great risk to yourself.'

'No, it's not like that at all. He understood I needed to be empowered, to be a co-detective. He thinks of me as a co-detective. I like that.'

Julienne frowned. 'Just give him the evidence and get out of there.'

She nodded. 'I will. But it's all right. Steve has gone away for a few days. Gold Coast.'

She frowned. 'Coincidence?'

Carrie shook her head. 'It was a conference planned weeks ago. He apologised. Said he would make it up to me next weekend.'

'Well, that's a relief that he's away. Gives you time to pack up some things and go. Do you have somewhere you can go?'

'I don't want my relatives to know anything; they're such busybodies. If I move out, they'll think we're fighting. And I don't want to arouse Steve's suspicions.'

'I have a room you can stay in for a few days.'

'Thank you. I'll think about it. I have the house for two days.'

'Just be safe, Carrie.'

'I know what I'm doing. I can do this, play this my way.'

On her way out, she remembered something the detective had said. 'Oh, and Julienne, the detective, Mike, told me a worrying thing – he said you might be in danger too. I should have told you right at the beginning, but I still don't quite believe it. He said not to tell anyone about the earring.'

Julienne narrowed her eyes. 'I haven't told anyone, you know that.'

'But if Steve knows you know...'

'Don't worry, Carrie, I can take care of myself.'

'Just watch out, won't you?'

'You too.'

27

MOOLOOLABA. SATURDAY NOON

As Carrie left the therapist's office, she walked across the road and sat on a bench facing the ocean and stared at the rough waves crashing onto the rocks at the end of the beach. A warm westerly wind was picking up and dark clouds were gathering in the sky. She hoped it would rain. Their garden needed it and their water tanks were nearly empty. Then she choked up at how she was using the word 'their'. She and Steve had built a life together, some measure of domestic bliss, and now she was going to turn him in to the police.

She felt as if someone was watching her, that eerie feeling when your skin gooses up. She turned around and again saw a flash of colour as someone, or something, ducked behind the building behind her. She should go.

Her phone rang.

'Hi, it's Mike. Sorry I couldn't get back to you before. You called me? How did you get on?'

'I have it.'

'Mwah. Excellent, my little co-detective. Brilliant. Let's meet at the Surf Club, Mooloolaba for lunch. You busy?'

'For lunch? Why?'

'I'm in the area and need a break for some food. I've been at it since early this morning. And it's a good spot overlooking the ocean. You have the earring, you say? Really?'

'Really. You doubted my competence as a private investigator, detective?'

'Not at all. But I am impressed. See you there in a few. And just to warn you, parking is a nightmare at the moment with all the holidaymakers.'

'See you soon.'

She was already in Mooloolaba, but she did not tell Mike that. She had parked by the public toilets only a few steps from the Surf Club. Mooloolaba beach boasted the Loo with a View, a toilet in prime location on the beach where you could pee and see a sweep of the ocean from Mooloolaba lighthouse all the way north to Mudjimba Island and further to Noosa Heads.

Mudjimba Island, so the Gubbi Gubbi/Kabi Kabi people's legends had it, was the head of a decapitated lover, Coolum, whose body was the Mount Coolum mountain overlooking the coast. A jealous warrior, Ninderry, so the story goes, had abducted the beautiful woman Maroochy who was betrothed to Coolum, and when Coolum rescued her, Ninderry pursued them and knocked Coolum's head off.

She was looking at another severed head.

She could not shake that image from her mind. How had Steve got to the point in his military career where he was associating with people who posed with severed heads and hands and tied-up prisoners? Had he had anything to do with these atrocious acts?

She walked along the bustling food area and looked out at the beach full of tourists and holidaymakers baking in the sun. Locals would avoid such a high UV index at midday, and she wore a large sun hat, and covered her arms.

The Surf Club was also full, but she spotted Detective

Sergeant Summers at a reserved table by the window over-looking the beach. His suit was crisply clean and ironed. He rose to his feet when he saw her and pulled the chair away for her to sit. Heads turned.

'How are you? I was worried,' he said, 'that I should not have asked you to get the earring.'

'It's my fault. I asked to be a fellow detective.'

'So, you have it? How?'

She smiled. 'A good detective does not reveal her methods.' She pulled out the sandwich bag and placed it on the table.

His eyes lit up. 'Excellent.' He picked it up, scrutinised it against the light. 'Did you touch it? How did you pick it up? Did anyone else besides Steve touch it?'

'I'm sorry – I told you I touched it many times. I didn't know it was evidence at first. Steve's fingerprints are all over it and mine, and someone at the market. And Julienne's.'

He raised his eyebrows. 'The therapist?' He made sure no one was watching – the restaurant was crowded and noisy, but no one paid them any attention. He pulled the photo out of the envelope in his briefcase. 'It's the DNA testing that will be crucial here in order to prove it is the victim's earring. And to find Steve's DNA on it too...'

'Or not.'

'Or not. But... whew, at first glance, this looks like an exact match.'

'I have more,' she said, pulling out the second sandwich bag. 'What's this?'

She lowered her voice but no one could hear the conversation as the noise in the restaurant had risen steadily to a roar. This was perhaps why he had chosen the Surf Club. Slot machines were dinging in the next room, a TV screen constantly announced winners for some Keno lottery game, and the ocean outside also contributed to the cacophony. 'A cutting of blonde hair. I found a snippet in his... secret room. In a box labelled 'souvenirs'.'

'Souvenirs? Good God, is this what I think it is?' He peered at the bag.

'Don't jump to conclusions, detective.'

'Call me Mike.'

'Mike. He says it belongs to his ex, an old girlfriend from years back. Someone called Mandy.'

'Mandy?' He looked sceptical. Thought hard. 'Maybe there is a missing person called Mandy. I'll have to check.'

'No, he seriously did have a girlfriend called Mandy, a high-school sweetheart. He never got over her, apparently.'

'So, this is her hair? Why are you giving it to me?'

'Because, as a good little private investigator, I checked out Mandy, and in all the photos of her at that time, and now, she's a brunette.'

'So, this may not be Mandy's hair. This could be another cover up, another lie?'

'I'm afraid so. I don't know. He always has an explanation for all these things – the earring, the blonde hair, the condoms...'

'Condoms?'

She shook her head. 'Oh, I didn't tell you... never mind.'

'Every detail is important, Carrie. Don't be embarrassed.'

She was embarrassed. She hadn't meant to share all the intimate details of her relationship with her husband. 'I found condoms in his office. And we don't use condoms. He had some excuse. But it just adds up to a secret life of his... that's what first made me suspicious.'

'You thought he was having an affair?'

'I did. But now. It could be worse. I... just don't know.'

'Murder?'

'I don't know. When you put it like that, it seems stupid. Of course not. He's not a murderer. I just want to clear his name.'

'Any history of violence in his past?'

'There is his military background.'

Mike's eyes lit up. 'Yes?'

'He won't tell me anything, but he was in the Middle East war. Afghanistan, Iraq, I don't know, one of those endless wars that Australia seems to be always tagging along with the USA in.'

'And?'

'In war there is always brutality, atrocity, killing, torture.'

'Carrie, what are you saying?'

'I think he was involved in some – how would you put it – atrocities.'

'How do you know?'

'I've seen pictures. Shocking pictures. Of dead prisoners, of mutilated corpses.'

'Mutilated, did you say?'

Carrie shook her head. 'What am I saying? I have no proof, and even so why should that make him a killer in civilian life.'

'That's exactly what would make him a killer in civilian life. It fits the profile of a serial killer perfectly.'

'A serial killer? There's only one dead girl.'

'There are others missing. All blonde, around nineteen years old, slim, baby-faced. A certain... type.'

'H-how many?'

'That's classified information.' Mike stared out at the roaring waves. 'Rough sea today.' The beach was dotted with tourists and sunbathers, and the waves were filled with surfers. 'This is beginning to make sense. I'm getting a profile here. A typical pattern caused by some earlier pattern of brutality and denial. A woman he never got over. Bloodied in a war, which makes it easier to kill again. And two nights ago, we received a report of someone who was harassed at the beachfront right here – by the parking down there.' He pointed past the Loo with a View to a parking area by the end of the beach, a rocky promontory, isolated from the bustling city.

'No.'

'It happens a lot here, Carrie, so I don't want to make any connections, but where was your husband last night around midnight?'

'He was at home.'

'Sure?'

'Of course.'

'And today?'

'He's at the Gold Coast at a conference.'

'Sure?'

'Of course.'

She stared at the beach where a trio of bikinied young blonde women paraded past the lifeguard stand, smiling up at the lifeguards.

She reached forward. 'Could you do me a favour?'

'For you, Carrie, anything...'

'Analyse the blonde hair, even if he says it's his ex. If you did a DNA test, we'd know...'

'Of course we will. That's the first thing we're going to do. But if I take this in, they'll immediately summon you, and then call in your husband for questioning. There is no way around it.'

'I want to know if he's telling the truth.' A DNA test could tell her that. With all this gaslighting, she needed something solid. 'I want to finally know the truth, find out what is really going on here. Whether he's innocent or... I want to clear his name.'

'Or incriminate him.'

'Exactly. I can't stand to be in this limbo, it's driving me mad. I have to rewrite the whole past I had with him. Is he who I thought he was?'

'You need to eat,' he said.

'I haven't been able to think of anything else except the dead girl.'

'I ordered for you,' he said, 'took the liberty. I hope you like seafood, they do a wonderful Moreton bug.'

'That's a little presumptuous. How did you know I'm not vegan?'

'A sensible lady like you? No way.'

'For a nice guy like you, you sure know how to offend people. I'm not a vegan, though I should be... We all should be.'

'Sorry. It comes with the territory. It's how we cops talk. And besides, you had prawns yesterday, so I figured you liked seafood.'

'So, what is the procedure? How long will it take to get a DNA sample analysed?'

'A week. But listen, this is how it has to work. This meeting never happened. You have to go to the station, give them the earring and the blonde hair, make a statement, ask to remain anonymous. Then if there is a positive match, you'll know.'

She took back the plastic bags. 'I told you I can't do that. I thought maybe you could run the DNA tests.'

He shook his head. 'That's not how it works. Everyone knows everyone's business. If they knew we had a lead, the whole district would light up. Your home would be under surveillance, Steve would be taken in.'

'Shit. What have I done? Please, Mike, just give me time to figure this out.'

'You'll be protected, I promise.'

'I still think he's innocent. Maybe it's just hoping against hope, but I still can't see it.'

'But then how would you explain his behaviour?'

'It could be he has some dissociative personality disorder, lives two realities.'

He nodded. 'Par for the course for serial killers. Did you

know Ted Bundy had a girlfriend and treated her with such gentleness and kindness, she had no idea and refused to believe at first that he was such a sicko, when his crimes were revealed? How he could be sweet to her, and then go out and murder young women?'

She sighed. 'Am I being an idiot then not to see what is obvious?'

The food arrived and the waitress smiled at Mike. 'Let me know if you need anything else, sir.'

He waved her away.

'What do you think? You don't know Steve, but as a detective, what is your gut instinct?'

'I think we've found our man. Thanks to you, fellow detective. The pattern is quite classic. Unrequited love, an old girlfriend he never got over, and he has to repeat the pattern, to get revenge, to deal with that void in his soul.'

'Even if he is happily married?'

He nodded. 'I'm afraid so. But this is still just speculation. We need a lot more investigation and evidence. Lots of things to do. This won't convict him on its own.'

She frowned. 'Is there any way you could have it... privately tested?'

'No.'

'Shit. I can't do this.'

'So, what can you do?'

'Just give me time. Let me talk to him some more–'

'Time is ticking, Carrie. 'The ute will need seizing and examining too. If there was a dead body in there, we'll know. Did he hose it down, anything unusual, take it to a carwash?'

'No. He does keep it clean though.'

'Where is it now?'

'He drove it to the conference on the Gold Coast. He's there for two days.'

'If he really is at a conference?'

'What do you mean? Of course, he said–' Then she stopped. 'No, I'm not sure, I'm not sure of anything anymore.'

'Text him. Call him. See if he really is there.'

'What, now?'

'Yup.'

'For real?'

He nodded.

She hesitated. She was not really prepared to let this man into her personal relationship with Steve.

But he sat with his arms folded, expectantly. 'You afraid that I'm right?'

'No.' She pulled out her phone, texted her husband.

How are you, Steve? Thinking of you. Love Carrie.

Showed it to Mike. He nodded. 'Let's see what he says.'

No reply.

She waited. 'He hates me interrupting his work life. He's always in some important meeting.'

'Sure.'

'Wait, he's texting.'

Everything all right, Carrie? In a meeting at the mo, can call you later, okay?

She showed it to Mike. He nodded, raised his eyebrows. 'Sure, sure.'

She texted back:

All good. Have a good day!

She snapped her phone closed. 'See?'

He just smiled.

'You think he's guilty, don't you? That he's lying, that he isn't even at a conference right now.'

'I've been in this business long enough to know a few things. To pick up signs. He may even be onto his next victim as we speak.'

'So, what do I do? The therapist thinks I have to move out. That he's gaslighting me.'

Mike's eyes narrowed. 'Does he suspect anything?'

'No.'

'Sure?'

'I'm sure not. He took the earring but not because he thought I would bag him. And he gave it back...'

He stared at her. 'Listen, I might be able to keep this undercover for a while. I have a mate who might be able to do some preliminary testing without letting anyone else know. Okay? Is that what you want?'

'Yes please, Mike.'

'Okay I'll try, okay? I don't think you're in danger, but we want to catch him at it. If we play it your way, you go back, I'll keep an eye on him, see what I can do. He should not suspect that you're onto him. My biggest concern is that you're safe.'

She finished her meal, pushed the plate away and reached across to touch his hand across the table. 'Thanks.'

'For what.'

'For doing things my way. Any other cop would have been heavy-handed. By the book. Thanks for being... sensitive.'

'It's how I catch the bad guys. By being sensitive, attuned, alert. And breaking the rules.'

She sipped her wine. 'He's going with me to the therapist. That's good, isn't it?'

He shook his head. 'Fuck no.'

'A criminal wouldn't subject himself to being analysed, potentially exposing himself, would he?'

Mike shook his head. 'If he's who I think he is, he can play the game so well, even take it as a challenge. Or if your shrink is right, he has a split personality.'

'He thinks I think he's having an affair.'

'Let him keep thinking that. Put him off his guard. But I think if he goes to the therapist, it's for a more sinister motive.'

'What?'

'He will want to know how much she knows, whether his cover is in danger. He can pull the wool over your eyes, but if you have told her about the earring, he may be worried she will spill the beans–'

'I still don't think he's that... devious.'

'Then Carrie, how do you explain the earring in his ute in the first place?'

'I can't.'

'Oh shit.'

'What is it?' She looked up in alarm at two hard, chiselled men who were standing at the bar and throwing hard looks at her.

Mike suddenly looked flustered. 'Excuse me a minute.' He stood and walked across to the two men in long-sleeve shirts, dark pants, same boots as Mike. Not in uniform but she could tell they were the same breed. Police detectives. He was right – you could tell them a mile away, even in plain clothes. She strained to hear above the buzz of conversation, but they spoke loudly, and she had no difficulty in hearing them.

One gave Mike a friendly punch. 'What the fuck are you doing here with this sheila? We've been looking all over for you. You haven't filled in the bloody homicide reports today.'

The other man took a swig of his beer. 'Yes, Summers, where the fucking hell have you been? Shelby wants to rip you another arse-hole. She wants you back at the office two fucking hours ago. We have witnesses lined up for statements. Who is this sheila anyway?'

'Adam, John...' Mike ushered them away out of eavesdrop-ping range, gave her a furtive look, and she played with her phone, looked away. She felt herself going beet red. 'I'm coming,' he told them. 'Just doing a little reconnaissance, that's all.'

'Reconnaissance, my arse. You want to pants her, don't you?'

When she looked up again, he was back. 'Sorry to be rude, but I have to get back to work. I'm on duty in a few minutes. And I have to get these analysed pronto.'

She stood too. 'Thank you. Who are those men?'

'Oh, the nice guys I work with. See what I have to put up with at work?'

'Did you...?'

'No. I didn't say anything. They don't know who you are. Let them think it's a date.' And he offered her his arm. She took it and they walked past the men. 'Ignore them. I'll walk with you to your car.'

Eyes followed him as he walked out of the club, and on the street, women's heads turned.

At her car, he touched his head in salute. 'I'll let you know as soon as I know anything. And please take care. Call me if anything happens, and I'll be there like a shot.'

'Goodbye, Detective Mike.'

'Goodbye, fellow Detective Carrie.'

28

MAROOCHYDORE POLICE STATION.
SATURDAY AFTERNOON

The major incident room upstairs at Maroochydore Police Station was crammed with intelligence analysts, intelligence officers, detectives, the arrest team, homicide squad members, the property officer and the overviewing officers. Some scratched on whiteboards, others tapped away at computer keyboards, and two were analysing photos, charts and diagrams on the wall. One photo was a COMFIT of a shadowy man in a sweater with the McDonald's logo clearly visible on the back and some writing on the front.

The homicide squad detectives working on this case had arrived, and now that the words 'serial killer' were in the air, everyone (to use Detective Senior Sergeant Shelby's words) 'wanted a piece of the goddam pie'.

She banged her fist on the table to start the briefing. 'Listen up, listen up. Now that we know it's a serial, we have company. I'd like to introduce Detective Sergeant Holmes and Chief Inspector Smith from homicide squad.'

The two dour men nodded, arms folded.

'Why the small team, boss?' called out Detective Inspector Jones. 'This is a major serial killer we have here.'

Detective Senior Sergeant Shelby fingered the air. 'Financial constraints, budgeting restrictions.'

Detective Senior Constable John Ribot, one of the men who had spotted Mike Summers in the Mooloolaba Surf Club earlier in the bar, chimed in, listing the people on his fingers: 'We have co-operation from the scientific section from Brisbane, pathologist, forensic unit and the Kawana scenes. Missing persons bureau is up here interviewing families. And we have Detective Summers, our chief investigator.'

'Where the fuck is Summers?' said Shelby. We've been working day and night on this and he's AWOL.'

'He said he's out "investigating",' said Detective Senior Constable Adam Lucas. 'We saw him having lunch with a floozy at the Surf Club.'

'Tell him to get his arse back here now. He hasn't even filled in the homicide log.'

'Detective Sergeant Summers does things his way,' said Jones. 'Always gets his man, apparently.'

'A maverick,' said John Ribot. More laughter.

'Not on my watch he does things his way. No mavericks here, you understand? Last time he nearly lost us the case with his maverick antics.'

Chief Inspector Smith shook his head. 'Is that how you Sunshine Coast CIB operate? Surf Club? Doing surveillance, no doubt on the beach.'

'I'll kill him,' said Shelby under her breath.

He had to dispose of the body, and had planned it all to the dot, to the tee. But after the latest incident, he realised that he needed to do something to show the world that he meant business. He took the knife and pressed down on her forehead. He had figured out how he would make the world sit up. He gouged the letters into her forehead, evenly spaced, symmetrical so that they complemented her bloody mouth.

He hated tattoos on women, but could see how this art was satisfying, to the tattooist at least, to leave your mark, to show the world who she was, and who he was. Or like graffiti. He hated graffiti but saw the pleasure it gave now, like a dog pissing on a piece of grass or a tree to claim its territory. Five letters. A woman's name.

He checked to see how her tongue was doing in the jar of formaldehyde. Fleshy, red, bloated. He didn't want it to dry up like that time a few years ago when he had been left with a dried-up black piece of jerky. No, this time he would be able to use her tongue again and again if he wanted to do the things he had made her do with it. But he was satiated for now. That ache was gone. Imagine what life would be like if he was always like this. Like a calm sea. He knew though, that this would not last a day. That drive, that core of his being that screamed *I want, I want, I want* would taunt him like a demon. But for now, tonight he would be satiated, happy, complete.

29

THERAPIST'S OFFICE, MOOLOOLABA. SATURDAY AFTERNOON

Julienne Van Tonder had had a long Saturday, and each client demanded so much of her, dragging the sessions over time so that by the end, her last client had to wait half an hour, and she was finishing so late it was almost six o'clock. And to make things worse, her secretary did not work on Saturdays, so she had to field all the calls, and get back to people in the breaks. So, the last thing she wanted as she was locking up was another phone call. But she felt obliged to answer it. She took her job seriously. People's lives were literally in her hands.

The call was from a private number. 'Hello?'

'Is that Julienne Van Tonder, the therapist?'

'Speaking?'

'I'm Carrie's husband. Steve Atwell.'

'Mr Atwell! Carrie said you would be coming in with her for our next appointment. How can I help you?'

'What did she tell you about me?'

'Mr Atwell, this is not the place, on the phone, to discuss my client's life. We can talk about this when you come in. I believe that is this Thursday at... 3pm?'

'Have you told anyone about what she told you?'

'Er, Mr Atwell, I am just on my way out of the office, and this is not an appropriate time or place to discuss–'

'Have you told anyone about what she told you?'

She put down her bag. *Whoa. This is not only inappropriate; it is borderline aggressive.* But she understood his concern, his vulnerability, so she did not hang up. She put on her smoothest, soothing voice. 'Okay, Mr Atwell–'

'Steve.'

'Steve, let me reassure you, as a professional, nothing my clients tell me goes outside the door. Everything we talk about is confidential. If you are apprehensive about this, we can always–'

'But you know everything.'

'Mr Atwell, I'm here to help you. I know it must be quite confronting, but I admire you for being willing to come in and discuss these issues with your wife. She is very happy that you want to talk with me–'

'Already analysing me, I see. What a presumption to think you know what I think.'

Julienne held back her annoyance. 'Why don't you come in for your appointment and we can discuss this?'

'That won't be necessary. But I have some therapy advice for you.'

A headache was beginning to pound. All she wanted to do was get home. But now she had to deal with an irate husband. This was too much. Carrie had told her that Steve was a kind, considerate man, even more so now that she had confronted him about what she thought was an affair. The man at the end of the line did not fit the picture she had had of Steve, but then they had discussed the possibility of a split personality disorder. And he had violently attacked his wife. Here was a cornered man who projected his frustration and aggression onto others, usually women. Not unusual. Therapists often took the blame for what emerged in relationship sessions.

'Mr Atwell, I don't think that–'

'Well, I have a suggestion how you can help me. Leave this alone. Stop prying into our relationship. If you know what's good for you, don't see her anymore. You make a report to the police about this and you're dead.'

She went cold. Did he just say what she thought he said? 'Mr Atwell? What are you talking about?'

'Say one word about the earring and the dead girl, and you will join her.'

Okay, more than passive aggression here. Death threats. She had had her share of these too, but this was almost an outright admission of... guilt. Why would he expose himself like this? She was silent. She fiddled with her phone. There was a way to record conversations, but she did not remember how to do it. She had to play it calm.

'Did you hear me?'

She did not know what to say. She wanted to yell at him, 'Is that a threat?' but his cold tone made her cautious. She had to humour this man. She took a deep breath, wiped her clammy hands on her dress, and stuck to the professional script. 'Mr Atwell, I can assure you that everything my clients tell me is in the strictest confidence. It is all confidential. I would never, ever tell anyone what I have heard in a therapy session. It is of the utmost...'

She found the app that recorded her phone calls and pressed the button, but she was not sure it was recording.

'Just a friendly warning then. I'm watching you. I know your every move. Don't talk to my wife again. Ever. Maybe you need to go away for a few weeks' vacation.'

'Mr Atwell, I can't possibly do that. I have dozens of clients who rely on me. Your wife is not my only client... And please don't threaten me.'

'This not a suggestion – it's an order. Unless you want to

disappear the same as those girls did, then you will take emergency leave. A family member is ill, and you will have to go away suddenly. Cancel your appointments.'

Those girls? Was he admitting something here even more than she knew?

'Please, Mr Atwell, why don't you come in and we can talk about this? That is what I am here for, to help you. Even now if you want.'

'Just do as I say. I'm watching you.' And with that he hung up.

She locked her office and tried to contain the rising panic in her chest. She stood on her balcony looking out over Marine Parade and the beach opposite. He said he was watching her. What – even now? Was he calling from across the road? Maybe that man by the children's playground with a phone to his ear, looking towards her? She did not know what Carrie's husband looked like.

She walked calmly down the steps, determined to show him that she was not fazed by his threats (if he was watching her). She made sure she had a getaway plan if he suddenly blocked her way. But the car park was deserted. She reached her car safely, and locked herself in, checking that somehow he wasn't crouching by the back seat.

As soon as she felt safe, she would call Carrie to warn her. Was this what she thought it was? *Carrie's husband had virtually admitted his involvement in murder, had threatened to do the same to her.* She had suspected all along that his actions had not been innocent coincidences, as Carrie tried so hard to believe. He had all the indicators of a psychopath. She drove slowly out of the car park and onto the beach drive. Mooloolaba was a safe town, and you could leave your cars unlocked, and sometimes people left their purses on the beach by their towels when they swam. But today she felt unsafe – most threats she had received were empty; she knew when it was just bluster or male bravado and pride. But this felt... real. Too real.

166

30

ATWELL HOME. SATURDAY NIGHT

Carrie got the call as she was eating supper by herself, thinking how nice it was to have the space and not have to worry about cooking someone else a meal. She tried to put the idea of Steve's possible secret other life out of her head. It just felt good to be on her own. It was not the first time she had thought this, but she lived for others – it was her nature – she had given herself the unfashionable role of helpmeet to her husband, always catering for his needs, adjusting to his mood swings, and never demanding that he adjust to hers. She was invisible most of the time, an accommodating chameleon.

She also tried to put out of her head the pleasant feeling when she thought of Mike, the lunch, the way he paid her close attention, as if she were special. Steve never did that. He was attentive in some ways; made her tea every morning, took out the rubbish, did the laundry, but somehow there was a disconnect – there had always been a disconnect. She had always excused it in him before – this is how men were, this is how Steve was... but now it unnerved her. Was this the chink in his two selves? Was he absent because a real Steve was somewhere else? Was someone else?

She jumped when the phone rang. 'Hello Julienne?'

'Are you all right?'

Carrie was surprised. Her therapist never called her, and especially at night. 'Yes. Why?'

'I hope you went straight to the police with the evidence. Did you?'

Carrie grew more and more puzzled. 'Yes, of course.'

'And?'

'He's going to do DNA tests on the earring and the strand of hair. It might take a few days. Is that why you're calling me?'

'Carrie... I'm sorry, I don't mean to scare you but... I hesitated to call you, but I think you need to know this. Your husband contacted me today.'

'Oh? Did he make an appointment? I gave him your card. Didn't he know I already made a time? Thursday.'

There was a long pause. 'Carrie, he... threatened me. He told me if I continued to counsel you, he'd... kill me.'

Carrie's breath caught. A chill went through her. 'No. Are you sure?'

'Carrie, I'm going to the police.'

'What did he say?'

'He said I'd go the way that murdered girl went.'

'Steve said that? To you? It can't be. He's never said anything threatening to me... ever.' She touched her neck, which was still painfully bruised, and she was still finding it difficult to swallow.

'Carrie, you have to get out of there. He told me if I went to the police, he'd kill me. That I needed to go on a holiday. Tomorrow. That he was watching me.'

'Steve said that?' Carrie repeated, and swallowed. Her throat was still raw from where Steve had strangled her. 'Why would Steve do that? I know he hates therapists and he absolutely refused to come with me... until just before he went away – he relented and asked me for your card. He said he would go with me if it made me happy.'

'He had no intention of coming with you. He just wanted my card so he could threaten me... and shut me up. That's why he asked for my card. He wanted my number. He said he's watching me.'

'Why would he...?'

'You told him that I knew about the earring.'

'But...'

'Are you sure he doesn't know that you went to the police?'

'No, of course not... I don't think so... No.'

'Listen, Carrie, I am going to disappear. If he asks, tell him you're not seeing me, that I've gone to Sydney, okay? I've told my secretary to tell the same story.'

'Are you?'

'No, I'm going straight to the police. But if he's watching me, he'll know I'm not going away.'

'Steve is on the Gold Coast. At a conference.'

'You sure?'

'Yes...' But she was not sure at all. 'Where are you now, Julienne?'

'At home.'

Carrie suddenly realised that she knew nothing about her therapist, who knew everything about her. 'You have family?'

'Yes. But not here. I have an apartment in Mooloolaba and it's quite secure, but if he's watching me, he might have followed me home. I did some detours and tried to lose any cars behind me, and so I think I'm okay.'

'Steve? I can't believe he'd be... watching you... or threatening you. He's... at a conference at the Gold Coast.' She said it to make it real. But her world was falling though a void.

'Carrie, how long will you be in denial?'

Carrie clutched her throat which was hurting more now. She

could hardly breathe. 'It's just... so... unlike him. What shall we do? I'm so sorry, Julienne, have I put your life in danger? This is exactly what Detective Sergeant Mike said would happen. He warned me to tell you your life was in danger.'

'I have had this happen before. A husband once threatened me, saying I broke up his marriage. But never a threat this specific.'

'Will you be okay?'

'Give me the name of your friendly policeman. If I go to him, he'll be very interested in this. Steve just about admitted guilt. He said he'd do to me what he did to the girl.'

'He did? Steve?'

'Well not exactly those words. Let me see... He said, "Say one word about the earring and the dead girl, and you will join her".'

Carrie did remember a few occasions when Steve lost his temper. He did make threats. But they were idle threats. When he had been drinking. Maybe he had had one too many at the bar in the Gold Coast resort, had riled himself up, told his mates about a therapist who was wrecking his marriage and they all had similar stories, urged him to call the bitch, tell her to shove it. So, alcohol fuelled, he had threatened her. 'It's just talk. Maybe he thinks you're breaking up our marriage. Maybe he thinks you're putting it into my head that he's having an affair. I bet his mates put him up to this. I bet he was drunk. Was he drunk?'

'Carrie, Carrie...'

'Yes, I can give you the policeman's number, here it's...' She rummaged through her bag for the card and read it out. 'But please... it's a delicate matter. Mike understands that.'

'I can take care of myself, Carrie. I'm just more concerned about you. Don't want you to be in any danger... If he has a temper as you say, and he's threatening me, a stranger, won't he come home and...'

'Steve has never laid a finger on me, Julienne.'

'Listen to what you're saying, Carrie. You're black and blue.'

'It was an accident. Listen, Julienne, do you want to come over here?'

'I was about to ask you the same question.'

'No, I'm okay,' said Carrie.

'You sure?'

'If he's watching you then maybe that's not a good idea.'

'Just take care and let me know if he returns. I'm going straight to Detective Sergeant Summers in the morning, and we'll go from there, okay?'

'Good night. Stay safe. Keep your phone on and be ready to dial triple zero.'

Carrie locked the doors, secured the windows, paced the house. It couldn't be. It seemed so unreal, and she could not imagine her husband threatening death to another person. But maybe he had been so drunk, and so incensed by what he thought was someone interfering in his marriage that he would pull off something like this. Should she call him, pretend everything was normal?

And Julienne was going to the police in the morning. She went cold. Steve would, without doubt, be arrested, or at least questioned and investigated. And it would all come out – how she had done this.

She could not quite face talking to Steve – her voice would be all trembly – so she texted him.

You okay? How's the Cold Ghost?

It was an old joke of theirs. On their honeymoon, she had had too much to drink and insisted on calling the Gold Coast the Cold Ghost.

He called back almost immediately, and she answered the

phone with dread. Tried to stay her fast-beating heart. 'Hey Carrie? What's up.'

He was his cheery self. Didn't sound drunk. Didn't sound like a threatening serial killer. Was there a way of tracing his call to make sure he was at the Gold Coast?

She wanted to ask whether he had called up the therapist but could not bring herself to do it. 'Conference going well?'

'Boring as hell, but some good leads.'

Now she was confused. She listened to a man she loved, who she knew. Those demons in her head – were they all demons? Could her therapist be lying? Surely not? Be mistaken? The woman she trusted and admired more than anyone else in the world?

Steve's voice was soothing. 'Godawful day, but we got the deal. Tonight, we're chilling with the bigwig – mad old guy, but I'm going to sneak off and have a swim in the heated pool. And my room has a spa!'

'Maybe I should have come!'

'Wish you were here. Next time, I'll make sure of it, though I'm in meetings all day and night. Listen, I'll be home by lunch on Sunday, or sooner if there's not much traffic. How are things there?'

She swallowed painfully. 'Fine. Quiet, as usual.'

'Love you, Carrie.'

'Love you, Steve.'

The words rolled off her tongue, and she wished, wished that this was the reality, that she had never found an earring, never found a lock of blonde hair. If she ignored it would it all just go away, and could she get on with her life as normal with Steve, this Steve, and obliterate these demons that clutched her heart?

She would know soon enough.

She sat but could not sit still for long. And like a scab she kept picking, she could not leave well alone. She googled the hotel he was staying at. And before she knew it, she had called reception.

'Hello?'

'Is there a Mr Steven Atwell staying there? I'm his wife.'

'There is no one of that name staying here.'

'Maybe under the company name? He's staying in a suite – with spa – there can't be many of those. Near the heated pool he said...'

'I'm sorry ma'am, but none of our rooms have spas. And our pool is not open at the moment, while it is being upgraded.'

Her heart was pounding. 'I see. Okay, don't worry, thank you.'

Maybe she had the wrong hotel. There may be more than one Radisson at the Gold Coast. She was about to call Steve on his mobile, but then decided not to. It would seem suspicious if she questioned the name of the hotel he was at. Again.

If she was a true detective, she would have put a trace on his mobile, to see where he had actually phoned from. She had to find out how to do that.

But she was too emotional. A true detective does not get emotionally involved. She googled other Radissons – yes, of course, there were several – but then did not call them. That had to be it. She had got hold of the wrong one.

She made sure the doors were all locked, and windows fastened, though she did not know why. He had a key. He could get in anyway. The night was dark – no stars, no moon, just those low black storm clouds and wind, and the house creaked and groaned. Branches scraped against the roof. Bats screeched in the gum trees; frogs croaked loudly in the retention pond. She could not rest.

His office door was open. He had made a pact to be open, but she was sure that he had carefully hidden anything he did not want her to see. She turned on the light, drew the curtains, and booted his computer. She was locked out, but she had an idea. Just maybe...

Password?

She typed the name MANDY.

Sorry wrong password.

It was stupid she knew, but she had to try.

Carrie.

Of course not.

Mandy with a capital M.

Wrong password.

mandy

The screen opened.

She was in!

Damn. It meant that he was still obsessed with his ex, or why would he use her name?

And she did not know what she was looking for. She did not want to find it, whatever secret life he had hidden on this computer.

What was she looking for here? A life of crime? A dark self? More war atrocities? Child porn? It would not be likely that anyone involved in such terrible crimes, or even just deceit would record any evidence on a home computer. But to have 'mandy' as a password meant he had a secret life. Or was living in the past. Mandy? So he was either still in touch with his ex, or there was a younger version, a blonde Mandy, and his ex was conveniently a good cover story. The darkness was limitless.

She found the usual office stuff, nothing strange. A boring

life. Steve as she knew him. He did not have any interests, hobbies, or friends, as far as she knew.

She typed 'mandy' in the Search Programs and Files box. If this was his secret password to another life, then he would label any secret files this way.

Bingo.

A file folder, ghosted, labelled OPERATIONS.

She clicked on it.

It was a hidden file, one which needed another password to get in when she clicked it, and so she typed in 'mandy' again, but the file folder would not open. She right-clicked and a series of ghost files appeared. Each was labelled a woman's name.

molly

beatrice

nora

She stood up, made sure the door was closed, that this time she would not be disturbed. She walked back into the living room, stared up the dark driveway, listened for the whine of his car engine. The road was silent. He was down at the Gold Coast – he said – 200 kilometres away. She bolted the front door this time so that even if he had a key, he would not be able to sneak in.

She felt sick to the gut. Could she even look in these files? She needed to be a good detective here. She found her phone, took a photo of the screen.

And then, deep breath, clicked open one file.

What did she expect? A Ted Bundy scene? Collections of... conquests? Souvenirs?

It would not open. It was password protected. She tried the 'mandy' password but this time it did not work. She could not open any of these files. Of course not. He would have chosen a more complex password to access these secrets. She tried his birthdate. His mother's maiden name. Nothing worked.

Perhaps just as well. Did she really want to know the darkness of someone's mind?

She scrolled down the files.

Was this evidence? Was this proof? Of what? Yes, evidence that he had a hidden, secret life he did not want anyone else to see. She knew the police could confiscate this computer, take the hard drive and decode it. She logged out of the computer, careful to leave it as she had found it. But if he looked closely enough, he would see a log on an evening he was not at home.

She settled into bed with her laptop and googled the names Molly, Beatrice, Nora + Serial killer + missing girls + Sunshine Coast. But came up with nothing. This was a matter for Mike. He had hinted that there were others.

The wind howled, the windows rattled, and she kept her phone on all night, with speed dial to the therapist, and to the policeman, and to 000, just in case. The storm broke around midnight, and she woke with the crashes of thunder. Lightning lit up the whole sky, and the world seemed malevolent. She slept fitfully after that, nightmares of those names haunting her. Crying to her. *We're the murdered missing girls! We're souvenirs!* The words whirled around and around her head. After a half tablet of Valium, she finally fell into a deep sleep and woke late in the morning. The storm had passed, and the yard was scattered with fallen branches and leaves, the turf sodden, the overflowing storm drain running violently down the road. The sun shone high and hot, as if this were just a normal day, and like the past when she was with a man she trusted, knew and loved. But she had opened Pandora's box, and there was no going back to that past.

31

ATWELL HOME. SUNDAY MORNING

S he called the therapist as soon as it was a respectable hour. She wanted to know what she made of this new information. But Julienne was not answering her mobile phone. At 8.30 she called the office. A voicemail informed her that Dr Van Tonder was on family emergency leave and would not be making any appointments for the following few days.

Damn. She had made her alibi watertight. Carrie did not know what to do. Had Julienne gone to the police?

A text from Steve at 10am cheerily said he was on his way home – a two-and-a-half-hour drive. Maybe they could go out for Thai that evening?

Sure, she replied, with a smiley face. She could handle this. Just go on as normal.

Next she rang Mike. He did not answer either and she left a message. At eleven, the phone rang, and she grabbed it and answered without looking. 'Thank God, Julienne, I wanted to speak to you urgently.'

'That's nice,' boomed a male voice on the other end.

'Oh detective–'

'Mike.'

'Mike. Sorry I thought it was a friend of mine–'

'And I'm not a friend of yours?'

'Yes, yes...'

'How are you, Carrie? I've been concerned about you. Are you all right? Is he still away?'

'He's coming back today. Listen, Mike, did Julienne call you yet? The therapist?'

'Why would she call me?'

'She wanted to speak to you about the case.'

She did not want to tell him that Steve had threatened her therapist. She could scarcely believe it herself. Let Julienne report it. And if she hadn't, well, maybe it hadn't been as bad as she had made out.

'No, sorry, I haven't been in, maybe my deputy took the message. I'll ask him when I get off the phone. Does she have any leads? What was it about?'

'It's better if she tells you herself.'

'I could call her. I have that card you gave me.'

'She's... away, but I'm sure she'll contact you soon or will respond if you call her.'

'So, any more detective work, Carrie?'

'I managed to get into his computer, and found some files, but I couldn't open them. I'll attach the photo. Do these names mean anything to you: Molly, Beatrice, Nora?'

'Should they?'

'Are they victims? Are they missing girls, or murdered women?'

'I'll check. What did you find?'

'Secret files on his computer labelled after these women. But I couldn't open them. I can't imagine what is inside.'

'Maybe correspondence from more ex-girlfriends?'

'I wish it were. Maybe it is. I should check. But I'm scared,

Mike. I have found out far too much, more than I want to know. It doesn't look good.'

'So sorry. But very brave of you, and brilliant detective work, Carrie.'

'I'm just trying to find out the truth.'

'Me too. Just be safe, all right. I'll keep my phone on, so if there is any trouble, please just call me, okay?'

'Trouble?'

'I don't mean to scare you but be prepared. Your husband is not the man you thought he was. He may become violent if he is confronted. So please beware. Act normal. Don't arouse his suspicions any more or bring up anything – don't for God's sake mention these girls' names in case it triggers something. If he knows you know, he may try to silence you.'

'But I know nothing.'

'I want you to be safe. When is he expected home from this so-called trip at the Gold Coast?'

'He said he'll be home for lunch.'

'Keep your phone on. Call me if he acts in any way threatening. I'll be here for you, okay? Act normal. He won't suspect you, or anyone at this stage. Is the computer as he left it? His office? And his secret man cave? He'll be wary as he has caught you in there before.'

'He left the key in the kitchen to show me he hasn't anything to hide.'

'He's clever, clever.'

'Or innocent.'

32

ATWELL HOME. SUNDAY AFTERNOON

S teve arrived in the heat of the day, and she opened the front
door, trying to be 'normal'. She did not have to try too hard.
The first thing he did was thrust a bouquet of flowers in her face.
She took them, stunned. He grinned at her. Kissed her, hugged
her tight. 'I missed you!'

'You were only away two days...'

'But I did some thinking, a lot of thinking. Things are not too
good between us, Carrie, and I have neglected you, not appreci-
ated you.'

She did not know what to say, so she turned and took the
flowers to the kitchen. He followed her and presented her with a
small box. 'A gift, to new beginnings.'

She took it, opened it. Tears came to her eyes.

'It's beautiful.' She pulled out a jade necklace, the stones
chunky and polished. He took it, placed it around her neck and
did the clasp at the back. 'Carrie, I'll spend more time with you, I
promise, I'll make time – I have been so... absent.'

She stared at him. He had never been like this before, well
maybe the first few months of their marriage, but then he'd slid
into neglectful absence. He had never given her a gift sponta-

neously, only on anniversaries and birthdays, and these felt to her like obligation and guilt more than bursts of feeling.

He pushed the box towards her. 'There's more...'

She pulled out a matching pair of jade earrings. And felt dizzy. Cold. Nauseous. 'E-earrings?'

He nodded. 'I realise with that whole earring episode that what you were asking was for me to pay attention to you. You deserve the best.' He touched the dangling earrings and she recoiled, then tried to smile.

Was this some kind of sick joke?

But he looked so real, so transparent. If he was gaslighting, he was doing a good job. Or maybe he was not even aware of his duplicity? That's why they were called dissociative selves. Or maybe it was all a chimera, and she should take this all at face value. Maybe he really was innocent. Had nothing to do with earrings and dead girls and secret files and gaslighting. Maybe he was the Steve she had married.

She smiled again, and he clipped the earrings onto her ears. His hands were cold, and she shuddered. 'Why... earrings?'

'I found them at the Gold Coast market. I was strolling down the street and realised that I never buy you anything.'

She had to ask. 'Did you ever find out who that earring belonged to?'

He hugged her. 'You.'

'No, seriously...'

She stared over his shoulder at his ute, and saw that it was cleanly polished, shining. He saw her staring.

'Nice job, huh? Betcha never saw it so clean before, hey? Part of the hotel valet service. They took the car and gave it back to me this morning sparkling new.'

He changed, had a quick swim, shower and then at lunch, where she arranged the flowers in a vase at the end of the table, he presented her with another small packet. 'And I found this at the market too. An anti-snoring device. The guy at the stall swore it would stop me snoring. I'll try it out tonight okay? Let's sleep in the same bed, like we used to, Carrie.'

She stared across the table. 'What has come over you, Steve?'

He laughed. 'You. I want to start again, make amends. Can we?'

His hangdog look made her smile in spite of herself. 'Steve...'

'Can we? I'm so sorry. I think I've been such an arsehole. Too caught up in work and my own stuff to realise how far we were drifting, for you to think I was having an affair. I had a long hard think and I don't want to be that guy anymore. Can we start again?'

She swallowed. 'I think we have to.'

33

ATWELL HOME. SUNDAY AFTERNOON

That afternoon Steve tinkered around in his office and she tinkered around in her office. Her new project was for an environmental professor, collecting data, and compiling info for a book the professor was writing on coral bleaching in the Great Barrier Reef and effects of climate change.

She wondered if Steve could sniff her presence in his office. But he said nothing. She thought of the hidden files on his computer, sitting there waiting for him. When did he view them? She should have checked his last access. What if he looked and saw they were last accessed the previous night? What if she confronted him about it? Mentioned the girls' names. How would he react? But she couldn't risk it. He was being so sweet now, and he was sure to have another excuse.

What was in those files? It was worse not knowing than knowing. Perhaps pictures of dismembered corpses. Perhaps – she was always hopeful – old girlfriends he had forgotten to tell her about. Even present girlfriends would be better than what she was afraid of admitting to herself.

He took her out to dinner that night as promised, and they brought a bottle of wine, sat at an outside table against the backdrop of a glorious red sunset over Peregian Beach and he held her hand.

But it made her more jittery, these signs of what might be a multi-personality disorder. He was behaving so strangely, putting on a new personality. And if he could do this, in such stark contrast to his usual withdrawn self, then he was capable of anything. She could not trust anything he said or did now.

While he was this romantic, contrite, soft self, she decided to push things a little. 'Anything more you need to tell me, Steve?'

He frowned. 'What do you mean?'

'I mean, maybe one day you can tell me a little about your military past. It must have been a traumatic experience. I saw some of your... army memorabilia on the wall... Medals, certificates... You got medals? For... bravery?'

He shrugged. 'Standard issue, for service.'

'What was it like? Why did you sign up? For how long?'

He clearly did not want to talk about it. He shuffled in his seat. He ordered the food. He sipped the wine. Then: 'It was probably the best time of my life. And the worst.'

'Oh.'

'It's hard to explain to civilians...'

'Oh, I'm a "civilian" am I?'

'I'd rather leave all that behind me,' he said.

In your secret room, she thought. 'In your studio.'

He nodded. 'Sometimes it feels as if it happened to a different person...'

She held herself together. 'I'm sorry to bring up old trauma. Same with... Mandy. I'm sorry.'

'Is that what the therapist wants to do?'

She tensed. 'What?'

'Bring up old trauma, explain my current personality by snooping into my childhood and my military years.'

'Only if you want to. She wants you to heal, and she's very discreet.'

He looked sceptical. She held her hands under her thighs. She was sweating. The subtext here was way too obvious.

'Maybe that's good then,' he said.

She left it at that. There was certainly a disconnect in his life. Which Steve was she talking to now? Certainly not the one who had threatened the therapist with death.

They ate the rest of the meal in silence, and clinked glasses every now and then in a wordless attempt at reconciliation. But she could feel the icy wind of a big void between them. He was displaying classic symptoms of dissociation. Or was a bloody good liar.

Back home, he turned on the TV and she sat with him staring at the screen at the breaking news. Another body had been found in the Sunshine Coast area, a young blonde female, with similar mutilations to the one found a few days ago and dressed in a local school uniform.

Fronting the cameras, in uniform looking reassuringly in control, but obviously rattled, Detective Senior Sergeant Shelby, standing by the rocks facing the quaint suburb of Noosa Waters. Behind her, Detective Sergeant Mike Summers stood with arms folded. 'It was here that the body was found,' said the reporter. 'Can you tell us about the condition of the body and why you say this is linked to the previous murder in this area?'

The senior sergeant detective shook her head. 'Sorry...'

Mike Summers pushed his way forward and spoke to the camera. 'A grisly crime. The girl's body was battered against the rocks. She has been identified as...'

Carrie held her breath. *Molly? Beatrice?*

'...Cindy Liptrot who has been missing for a week. Her next of kin have been informed.'

She dared not look at Steve who was beside her, holding her hand, watching with an expressionless face. She could not read him at all, but his grip on her hand was tight, and her hand was clammy.

'Is the modus operandi the same...?'

The reporter, and the audience, and Carrie all wanted to know – was she disfigured? Had this killer mutilated her body like his first victim?

Mike was about to say more but Shelby pushed him back. 'If you have any information please call Crime Stoppers.' And he gave the number.

'Who is that cocky guy?' Steve pointed at Mike Summers on the screen. 'He seems to enjoy his role here.'

Her heart raced. The most innocuous questions from Steve could be read in another way. Why did he want to know? She shrugged. 'The chief investigator of the case.'

She wanted to call Mike that night and find out more about this next victim. He was sure to tell her. But she could not while Steve was here. It would have to wait until morning when her husband left for work.

She was so absorbed by the news that when Steve suddenly reached for the remote and turned off the TV, she stared at him. 'Steve, for fuck's sake?'

'What?' he said.

'I was watching that.'

'Enough bad news. And that arsehole of a cop is too smarmy, makes me sick.'

'But Steve.'

Steve shook his head. 'Always bad news. I'd rather talk. Enough of these devices, phones, screens.' He turned towards her. 'So, what were you up to while I was away?'

She tried not to turn red. 'Nothing much. How was the Cold Ghost?'

'I hate it. Too built up, like Miami. Give me the Sunny Coast any day.'

'But you had a good hotel? Room with a spa. Heated pool? Sea view?'

'The hotel was the only good part about it.'

So, he was going to perpetuate the lie. If it was a lie.

Usually at bedtime, they separated, but Steve crept into her bed and waited for her to brush her teeth. 'Come, Carrie...'

'This is a nice surprise,' she said. But she felt dread.

She took off her clothes and he stopped her taking the earrings off. 'No,' he said, 'leave those on... and the necklace, it's sexy just wearing those. Sort of... kinky.'

This was definitely not Steve. She lay naked, the earrings pulling at her earlobes as she lay down, the necklace choking her neck, her throat still feeling raw where he had bruised it with those hands that were now gently, ever so gently, caressing her breasts.

'Sorry, I can't do this, Steve.'

'What's wrong, honey?'

'Just not feeling good.'

He sat up, sighed. 'I know what it is.'

'What?'

'You're still suspicious of me, aren't you? I'm not stupid. You think I'm having an affair.'

'No, Steve, I don't.'

'You've been distant and wooden all evening. You think... the earring, the perfume, snooping in my office, my studio, my computer.'

She went cold, pulled up the duvet around her. As if that would protect her. So, he knew she had hacked his computer.

He caressed her hair. 'I don't blame you for checking up on

me, but at least be honest. Talk to me. Don't do things behind my back.'

Honest? Then tell me you called up Julienne and threatened her. Tell me who those girls are in your computer files. Tell me if you were really at the Gold Coast. 'No. I...' She could not bring herself to speak. She pulled the duvet right over her.

He sat up on his elbows, gripped her arm. 'It's okay, Carrie, it's understandable. I'm sorry that you feel like this, that you're suspicious. It's my fault. I do have skeletons in my closet.'

She pulled back the duvet and stared wide-eyed at him.

'Skeletons?'

He smiled. 'So to speak. There are things in my past – yes, my military career, old wounds from ex-girlfriends – I never shared with you. I wanted to put my past behind me. And there are things I do not share with you. Work-related things... I don't want you to stress about my issues. But, Carrie, I swear I'm not having an affair.'

She hugged herself, did not respond.

'Believe me.'

She turned. 'I'm sorry, Steve. I'm just feeling insecure with all this stuff.'

'I understand.'

Her mind was spinning. 'Will you tell me about your secret life?'

'I will. One day. But not now. I need to sort out a few things first.'

'Oh?'

But he said nothing more. She wanted him to go to his room, but that night he was determined to stay. He wanted to prove he loved her, that he was repairing their relationship, that her suspicions were unfounded. He wore his snoring device, a clamp on his nose, and settled on his side.

He was asleep almost immediately. Steve could do that, but

she lay awake, tense, listening to him breathe. After a few minutes he began snoring, loud, and she pulled a pillow over her ears. She nudged him and he turned in his sleep, stopped for a while then started up again like a monster.

She nudged him again. He sat up, angry. 'What, Carrie?'

'You're snoring so loud I can't sleep.'

He pulled the device off his nose. 'Well, that's thirty bucks for nothing. Damn.'

He gave her a hug, kissed her on her cheek and stumbled out of the room to his office. 'Love you, Carrie...'

'Love you too.'

She made sure her door was locked and settled back into bed, but she could not sleep. It was past eleven, but she texted her therapist – checked Facebook to see who was online. Her husband, tired as he said he was, showed up as active. What was he doing?

She texted Julienne:

I need to see you tomorrow

She hoped that maybe she was awake and would respond, but she did not.

She also texted Mike.

Terrible news, isn't it? I'm fine.

But no reply there either.

She lay down again but could not sleep. She googled 'dissociative personality disorders' for the umpteenth time. Read all the symptoms and checked them off one by one: he matched them perfectly.

Dissociative identity disorder is characterised by the presence of two or more distinct personality identities. Each may have a unique name, personal history and characteristics.

Treatment is talk therapy. Memory gaps are usual too, when the subject does not remember events or else makes up stories to cover these gaps. This is called rationalisation. These are not lies: the subject really has to believe them in order to hide the disorder.

34

ATWELL HOME. MONDAY MORNING

In the morning Carrie heard him getting up and putting on the kettle: he brought her tea, told her he loved her, placed a flower on her pillow. Not like Steve at all. He was really trying – perhaps too hard. She wanted to feel good about this, give him the benefit of the doubt, but... the earring, the computer files, the perfume, the photos of body parts... And his strange reaction to the news of the deaths. She could almost believe him, but then how did she explain his threatening of the therapist?

Today, she felt strong enough to confront him on this. He had, after all, promised to tell her his 'secrets'. But she needed to keep up that illusion of her ignorance. She took a deep breath. Here goes. 'Just a reminder that I've booked an appointment with the therapist for Thursday. You still okay with that?'

He did not react in the way he would have if he had threatened her. He reached forward, squeezed her hand. 'Absolutely. You know I don't believe in that quackery, but if it makes you happy, if you think it will help our relationship, I'll do it.'

'It's not just for me. It's for you too, Steve.' She watched him carefully. He looked so penitent, so aware of her pain, of his supposed crime, which was neglect. Not murder. Not rape. Not threatening her friends with death if they didn't shut up. How could this man be that man? She almost felt safe in his arms today, though she knew not to trust that ghost memory.

'Where is this therapist of yours, anyhow?'

'Mooloolaba Beach. I gave you the card.'

'Not far from here?'

'Not far.'

He kissed her. 'Honey, I got to go. Have a good day, and maybe we can go out to a movie later?'

'That would be nice.'

She watched him drive off and called the therapist's private number again. No answer. Tried the receptionist to confirm her appointment.

'Sorry, Mrs Atwell, but all appointments for the next two weeks have been cancelled. Would you like to reschedule?'

'Listen, Julienne told me I could call her, that I was the one person who could.'

'Sorry,' said the receptionist, 'she hasn't been answering my calls either.'

'Well, when you do get her, please tell her I really need to speak with her urgently.'

She scoured the internet for news of the newly found victim. The media was also obsessed, and because the police hierarchy and Detective Sergeant Mike Summers had given no concrete information, speculation was rife.

The headlines:

Another mutilated body.

Ocean dumping serial killer strikes again.

Which body part this time?

It sickened her, all this morbid fascination with death. Detective Sergeant Mike and the others had been right not to tell anyone. People fed off vile perversions, loved the gory details.

But the few facts given were enough to confirm her fears and confirmed what looked like a pattern – another young blonde woman murdered, dumped in a waterway to destroy any traces of her killer, four kilometres away from the last body drop, and mutilated in a similar way to the first victim.

The phone ringing made her jump.

'Mike, I'm so glad you called.'

'Can you speak?'

'Yes, he's gone to work.'

'How are you? I've been worried sick about you.'

'I texted you last night. I'm fine.'

'Yes, I saw your texts, but I was working on the new case last night, as you must have seen. How horrible is that?'

'I saw you on TV last night,' she said. 'But you didn't tell the public anything.'

'I can't, Carrie... it's too terrible. And we're in the middle of an investigation so I am not supposed to give out any information, only enough for the public who might have seen something.'

'But I'm part of the investigation, Mike. You can tell me. Was this similar to the last victim? Are we talking about a repeat killer, a serial killer as the media are telling us?'

'I'm afraid so, Carrie. Yes. She was mutilated, body parts cut out of her.'

'Tell me.'

'I don't want to say.'

'Tell me.'

'That is classified–'

'Bullshit. You know you can tell me.'

'Clitoris this time.'

'No!'

'And ears disfigured. Earlobes slashed, and earrings removed.'

'Earrings.'

'And we're connecting the dots to other potential victims we did not know were related. There are missing women who fit the same profile. Blonde, late teens... from Coolum, Maroochydore or Mooloolaba.'

'How many?'

'At least two. There may be more.'

'Are their names Beatrice? Nora? Molly?'

'No. But tell me about you. How did you manage with your husband? Is he suspicious of you? Are you safe?'

'He thinks I suspect him of an affair, and he is sweet to me.'

'What do you mean?'

'He's trying to make up. And he admits he has secrets and wants to tell me about them.'

'What did he tell you?'

'Nothing so far. He says when the time is right.'

'You should press him. If he will talk to you, you can bring that in as evidence. Can you record your conversations with him on your phone?'

'I don't know about that.'

'It would be crucial for the case. Ask him what his secrets are, he seems to trust you.'

'I will.'

'Just be careful, Carrie, okay?'

35

ATWELL HOME. MONDAY EVENING

It was the last thing she wanted to do that evening, but Steve came back from work with flowers, a bottle of wine and a reservation for Italian and a movie at Noosa Junction. He was trying hard, and it made her feel much worse. She still clung to one fine thread of hope and could not betray him. If she had that one thread then he still may be innocent. Or if he had a multiple personality disorder. She had to, for her own conscience, give him the opportunity to turn himself in.

She had set up her phone so the record app was ready to go at the tap of the screen. She would keep it on and hide it in her pocket so that at any time if he decided to confess his 'secrets' she would be ready.

She felt guilty for betraying him. If 'betraying' was even the right word. Dobbing him in. Ratting on him. But this is just what the therapist had told her – he was the one betraying her, yet she was the one feeling guilty.

That evening, he was even more out to impress. He ordered for her. 'Cannelloni, right?'

'Special occasion?' said the waitress when she saw the flowers he had placed on the table.

'We're renewing our vows,' he said.

'Ahh, so sweet.'

Carrie stared at him. 'Steve, what has got into you? I really don't know how to respond. For years you ignore me, you're too tired to go out with me anywhere, and suddenly you're back with this... guilt trip? What are you hiding?'

There, she had said it. He looked hurt. 'Carrie, Carrie, I just want to make up for neglecting you. I let my work take priority... I want to make up for everything. Will you let me?' He clasped her hand.

'Only if you're honest, straight with me. Those secrets you spoke of. I need to know them, if we are going to renew our vows.'

'I will tell you everything, Carrie,' he said.

She fumbled with the phone under the table.

'But not now. Not here. But I have to repeat that I'm not having an affair. That's not the secret.'

She took a breath. 'Steve, I have to be honest. I still don't believe you. I am still not convinced you're telling me the truth. And it's hard for me to suddenly switch from the shock of finding out about the earring, the condoms, an ex-girlfriend's hair you still keep. And I have something I need to ask.'

Steve looked pained. 'What, Carrie?'

She braced herself. 'That earring.'

'Still the bloody earring. Carrie, Carrie.'

She lowered her voice. 'It's the same one that was found on the dead girl.'

'What dead girl?'

'Mary Stevens. It's her matching earring.'

She was careful now, had deliberately chosen a public place, had her hand on her phone, ready to speed dial and ready to hit record if he started to confess. She had no idea how he was going to react. But she felt it was the right thing to do. She had to be open. If she was going to dob him in, she was going to give him one chance to give himself in first.

He looked confused. 'What are you talking about?'

'It's the same earring. Matching earrings.'

His eyes were wild. 'How do you know?'

'I saw a photo of her on the news and...' She pulled out her phone, scrolled to the photo and zoomed in with two fingers. Showed it to him.

He squinted at it. 'Frankly, I can't remember the earring.'

She was playing a dangerous game here, but she was not accusing him. She was playing innocent, acting as bewildered as he was, asking him to decide what he thought. Asking him to be on her side.

'It's exactly the same. If I had it here, I'd show you.'

'Maybe, maybe, but... surely there must be thousands of earrings like this. It's a common enough earring. Where did you get the crazy idea?'

She shook her head. 'Steve, I think we should go to the police.'

He threw his hands wide. Looked at her as if she were mad. 'Why? Because of a fucking earring?'

The family at the next table looked up.

'This may be evidence, a clue.' She watched him carefully. He ran his fingers through his hair, looking distressed. He swallowed and his Adam's apple bulged. 'I don't think so.'

'But don't you think...?'

'Carrie, I'm sorry but what planet are you from? You find an earring and you suddenly imagine it belongs to a murdered woman? It's a common earring.'

She could not tell him what she knew.

'Carrie, do you still have this earring I gave you?'

'Yes,' she lied.

'Let's see it. Let's compare. But even if...'

'It's at home.'

He was silent. The food arrived and they ate without speaking. In the middle of her main course, her phone buzzed. A text from Mike. *Call me.* She turned off her phone. Steve saw her face redden. 'What's up?'

She shook her head. 'Nothing.'

Something changed in him, instantly. Had he seen the text? His face was red, and his voice was raised. 'Carrie, why...' The other patrons looked up at them in alarm. '...Why is this all going on? I wanted a reconciliation. You feel so far from me.'

She reached out a hand to try to calm him and spoke quietly, aware that everyone was listening in. 'I'm just worried about a lot of things. That earring...'

He slammed his fist on the table. 'You're so obsessed by that fucking earring. You're making a mountain out of a molehill. I have no fucking idea about that fucking earring. And let's get it straight, we're not going to the police over some fantasy you've dreamed up.'

'We have nothing to hide...'

'Of course we have nothing to hide.' He stared at her with such anger, she shrank back. 'You think...' He kept his voice low and hissed at her. 'You think I had something to do with the dead girl?'

'No, no,' she said, desperately, afraid at what she had just done. 'Don't be stupid. Please, Steve, I'm just trying to do the right thing. Crime Stoppers say that if there is anything... and the earring is something...'

'Fuck the earring.'

The waitress stood by the table. 'Is everything all right, sir? More... water?'

Steve blinked, suddenly realised that people at nearby tables were staring wide-eyed at him. 'Fine, fine. Sorry.' And to Carrie: 'We'd better go.'

They left the food unfinished. He paid the bill and she waited outside, ashamed, and fearful. She did not want to be alone with him. For the second time, she was afraid to be with her husband. But he walked out, held her hand, and gave her a warm hug. 'I'm so sorry.'

They walked to the car. 'I think we'd better go home and discuss this.' He was suddenly contrite. 'I'll do anything to make this relationship work. Even go to the cops, the therapist.'

She squeezed his hand. 'I think that is exactly what we should do.'

'But... you are being paranoid, you realise that. From the outside, you are acting really weird.'

She opened her mouth to object, then realised this was the opportunity to backtrack. To humour him. She should never have suggested the cops. The reaction was vitriolic, no matter how he was trying to mask it now. 'You're right, Steve.'

'Tomorrow we'll call them,' he said. 'Okay? If it makes you happy.'

She was trying to humour him but had the impression that he was also humouring her, as you would a mad person. 'Thanks. We can just– I can just give them the earring and that will be the end of it. They can judge if it's at all relevant to the case.'

'Which I am sure it isn't. But it may put an end to your paranoia. Christ, first an affair, then you think I'm a murderer. Is that what you really think?'

'No, Steve, no. Of course not. I never said that. I don't think that. But you said you had secrets.'

He squeezed her hand. 'I will tell you everything.'

They drove home in silence. 'Sorry about my behaviour tonight,' he said. 'And sorry about the movie... I was not in the mood. I'd rather just snuggle up with you and talk, listen to you... tell me everything, how you feel, what's bothering you,

how I can help, what I can do to change. And I'll tell you about
my military life. There is stuff you need to know that may help
explain things.'

'That would be good, Steve.'

She stared at him as he drove. He looked sincere. Contrite.
And unhinged.

36

ATWELL HOME. MONDAY NIGHT

At home, a text came through and he swore as he read it. 'Damn, Carrie, an emergency came up at our latest project. There's a toxic spill and I have to talk to the engineer.'

She wanted to see the text, but he flipped his phone closed. 'What project is this?'

'The airport expansion. You must have heard me swear about it before. A bloody nightmare with those environmentalists blocking us at every turn.'

So instead of a cosy night where she told him everything, and he would tell her about his military background that he said would 'help explain things', and his 'secrets', he was kissing her goodnight at the bedroom door. 'I love you, Carrie, you know that. I am so sorry; I want things to work out between us. I feel so bad, so... guilty having to go off like this.'

'It's fine, Steve. Another time.'

'I might be out late. And dammit, an early start tomorrow. That's if I can get this sorted. Doesn't look good.'

'Drive safe,' she said.

'When I get back, we'll talk, I'll tell you everything.'

~

She could not sleep. She tossed and turned, tried not to wait up for him, not to listen for his car. She googled Sunshine Coast Airport expansion, and yes, Steve's company was contracted to lay the concrete, and there had been problems with water contamination, and there had been environmentalist protests. He was telling the truth. Maybe. He was always telling the truth. Or half-truth. The only way to know was if she followed him or bugged his car so she could track him. She called Julienne again. For the umpteenth time. But no answer.

Just as she was dozing off, her phone rang.

'Mike!'

'Carrie, sorry to call you so late. Are you okay?'

'Steve is out on some project.'

'I called you because I have some news about the DNA test.'

'You got it done?'

'Yup. Carrie, you don't know how difficult it is to do this under the radar. Very difficult. But I do have contacts in the scenes-of-crime office. The forensic officers did me a little favour.'

'And?'

He hesitated. 'Some preliminary results came back from the subsample. It still needs to be forwarded to DNA management section in Brisbane for the final analysis and confirmation, but we won't do that until you come in and give a statement. So, nothing official or conclusive. But we have something.'

She held her stomach. 'Tell me. Good news, I hope.'

'Not so good.'

'What do you mean?'

'The earring has been wiped clean. Disinfected. All traces of DNA removed. They cannot tell if it is a positive match or not.'

'Disinfected? You mean...?'

'That's why he took it from you. He cleaned it up, removed all traces of the girl and his DNA. I wondered why he gave it back to you. He knew now it was safe. He's been tampering with evidence.'

'Shit. That's what Julienne suspected too.'

'The DNA lab technicians want to know where I got this from. They want me to officially declare it and send this off to Brisbane. But I cannot do that unless you come down to my office to give a statement. You'll also need to be careful that he does not know you're part of the investigation.'

'What are you going to do? Arrest him?'

'If he does not come in voluntarily, he needs to be arrested under the PPRA – Police Powers and Responsibilities Act.'

'No, no. Please. What about me? What will happen?'

'We can protect you.'

'I was just beginning to think it was all a horrible mistake. It is. It can't be. Just because her earring was in his vehicle doesn't mean he's involved, does it? Is there any chance he is still innocent, that this is a big mistake...? I mean, if they don't find his DNA on the earring, then...?'

'He is innocent until proven guilty. There is insufficient evidence to arrest him for murder at the moment – it's all circumstantial. But... things are looking pretty clear. He is a likely candidate to be arrested for possession of tainted property, and tampering with evidence – namely the earring.'

'And the hair?'

'It sure looks like her hair. Mary's hair. I did a visual match and it fits. But I can't send this for forensic DNA tests at scenes of crime without them asking all sorts of questions. I am pushing my luck here. I could get into serious trouble for not doing this officially.'

'I'm sorry.'

'We have to go through official channels, all right, Carrie?

You come in, present the evidence and they will do a thorough DNA test on both the earring and the hair.'

'Why did he label the envelope 'Mandy'? His ex, Mandy?'

'I think that was just a subterfuge, Carrie. In case someone did dob him in. He had a story already prepared. Or worse, he misheard her name. Mary... Mandy. Maybe he has attacked so many women he can't remember their names, or their names are not important. Or he has his own names for them which he gives them. That happened with a case in the US not long ago. He gave them new names, names of women who had hurt him in the past and he wreaked revenge on these ones.'

Beatrice, Nora, Molly.

'Dissociative personality disorder,' she said aloud. 'Subjects make up stories in order to reconcile their different selves.'

'You could be right.'

She thought back to the photos of a brunette Mandy. 'But he hadn't expected anyone to find that envelope.'

'I know how their minds work. But Carrie, I'm worried about you. Now you know he's... he's... involved in something terrible, what will you do? You should maybe go and stay with someone and let us sort this out. If he finds out you're involved, hell, he may already think you're involved and he's playing you.'

'Gaslighting, Julienne calls it.'

'Exactly. You don't want to be there when he gets home. You won't be able to look him in the eye. Is there anywhere you can stay?'

'My mother. Funny, the therapist also told me to move out.'

'He did?'

'She. Julienne.'

'Oh yes. You gave me her card, sorry.'

It was time to come clean. 'You have to talk to her. I am not sure why she was going to contact you urgently, not sure why she hasn't yet.'

'About the earring?'

Carrie swallowed.

'You still there, Carrie?'

'She told me that my husband threatened her, said that she would go the way of the other women if she didn't get off his case. She... had to lie low for a while.'

'Shit, she told you that? My God. Why didn't you tell me? Carrie, that's evidence enough to arrest him on the spot. We have to get a statement from her immediately. You say you can't contact this therapist?'

'I haven't managed to get hold of her. She told me she had to go into hiding. But she said she was going straight to the police. Hasn't she called you?'

'No, as far as I know, she has not filed any report or contacted us. Good God, Carrie, you know what this means? Steve has committed *using a carriage service to menace, harass or cause offence* – an offence under Section 474 of the Commonwealth Criminal Code. This is looking very bad for him. You have to come to my office and give a statement immediately. First thing in the morning.'

'I suppose I must.'

'It may be hard for you to accept this, but we're talking about a serial killer who has threatened a witness. If we had arrested him when I first knew about the earring maybe this latest death could have been avoided. And if he is now going after witnesses, then we have no time to lose. And Carrie, you're also in danger. Has he ever threatened you or shown any violent tendencies towards you?'

She hesitated again. 'No. He will never harm me, I know that.' *Why was she lying to him?* 'He's been sweet, giving me flowers, taking me out on dates.'

'I'm also worried about the therapist. What was her name again?'

'Julienne Van Tonder.'

'In the light of what you've just told me, we have to make sure she's safe. Why hasn't she come to us? Give me all the details you know about her... we're going to find her, obtain a statement from her and get her to a safe location.'

'I don't even know where she lives, but here's her mobile number, and I'll try to call her again too. But please don't do anything to Steve.'

'Carrie, the procedure is clear. We need to arrest Steve immediately, get a search warrant for his house and the ute–'

'What will happen to him?'

'He'll be lodged in the watch-house in a cell for eight hours while we investigate and forensic officers and scientific section from Brisbane examine the house. We'll interview him, and if we need more time, we can also get a four-hour extension from a magistrate.'

'I'm sorry – I should have told you this before.'

'Bloody right. The detective senior sergeant and detective inspector would have my balls for this delay. We have to arrest him now. It was difficult enough getting the earring examined without all those prying eyes. I could get into serious trouble for this.'

'I'm so sorry.'

He laughed drily. 'I could be charged under the Police Services Administration Act and maybe under the Criminal Code – *Attempt to pervert the course of justice.*'

'Mike, I'm sorry, I will come over first thing in the morning.'

'I'll make sure you're protected. You sure you are all right there tonight? Maybe go stay with a relative?'

'I'll be fine.'

'Meanwhile, I'll get hold of this therapist of yours. Urgently.'

37

MONDAY NIGHT

He picked up the therapist's phone which was buzzing. Another message from Carrie. He was inclined to respond, and began typing in the therapist's password, then stopped. For his plan to work, he had to keep mum here. He wiped the phone with a sanitised tissue – there was still a little blood on the screen from his coercion – well, he had to get her password somehow, didn't he?

It had been a fun night. After he called her at work that day, he watched her on her office balcony looking at the beach. Looking for him! Then she drove home, and he followed, watched her park, watched her lock her apartment and draw the curtains. He made sure she was alone – waited for the right moment and knocked on her door.

'Wh-who is it?'

'Carrie's husband, Steve. We need to talk.'

'I'm calling the police. How do you know where I live?'

He knew how to sound disarming, contrite, victim-like. 'Please Julienne, I need to talk. I... followed you from the office. I know this is weird, but I'm sorry... I panicked; I want to apologise for that phone call. I just need to talk. One minute.'

Something must have changed her mind – maybe the crocodile tears – because she opened the door a few centimetres, but with the safety latch still on. Looked at him. Her phone was in her hand, ready to speed-dial the cops.

'Hello Julienne. I really do appreciate you helping Carrie with her issues, but I just wanted to put forward my side.'

She frowned, trying to assess him. 'In my office, not here.'

'Just hear me out, please. I just need a minute. I'll make an appointment to see you at your office too. But I feel terrible. I have to apologise. I was out of line, way out of line. Please forgive me. I didn't mean any of those things I said.'

Her eyes were wide, but she was putting on a brave face, holding her panic at bay. She was a brave one, this. He liked brave ones. She was not his type. But she needed to be dealt with. It was all part of the plan. If he was to continue with his lifestyle of choice, she had to be silenced. And he may as well have a bit of fun on the way. There was nothing he liked more that the terror in their eyes. 'I'm sorry, I lost it there on the phone. I have issues.'

'Listen, Steve, we do need to talk, but not here. I can help you. That's what I'm trained to do. I'm on your side, even though you don't think so. I can help you.'

He wiped away a tear. 'Really? I'm a mess, Dr Van Tonder, and my wife thinks I'm having an affair.'

He reached out his hand through the doorway, and she, like a fool, shook it. Quick as the devil, he yanked her arm through the opening. Twisted it. Then he stood back and threw himself against the door with his shoulder. The flimsy door chain broke, and he was in. He pushed her onto the floor, closed the door behind him and held her in a vice grip.

'You can help me? You didn't do as I asked, did you?'

'Please, Mr Atwell, you're hurting me. My arm...'

Wily one, this. She was still clutching her phone and with one hand had pressed speed dial. She had it on an emergency number and was prepared for him. He grabbed the phone and cancelled the call. Threw the phone onto the floor. 'I told you to call no one. The first thing you did was call the cops.'

'No–'

He twisted her arm behind her back, and she winced.

'Please, you're hurting me.'

'If you think this is hurting, you ain't seen nothing yet, baby. And hurting is the whole idea, you silly bitch.'

She bit her lip.

'What did my wife tell you about the earring?'

The phone began ringing on the floor, and because it was on vibrate, it began to dance along the tiles, as if it was trying to get to her.

He ignored it. 'Well?'

The therapist glanced anxiously at the phone. 'She was worried about you, she never doubted you, she loves you, she was upset and thought you were having an affair.'

The phone continued to buzz. He looked at it. 'Shit. Look what you've done. You dialled triple zero. Even if the person hangs up, they'll follow up on the call. And if there is no reply, they'll trace the call and come find you. Is that what you want?'

A sparkle in her eyes. She thought she was going to be rescued.

'If they come here, they'll find a corpse, and I'll be long gone. I want you to answer that phone and tell them you made a mistake. Wrong number. You dialled the wrong number. Got it? Then you'll live. If you don't, you die here and now on the floor, and I'm gone. Before they investigate. Get it?'

She nodded. But he could see she would yell out help or scream into the phone the moment he let her answer it.

'Here.' He let her go, and she scrambled for the phone. But as she swiped the answer button, he pulled out his knife and sliced it across her cheek, gently, so it just left a trail of blood. Then he wiped the knife on her hand, so the blood left a smear on the phone.

'Shit,' she said.

Still holding her other hand behind her back, he carved a little smiley face into the skin on her hand holding the phone. 'Answer it, Julienne. And tell them it was a misdial. Be a good girl, okay? One scream or false move and you're dead, and I'm out of here and they will find only your corpse when they get here. Got it?'

She nodded. He pressed the blade to her throat and drew a pretty line across her gullet, light, and bright blood dripped onto her shirt.

'Go for it.'

She held the phone to her ear, but he could hear the dispatcher's voice clearly.

'Hello, we had a triple-O hang up from this number a minute ago. What is your emergency?'

He felt her tremble in his arms. He knew she wanted to scream, but he forced her to look him in the eye so she could see that he meant business. The knife pressed into her throat and he whispered, 'Do the right thing and you live, honey.'

'S-sorry, this was a mistake. I misdialled; I was trying to call my sister... I'm sorry.'

He pressed the knife into her gullet, and she cried out.

'Ma'am?'

'Sorry, please, it was a wrong number. I'm okay.'

'Are you sure, ma'am?'

She looked at him, her eyes pleading. What, did she think he would nod and let her tell the cops that she was about to be murdered? He tightened his grip on her arm and she winced.

'I'm fine. So sorry to bother you. You guys are doing a great job. Thanks. Goodbye.'

He eased up the grip and pulled the knife back as she ended the call.

'Brilliant, Julienne, such a good little girl, aren't you? When you try. Well, you know what's good for you. Maybe even made up for that call you made to Carrie yesterday when you told her I was a serial killer.'

'I didn't say that.'

'I monitor her calls, my dear. As I do yours.'

'You're... spying on me?'

He released her and she fell to the floor, holding her arm. He held the knife at her face, in case she tried any more clever tricks. He was not sure she did not have a panic button anywhere in her apartment.

'It's a pity you're not my type,' he said. 'But I suppose we will have to make do.'

'Please,' she said, 'I did as you said. I cancelled all my clients. I'll disappear for a while. Go stay with my relatives in Perth–'

'Good, good. But first we are going for a little drive. Get your car keys.'

38

ATWELL HOME. MONDAY NIGHT

C arrie slept badly, tossed and turned and deliberated, still tried to find a path out of her betrayal of her husband. Wasn't she supposed to stick with him through thick and thin, in sickness and in health? Even if he was a liar, an adulterer, even if he was a serial killer, he was mentally ill and needed help. He needed her support. All this kindness was his cry for help, telling her he was a good person at heart and needed her.

He wasn't a serial killer. He was at worst having an affair, and this was all just coincidence. She would be so relieved to hear his confession that he was having it off with the secretary – that it was her earring, her perfume, the condom for her, the Gold Coast hotel a fling with her. He had wiped the earring to rid it of his secret lover's fingerprints. She would hug him and say *thank God*, if that was the truth. Anything but this nightmare. It had to be all a bad mistake – surely he had nothing to do with those dead bodies in the ocean? She could explain the threat to her therapist – he was just upset that his affair would be found out, that his marriage would be on the rocks.

She should just ask him. *Come clean, Steve, tell me it's an affair.*

I know you are obsessed with your exes. Molly, Beatrice, Nora. Mandy. It's okay. Let's work this out.

She was so convinced that she took a Valium and settled into a deep sleep.

39

ATWELL HOME. TUESDAY MORNING

C arrie woke late in the morning, the sun streaming into her window. She felt drugged. The phone was buzzing. She looked out of the window. Steve's car was gone. He was either not yet home or had got back late and left early.

'Carrie, it's me again.'

'Mike? What time is it?'

'8am. Are you coming into the station? You have to get out of there. Where is your husband?'

'He's at work.'

'Sure?'

'Sure.'

'Carrie, turn on your TV. Haven't you seen the news?'

She stumbled into the living room, holding the phone to her ear, found the remote and turned the TV on. At first, she could not make sense of it. A car being dragged out of the ocean just above Yaroomba and Luther Heights. Flashing lights, ambulance, police cars, fire engines. Media. Excited newsreaders with mics, waving arms, pointing to the high cliffs where a piece of the wall was missing.

'Mike, God no. Another victim?'

'Carrie, listen to me. I have some bad news, I'm afraid. We haven't identified the body, so this is not official and do not say anything to anyone, but I'm sure this is your therapist.'

Carrie was still slow, and her head pounded. She hated what Valium made her feel the next day. She needed coffee. 'What is?'

'Her body was found at the bottom of the ocean in her car. She apparently drove off the cliff.'

Carrie stared at the fifty-inch screen on her wall. 'What do you mean, her body? She's... dead? You sure it's her? She had a car accident?'

'Please don't say anything at this stage, we can't tell the media, but this was no accident.'

'What do you mean?'

'Preliminary examination of the body shows signs of... mutilation.'

'No! I can't believe it. Julienne? You sure?'

'I'm sorry, Carrie, I know you two were close. Friends even.'

'Yes.'

'The signs are clear – it's the killer. Same modus operandi.'

'But... why?'

'Come on, Carrie, you told me yourself yesterday. She knew too much. She was going to the police.'

She stared at the TV.

'Carrie, you need to come to my office right away and make a statement. If not, I will have to bring you in. You're a substantive witness. You have very important information.'

She felt the world spin. 'I'm coming in. I'm coming in. I'll be there...'

'Come straight here, Carrie. CIB office, Maroochydore Station. Or do you want me to come pick you up?'

'No, I'll come now.'

'I just want you to be safe, Carrie. Listen I am sorry, but I had to put this in the report. The guys at forensics were asking questions.'

'What did you do?'

'I had to let the other members of the investigation team know about you. I have had to list you as a witness on the QPrime report for the homicide, and I must issue you with a field property receipt for the earring and the strand of hair. That we met and you presented me with the evidence.'

She slumped. 'So that's it, the point of no return.'

'The point of no return. Keep your phone on, and come straight to the station, okay?'

She turned up the sound on the TV. Made herself a strong cup of coffee. She felt like throwing up. She splashed her face with cold water. Drank the coffee so hot it burned her mouth.

According to the news reporters, the body had been found early in the morning. Two fishermen on the rocks had seen a car submerged in the surf and foundering on the rocks and had seen a body slumped at the steering wheel, trapped by her seat belt. Seeing the broken fence at the top of the cliff, they had assumed an accident, and had called the police. But now the vehicle had been towed out of the water, the police had declared it a crime scene.

'Why?' asked one reporter on camera to Detective Senior Sergeant Shelby. 'What have you discovered?'

The senior sergeant detective refused to comment on an ongoing investigation, but the media had already found out by interviewing witnesses that there was evidence of murder.

'The fishermen told us that the woman at the wheel was naked, and that her head looked as if it was split open. Any comments?'

'No comments. This is all conjecture at this stage.'

'Do you think this may be related to the other cases in the area recently?'

'Not at all,' said Shelby. 'This woman was middle-aged, dark-haired, and that is enough questions for now. Thank you.'

Carrie dressed, had another cup of coffee. Her mind was racing, trying to find an explanation, any other explanation. But found none. She could not believe Julienne was dead. Had been mutilated, tortured, killed... NO!

She could hardly drive, she was so jittery. Maybe it was the coffee. She could not think too much about what she was doing. But on her way down the Sunshine Motorway, the world rearranged itself. Yes, she was in denial. It was obvious now. He's been gaslighting her, living in two realities, and the only thing she did not know was whether these two realities were entirely separate, whether he knew exactly what he was doing, manipulating her, or whether his good side did not even know what his dark side was doing. How she wished she could talk to her therapist now! Julienne, dead? She couldn't deny it any longer. Her husband was a killer.

And it was her fault that the therapist had died. Julienne had been killed by her delaying, by giving Steve the benefit of the doubt. Why had she told her about the earring in the first place? Why had she told Steve that she knew about the earring? *Why? Why? Why?*

The traffic was slow, lethargic, and laid-back. Holidaymakers here for fun, off to the beach or Australia Zoo, or Noosa. This was the prime tourist spot for Australians and particularly Melbournians, as she could see by all those Victoria number plates. And a pain in her heart cramped her so she could hardly drive. *Steve! What happened to you? Did you always have a secret life? How come I never once suspected you?*

And all these happy people: she was impatient, trying to overtake, but the Sunshine Motorway was still only one lane each way and she saw the snaking queue of cars jamming up all the way to Maroochydore. How could the world be a happy place for these people when such terrible things were happening? She tailgated a car with children smiling at her from the back seat and a big yellow surfboard strapped on the roof.

She called Mike on the speakerphone. 'I'm on my way. Sorry, held up in traffic.'

'You're doing the right thing, Carrie. I know it must be hard for you. Well done. When you get there, ask for Detective Senior Sergeant Shelby. But in a case like this, it'll be more likely a detective sergeant from homicide squad.'

'Aren't you going to interview me? I thought... I don't know. I need you to be there.'

'It's better to have an objective and independent interview,' he said. 'We have to play by the book. And I'm busy here at this Yaroomba crime scene. I'm working long hours on this investigation.'

'But what shall I say when they ask why I didn't come in before?'

'Just tell them the truth, that you spoke to me informally and that I advised you go immediately to report this. That you presented me with the evidence. Don't mention that I conceded to a delay, that you played detective, nothing like that. I did that for you, Carrie, but it was not correct procedure. And we could both get into serious trouble.'

'Okay,' she said, confused now.

'Just tell them the facts.'

40

MAROOCHYDORE POLICE STATION.
TUESDAY, LATE MORNING

C arrie was met at the counter by Detective Senior Sergeant Shelby, the short, pudgy woman with her hair in a bun who had given all the media statements on TV. A no-nonsense woman, she could tell, and she would get no sympathy from her.

She took Carrie upstairs to the CIB office and ushered her into the same cool, green-walled, well-lit room with what she suspected was a one-way mirror on the left-hand side where Mike Summers had first spoken to her. Carrie took a seat at an L-shaped desk and Shelby sat adjacent to her and close to a TV monitor and some electronic recording equipment.

'Carrie, I am Detective Senior Sergeant Shelby, the officer in charge of Maroochydore CIB. I intend obtaining your witness statement today and I will be electronically recording everything you say. Do you understand that?'

She nodded. Shelby got out of her chair and turned the recording equipment on. 'Now Carrie, the purpose of this interview is to obtain a witness statement from you in relation to a current investigation. For the purpose of voice identification would you please state your full name?'

'Carrie Jane Atwell.'

'You don't have to say anything unless you wish to do so, as anything you say will be recorded and anything you say may later be used in evidence in court. Do you understand that?'

Carrie's heart was exploding in her chest. 'Yes, I understand.'

'So, do you mind if I record this?'

Carrie shook her head. 'No.'

The detective's eyes narrowed.

'I mean, no, I don't mind.'

'Detective Sergeant Summers tells me you approached him informally with some information that might have bearing on the investigation.' She was cold, unemotional, monotone. 'He also tells me that...' – she read from a report in her hand – '...he issued you with a field property receipt for an earring and another item, which is now being analysed, that you are listed as a witness on the QPrime report, and that he urged you to come give a statement. What can you tell us? From the beginning.'

Carrie sighed. 'I thought my husband was having an affair, I still don't know if he is, and whether this is all just coincidence.'

'Just give us the facts, ma'am, and we can decide how relevant they are to the case.'

She was going to get no sympathy from this woman, Carrie could tell. 'Okay.' She breathed out. 'I found an earring in my husband's ute that looks as if it matches the dead girl's earring.'

'The dead girl?'

'Mary Stevens. The first murder victim.'

She nodded. 'How did you know it matched?'

She was confused about what she was supposed to say and what would expose Mike's breaking of protocol. 'I saw the pictures in the media, and so I asked Detective Summers about it. He told me to come to you.'

'What? Summers? Why didn't he report this?'

She had already said the wrong thing. She didn't want to get Mike in trouble. 'I thought my husband was having an affair. But then I thought it could be much worse. But I couldn't believe he would be involved. I wanted to clear him of any suspicion.'

'So why are you coming to me now? Why didn't you come to me straight away?'

'I didn't really think he was involved. I thought I was being stupid. But it just got worse. I told my therapist everything. Julienne Van Tonder.'

The detective senior sergeant jolted in her seat. But she said nothing. This woman knew who the latest murder victim was, but it was not official yet. Carrie, as distressed as she was about the news, could not let on that she knew her therapist was dead.

'And?'

'I told her about the earring, and she urged me to go to the police. I told my husband about her and he was upset that I had told her. A few days ago, she called me and told me my husband had threatened her to keep quiet and threatened to kill her if she didn't. Then she disappeared. I haven't heard from her for two days.'

Shelby's face was animated. 'He threatened her? What did he say? Was she worried?'

'Yes, she was going to pretend she had left town, as he suggested she do.'

'And you think this implicates your husband further?'

'Yes. Why would he threaten her? But maybe it was not as bad as she said. Maybe he was just upset. I don't even know if it's true.'

The woman nodded. 'It's true. She called the police and left a message, reporting a death threat from your husband. Said she had made a recording of it and would send it through. But we never received it.'

'She recorded it?'

'Yes. We also discovered that she made a triple zero call last night from her apartment in Mooloolaba.'

'Last night? What, before she was murdered?'

The woman frowned. 'Whoa, whoa. Who said anything about her being murdered?'

Carrie bit her lip. 'Damn. It's obvious. The car crash last night. I knew it was her. Her car. And it was no accident.'

The woman nodded. 'We have no official confirmation yet that it is Julienne Van Tonder. But that is a pretty good deduction.'

'I'm scared. That's why I came to you. Until now I could still fool myself, but this points directly to my husband. I don't know what he's done, but it looks bad. And if he... or someone will murder Julienne because she knows something, then... what about me?'

'We can organise protection for you, Mrs Atwell, if your life is in danger. Has he threatened you?'

'No.' She touched her neck and tried to hide the bruising.

But the detective was too sharp-eyed. 'He did that? For the record, I see bruising on your neck.'

'It was an accident. I had an accident.'

She wrote this down. 'He knows you are suspicious of him?'

'I told him last night that we should go to the police about the earring. He was angry, said I was mad, and since then he's been away from home, a work emergency.'

'Is he often away from home?'

'His work is very demanding.'

Detective Senior Sergeant Shelby leaned forward. 'Carrie, there is something you should know here. In confidence. First, yes we are 100 per cent certain that the dead person in the car accident is your therapist.' She reached out her hand and Carrie took it. 'I'm sorry.'

'Have you positively identified the body?'

She nodded. 'The autopsy has not yet been done on her, but Detective Sergeant Summers found her ID in the car, the car is registered in her name, and she is missing from her apartment. Neighbours saw a man in a McDonald's University sweater violently enter her apartment and leave a few minutes later in her car. Where was your husband last night?'

'A McDonald's University sweater?'

Detective Senior Sergeant Shelby was hawk-eyed. 'Does that mean anything to you?'

'My husband wears a sweater like that.'

'Where was he last night?'

'We went out to supper.'

'And was he with you all night?'

'We sleep in different rooms, and I went to bed early. He had to go to work – the emergency I was talking about.'

'He was out last night? Do you know when he returned?'

Carrie gripped the table. 'He hasn't returned. He's not a killer, detective, I can't believe it.'

'I'm just looking at all possibilities; no one is accusing your husband yet–'

'Are there any other suspects?'

'I am unable to divulge that information to you.'

'It's my fault, isn't it? I should have come in earlier when Julienne told me he threatened her. And now she's dead. I thought he was having an affair.'

'No one is accusing you, Carrie. Here.' She passed her a box of tissues. 'We're just investigating. But we'll have to bring him in right away.'

She shuddered. 'My fault again. I wish I'd never found that damn earring.'

'You've saved people's lives, Carrie. Think – if that killer isn't stopped, how many more young women's lives will be lost?'

'It still doesn't seem real.'

'Secondly, Detective Sergeant Summers had the foresight to

send the earring for testing, and we have preliminary DNA results on that and another piece of evidence you gave him.'

Carrie was not sure if she was supposed to know the content of the report, so she feigned ignorance. 'What did you find?'

'The earring has no DNA traces. We suspect it has been wiped clean. Did you or your husband disinfect the earring or tamper with the evidence before handing it in?'

'I did touch it, before I knew it was evidence, it probably has my fingerprints and my husband's on it, but no, I didn't–' She stopped.

'What?'

'When my husband knew I had it, he took it from my drawer and returned it to me a day later. He said he was taking it to a mechanic who he thinks left it in his car. He could have wiped it clean then.'

She wrote this down. 'Mrs Atwell, you should have come to us before when you first found the earring and suspected that it was a match.'

'I'm sorry – but I still did not know for sure – I thought he was having an affair, and this was his mistress's earring.'

'I'm not blaming you, Carrie. Detective Summers speaks highly of you, and said you were very co-operative.'

'And what about the blonde hair?'

'The blonde hair was not tampered with. And we found the results were negative – it is not a match with the deceased.'

'Oh. That's good then?'

'Further, the hair is not in any way associated with any of the victims. But who knows what other victims there are out there that we do not know about?'

'Others?' she heard herself say.

'There may be others. This blonde hair sample might lead us to others.'

'He said it was his old girlfriend's hair.'

'Carrie, we're concerned about your safety. Detective Sergeant Summers considers you to be at grave risk.'

'Me?'

'If your husband finds out that you came to the police, and if he is the one who killed the therapist on suspicion that she would go to the police, then you are in a dangerous situation.'

'I never thought that Steve would do anything like that.'

Detective Senior Sergeant Shelby corrected her. 'The Steve you know would never do that. But the Steve you don't know...'

Carrie wiped her eyes on a tissue. 'What do I do?'

'When is your husband coming home from work?'

'Six.'

'Does he suspect that you have come to the police?'

'No. He thinks we're reconciling, that we need to get back to fixing our relationship, and he's looking forward to seeing me. Sends these texts...' She pulled out her phone and showed Detective Senior Sergeant Shelby the series of *I love you* texts that had been pouring in. 'Something is up, because he has never been so attentive.'

'Do you have family to go to, somewhere you can visit tonight?'

'Why?'

'We have sufficient evidence after what you've told me to arrest him. And the sooner we do that the better. Tonight. I will have a statement typed up from the information you provided during this interview and I will get you to come in and sign it.'

'Okay, sure.' Carrie took another tissue from the box with a trembling hand.

'It's okay, Carrie. Well done. I know this must be hard for you, but you've done the right thing.'

'Can I speak to Mike?'

'He'll be in touch as soon as I attend to some correspondence – he's busy with the Yaroomba case.'

The detective senior sergeant stood and shook her hand, and as an afterthought, gave her a stiff hug. 'Take care, Carrie, and find somewhere to stay this evening. Do you have any place to go?'

'My mother.'

'But your husband knows where your mother lives?'

'Of course.'

'Then we may have to find you a place of safety. Mike will contact witness protection and arrange that as soon as possible.'

'Maybe that would be better.'

She was not in a state to go home so she walked on the beach at Maroochydore, pushing through the crowds of tourists, dragging her toes in the warm water, and in a bid to get away from people, ended up at the far side of the beach by the rocky promontory at the river mouth.

She tried calling Mike, but as expected, his phone was busy, so she texted him.

I need to talk to you.

He called back immediately. 'Hi Carrie, how did the interview statement go?'

'Good, I think. Mike, she's going to arrest him and she wants me to stay somewhere else tonight.'

'I know, Carrie, I'm in charge of this investigation and I will be the arresting officer. And yes, I am going to arrest him. Please don't say anything to him, or do anything to alert him, okay? We have to go by the correct procedure. Sorry to put you through all that. Detective Senior Sergeant Shelby is a little abrasive.'

'She was fine. Even gave me a reluctant hug at the end.'

'How are you feeling?'

'I feel terrible and scared and I don't know what to think. Mike, I think he wiped the evidence from the earring. I wondered why he took it and then gave it back. I was such a fool. I believed him. He was so nice to me. It's all unreal, I still can't imagine him doing all those things.'

'Carrie, listen to me – he mutilated another body here. We're just getting the picture now – he stabbed your therapist multiple times, and – are you ready for this? – sliced open her brain and removed part of it. We found her naked with part of her brain missing, and lacerations all over her body. Then he must have driven her into the sea. There is no doubt here.'

'What?'

'He's sick, he's deranged. And he's done this to two other women, maybe more. We don't know yet who the blonde hair you found belongs to, but we're afraid there may be other victims out there and there will be more if we don't stop him now.'

'You're talking about someone else, not my husband.'

'Maybe – if he's a split personality or whatever the term was your therapist used.'

'Dissociative personality disorder. Listen, Mike, I'm on my way home via Coolum Beach. Are you still there? I could stop on my way?'

'Sorry, I'm finished there. I'm at the morgue with the body. We've positively identified her as Julienne. I'm so sorry, Carrie, she was more than a therapist for you, wasn't she? More of a confidante?'

'I can't believe she's gone. She told me he'd threatened her with the same fate as the other girls, but neither she nor I believed it. Why didn't she just go away like he asked her to?'

'I think he would have got her anyway. What alternative

arrangements did Detective Senior Sergeant Shelby make for this evening?'

'She told me that you would organise something like a safe house through witness protection.'

'Good. And yes, that was my idea. I have already organised it. Don't go home. Send your husband a text that you have been called away – a relative is sick.'

'I could say I have to go to my mother's?'

'Perfect. As long as you don't arouse suspicion. It won't be safe at home tonight for you. Actually, better not send him a text. Go home, pack some things, leave a note on the kitchen counter that you had to urgently go to your mother, and leave the front door open. And don't be alarmed, police are already casing out the house. I'll warn them that you will be coming home.'

'Where do I go?'

'I have arranged a place for you to stay. Not an official safe house but safer than anywhere. The red tape to get an official place of safety would take too long so I've got one for you.'

'Thank you.'

'As I said, go home now, pack a few things, and drive to the following address: 260 Verrierdale Road. Key in this PIN to the cottage: 435435435 and then lock the door behind you. It's totally safe and he won't find you there.'

'You sure? I mean you think a safe house is necessary?'

'Absolutely. You must not be at home tonight. I don't want another mutilated body in the ocean to fish out.'

'But you're going to arrest him?'

'He might put up a struggle. I don't want him to use you as a hostage. Just to be safe.' He gave her a few other details and then cut the call.

∼

She drove towards Yaroomba and pulled off at the parking on top of Luther Heights where the murder of her therapist had taken place. The area was cordoned off with blue-and-white tape – *police line do not cross* – but the area was now deserted. She parked and walked to the police line. She could see tyre marks to the edge of the cliff, the barrier smashed. She ducked under the tape and walked to the edge and stared over into the sea below. The car had been removed, and there was no trace of any trauma here or accident, or murder. But the words Mike had said were bright images in her head – knife cuts, naked body, skull sliced open and brain removed.

It could not be her therapist. Not Julienne. Julienne was still so alive to her, her voice in her head, her sound advice.

She closed her eyes, said a goodbye to her. 'Julienne. I'm so sorry,' she said to the air.

'Terrible thing, hey, lady?'

She turned in fright to face a withered older man, bronzed to a stick of jerky, holding his surfboard. He pointed to the swirling currents below. 'Terrible accident here last night.'

'She was a friend of mine.'

'Sorry, lady,' the man said. 'I live opposite' – he pointed up at a high-rise perched on the rocks – Coolum Point – 'and I saw everything.'

'You did? Did you tell the police?'

He smiled to reveal blackened teeth. 'They didn't ask me.'

'What did you see?'

'Car pulled up; I was awake. Around midnight. Saw two people in the car, struggling, but at the time I thought... couch rugby, you know.' He winked. 'Then after a lot of kerfuffling, the man leaps out and the car drives through the barrier into the sea.'

She shuddered. 'Did you see the man?'

'Not at that distance. And it was dark. But he was wearing a sweatshirt with a hood so you couldn't see his face. I could see that. Like a Big M on the back.'

She held onto the railing. Closed her eyes. Her husband's hoodie, his favourite one for messing around at home in. Not that she needed proof, not anymore. But it brought it home to her. No doubt. 'You should go to the police. Or call Crime Stoppers.'

'Sure, sure. The pigs are my friends,' he said.

'What did he do, this man?'

'He looked as if he was trying to stop the car, I thought at first, but he actually pushed it into the ocean. Not sure actually. I was a little... you know... psychologically enhanced, if you know what I mean.'

'Is that why you won't go to the police? But you're sure of what you saw?'

'Sure as I'm standing here talking to a beautiful woman. But that might be an illusion, too. Can you pinch me to make sure you're real?'

She pulled away from him. 'No!'

'Sorry,' he said, showing his blackened teeth. 'But I saw it all clearly.'

'What did he do next, this man?'

'He leaned over the edge and watched it fall. Then he walked away. I thought he would go for help, but he calmly walked off, and disappeared into the streets opposite. Then I heard the roar of a car, or truck.'

'What car was it?'

'I don't know. I didn't see it, just heard it.'

'You have to go to the police and tell them this.'

'No way.' He reached out his hand. 'I'm Andy by the way. Everyone knows me around here. And if you knew me, you'd know why I won't go to the pigs.'

'Carrie.' She held his hand weakly. She wanted to be left

alone, to think, to mourn, to let the events catch up with her, not to have the nightmare confirmed. Detective Senior Sergeant Shelby had mentioned the hoodie. A man had visited Julienne at her apartment wearing a McDonald's University hoodie. How many of those were around this area? Only one, she feared. Her husband had always worn it around the house as a joke. McDonald's University? Apparently though, it was a real place in Chicago somewhere and he had acquired the hoodie from a friend in the States. And now a man in that exact hoodie had visited Julienne, and then murdered her. She would have to go home and find if it was still in his closet.

'What did you see was happening in the car?'

'It was dark. Just some rocking. A lot of leaning over... wrestling... of course I thought... you know.'

'How horrible. You saw something terrible. Didn't you think it was suspicious? And didn't you go out and do something, or call the cops?'

He laughed. 'It happens a lot up here. If this van is a rocking, don't come a knocking. Not that I'm a voyeur or anything... You say she was your friend? Who was she?'

'She was my therapist. She lives– lived in Mooloolaba. Julienne Van Tonder.'

He shrugged his shoulders. 'She was your shrink?'

'Yes.'

'My shrink comes in a pipe.'

'I gathered. Listen, Mr... Andy... I'm not feeling that great. I'm still in shock.'

'I understand,' he said. 'Listen, I know how to help. How to numb the pain, at least.' He offered her a small packet of grass. 'You smoke?'

She shook her head. Turned and walked unsteadily to the car. Andy stared at her as she turned the car around and drove out of the car park and gave her a peace sign. She waved back.

It all felt like a nightmare, even this wispy, white-haired, black-toothed, ageing hippy surfer, like some underworld demon come to taunt her, to confirm that her husband was a murderer. *That was my husband you saw,* she wanted to tell him, *and you saw him murder my best friend.*

It was too real now, too close to home, too much detail. No longer circumstantial evidence but hard fact. If she could trust a stoned hippy. But he had seen the hoodie. *You can't make that up.* It was something maybe she should report to Mike. But it looked like they had enough evidence already.

She drove north. She did not want to go home yet. She had one more thing to do. She drove all the way up David Low Way, took the Sunshine Beach turn-off, and climbed the hill to the end of the road, into a cul-de-sac that abutted the Noosa Reserve.

The site of the first murder.

Mary. Whose earring she had held.

She had to see this place too. She had to take it in, make it real, if she was to be able to live with her conscience and what she had done to her husband. Or what he had done to her.

He certainly knew how to pick the best spots for body-dumping. In a relatively densely populated area, this cul-de-sac was hidden from view and surrounded by wild bush, eucalypts, and the crashing ocean. She pulled up by the drain. There was no sign that this was a murder scene anymore. No doubt it had been cordoned off too and bustling with detectives, forensics, reporters, but now it was a haunted, lonely site again.

The drain was large enough to stuff a body down, but it was dark and slimy, green with mould. She shuddered to think of a body being stuffed down there, falling into the jagged rocks beneath and tumbled by the high crashing waves. It was high tide and the ocean swelled and sent a spray high in the air like fireworks.

And then it hit home: she could be next. She would be shredded on those black, gleaming rocks, torn apart, mutilated. She had to get home and out of her husband's clutches. She needed to get some distance. She had to let go what she was holding – it was out of her hands now. Let the wheels of justice turn.

Brain looks like coral, grey coral, with its rivulets and trenches and ridges. So this is what a therapist's brain looked like. He had dried out and cleaned the section he had sliced out of her, and now placed it on the altar next to his other trophies. Tongue, ear, lips, clitoris, toes, fingers. A fine collection. A veritable work of art. He saw it as a collage. Not at first but as the souvenirs began to pile, he decided to display them, to give a shape to his desire. A composite girl at pride of place at the shrine. HER. Now with blonde hair draped over her makeshift face – the lips, the eyes, almost complete. The dull ache was the shape of the demon in his soul. Her. The one who had destroyed his life, the one he now took revenge on, her copies, her shadows, her images, her sisters. All HER.

He knew exactly what he was doing. Healing. Sexual healing. He felt better each time, fulfilled, by doing, being, existing, acting out what he wanted to do as a young teenager but had never been allowed to.

And they would never catch him. He knew exactly how to do things. Highly evolved, one step ahead. No trace on any of the bodies. Seawater was his friend. Wiped the evidence from the earring. He had planned his next victim, and she would be the best, he knew. He had been hanging out at the Sunshine Plaza for weeks, looking for the right one. And he had found her. Coffee barista at Coffee Time, with cute cap, apron, earrings to die for. And he had ordered coffee from her, had chatted, and he knew she liked him. He had even remarked on the earrings and she had felt flattered. She would be the best, and she had no clue what he was going to do to her. He had planned all sorts of tricks.

That therapist had talked about dissociative personality disorders. She was wrong, dead wrong. There was nothing wrong with his mind; he was perfectly tuned, an evolutionary marvel, at the peak of his powers, all man could achieve. And what was man at his prime? Predator. Sexual king. He had sharpened his biological impulses, super-tuned them to a fine art. If he had lived a few thousand years ago, he'd be a hero, the king of his tribe, for his sexual exploits. Cavemen clubbed women and dragged them by their hair back to their cave. Could do what they liked with them. Ate their flesh, dismembered them, all in a night's fun. Only in today's society was that a crime. If a lion caught its prey, played with it, dismembered it, you would just say it was the lion's nature, its instinct, not an immoral act.

But if a man does it?

And so, aware that he lived in a weak, emasculated society, he had to bide in a mask of civility, pretend to be the gentleman, to fit in. Play their rules. And he did it so well. So well.

41

ATWELL HOME. TUESDAY AFTERNOON

The first thing Carrie did when she arrived home was lock and bolt the doors behind her. She caught sight of a car in the back driveway. Police. The detective in her head had made a decision, a logical, rational, objective decision based on evidence that this man Steve Atwell was a dangerous serial killer.

The sweater, the earring, the wiping of evidence so that a DNA test would not point to him, the threatening phone call, the witness, they all pointed to his guilt. If she were a police detective in charge, she would arrest him. But of course, the wife of this husband was still fighting for any seed of evidence to the contrary. The wife of this man, she could see, was in denial, clinging to strands of hope, like his kindness, his excuses. He was innocent until proven guilty. But even she as a wife could see she was being gaslighted. He was not telling the truth about anything – the hotels he stayed at, the work emergency, why he had taken the earring from her drawer... *Wake up, Carrie to the truth!*

The second thing she did, both as a detective and as a wife, was rummage through his drawers to look for the McDonald's

University hoodie. Maybe it was sitting here, newly washed, folded in his drawer all this time. Okay, so a witness, two witnesses, had seen a man in this very hoodie, but who says it was his?

She searched every drawer. She could not find it anywhere. She checked the laundry basket, the washing machine, the dryer, even the rubbish bin. Maybe she'd find a bloodstained, scrunched-up hoodie in the bin! But no, it was nowhere.

He was wearing the damn thing. Had it in his car.

She sat on the laundry room floor and cried. It was over, then. It was true. She could not hold back the floodgates any longer. Give it over to the cops. Let them arrest him. She needed to step back and watch the wheels of justice turn. And if it was true that he had killed all these women, and he suspected she knew, he would of course come after her and kill her. That's what any cold, calculating, self-preserving serial killer would do. He had killed a witness. And she was next.

She packed her bags. Locked the doors but left the front door open as instructed so the police could gain entry. How did she feel? Dirty. A betrayer. But she settled herself. She was in denial, even now, she knew it, still with that faint glimmer of hope that this was a ghastly mistake, that Steve was innocent, wrongly accused. But the detective in her knew otherwise. She could feel it in her gut. She felt sick.

She wrote a note, placed it on the kitchen counter, and left the house as instructed.

Dear Steve, Mother is unwell. Sorry, had to rush over to her house for the night. Plenty of food in the kitchen. Make a toastie. Bread in fridge. Love you Xxx

She placed the note next to the flowers on the table. She felt sick writing it. She was gaslighting *him* now, weaving a web of deceit and lies around him so he could be ensnared. So many lies! Is this how life played out? She had started out honest, wanting truth, and now she was part of the lying game too.

But she felt better as she drove away, with her suitcase, her laptop, and her passport. As if she was making a clean break, like she did when there was a bushfire emergency or a flood, leaving it all behind, thinking: *what do I really need anyway from that life?* She mapped the way to the safe house on her GPS – it wasn't far, in Verrierdale, but felt secluded and tucked away, in the multi-acre properties in the hills behind Peregian Beach. She loved this area, the rustic setting of millionaires and gentleman farmers, architectural wonders perched on top of the rolling green hills overlooking the Pacific Ocean and Mount Coolum, forests, horse paddocks, lakes.

Mike had told her to be careful – *make sure no one is following you. If there is a car behind you, double back to Peregian Springs, drive around, do some shopping or something until you lose them.* But she was alone on the road. She found the address and at first drove past because the entrance was hidden in the bushes. No sign, no clear driveway or gate. A small overgrown dirt road, full of ruts and puddles. She wondered if her little Honda Jazz could take the bumps, so she drove around on the grass verge as much as she could.

She passed through a thick eucalypt forest up a long dirt driveway, past a macadamia nut farm, past a paddock where beautifully groomed horses swished their tails and came up to the fence as she passed, and then she saw the sign to the safe house, 260 Verrierdale Road, a rutted driveway leading to a cottage. Her small city car hit rocks and spun dirt and she tasted red dust that caught up with her as she parked by the gate. She pulled it open and then saw the note: LOCK ME AFTER YOU

ENTER. She clicked the chain lock and pocketed the key, drove to a cottage in a small clearing.

She felt grateful to Mike. He had found her a place because they did not have time to organise a police safe house. Had he organised this personally for her? She was flattered. But was it safe? The cottage looked beautiful from the outside. Rendered in an ochre wash, it was like a Hobbit house, with rounded windows and doors. But the fairy-tale look was deceptive. There were security cameras on the roof, and above the front door, a red flashing light above each window.

She had seen movies about witnesses secluded away in protective custody, so she expected a guard at the door. But it was deserted. She parked her car out of sight around the back, as instructed, found the key in the key safe on the side of the house, and tapped in the code she had been given. She pushed open the door and saw a light flashing in the passageway, which meant that she had twenty seconds to turn off the alarm in the house. She fumbled into the dark corridor to the alarm system, punched in the code she had been given, and the red light stopped flashing.

Whew. She flipped on the light switch by the entrance and the cottage rooms glowed with warm light. She looked around, in relief. She had envisioned an austere hiding hole, but not this! *What a nice place.* Had Mike especially found this cottage on Airbnb for her? No, of course not. It looked like a fortress. He had planned this weeks before, probably, especially set this up for her when he first realised that she was in danger.

She fetched her suitcase and laptop and took a tour of the property. Outside was dense forest, and the cottage was in a small clearing, bordered with a high electric fence. Inside, the kitchen was modern: white marble countertops, new oven and microwave, humming white fridge, and a round dining room table with four chairs. A living area with flatscreen TV, comfy sofa and a mini bar, fully stocked. A passageway led to a bedroom with cosy earth-rendered corners and a low ceiling with a wooden fan. Each window was alarmed, and faced into the forest, but she noticed motion detector lights and cameras positioned around the house that were, she assumed, triggered to set off an alarm if any intruders entered. This was a safe house all right, with alarm panic buttons placed at intervals.

On the kitchen counter next to a bowl of fresh mangoes and lychees, a welcome note from Mike:

Make yourself at home. Food in the fridge. Bar stocked. Remember to keep the doors locked.

And so, a new life had begun. She sighed. Whatever would happen now? How long would she be here?

Detective Senior Sergeant Shelby watched the video of her interview with Carrie Atwell. Poor woman. But there was something not quite right here. She could always tell when they were lying. Whenever Summers' name was mentioned she shuffled around, averted her eyes, looked flushed. Summers, the fool. He had been messing around with witnesses. Was it a mistake to send him to arrest the husband? Probably.

'If you fuck this up, Summers...' she said aloud.

But still. A thrill of pleasure went through her when she thought of the noose tightening around Atwell. Summers had delivered her the serial killer, in spite of his unconventional methods. She had to give him that. And she was enjoying this. Not that she wanted a serial killer loose. But the Sunny Coast had never seen anything like this before. This was the most significant homicide investigation the Sunshine Coast had ever seen.

International media and swarms of national media were all over the place. The mayor had called her, concerned about tourism, tourist operators were freaking out, women had been cautioned not to go out alone – no more jogging in the park or on the esplanade. As soon as the major incident room had Steve on their radar as the suspect – and this had happened even before his wife had come in to give her statement – a myriad of measures had been put in place.

The interception and arrest of the suspect was meticulously planned, organised and overviewed in liaison with homicide squad members... and Summers. He wanted to be at the front of the pack, and he had earned it. She had lined up SERT – Special Emergency Response Team – to be on standby near the house. Two detective cars and a uniform car were parked around the street near the house.

She had deliberated nabbing Steve Atwell before he got home. There was always the danger that he might run into the house and start a siege situation. He might have weapons there. She wanted heavily armed SERT members to intercept him while he was walking along the street about to get into his car. But Summers had insisted that he be apprehended at the house. 'He's mine,' Summers had said. 'I found him, didn't I? I got the woman to give a statement, give the evidence over. Trust me on this one.'

'Trust you?' she had sneered. 'I don't trust you. I disapprove of your Casanova methods. Have you organised witness protection?'

He nodded. 'I've organised a place of safety for her.'

She stared at him. She did not trust him, did not approve of his methods, but he got the job done. He had delivered the evidence, had persuaded the suspect's wife to come forward. She would go along with him this time against her better judgement. But she would give him this one last chance to prove himself.

The house and Steve had been under surveillance for a day by the Bureau of Criminal Intelligence in Brisbane. They had followed Steve all day in two cars, taking turns to follow him. They had engaged a telephone intercept on his mobile too.

42

MAROOCHYDORE POLICE STATION.
TUESDAY EVENING

Detective Senior Constable John Ribot, Mike's assigned partner, and Detective Senior Constable Adam Lucas, waited for Mike in the unmarked grey CIB car.

'Mad Mike is all wired up for this mission.'

'He's been waiting for this moment. Have you ever seen him arrest anyone? He's like a salivating dog about to pounce on his prey.'

'So why did he wait for so long for this one? He had the evidence.'

'Not really. He had to make sure. Too many times the bird has flown the coop, as Mike says. He has the killer's wife, can you believe it, eating out of the palm of his hand.'

Adam frowned. 'I've seen her. Pretty little thing, ain't she? Perfect for Mike. He's a ladies' man, worked her so well, made sure she talked.'

'Speak of the devil – here he is now.'

Mike Summers bounded down the steps of the station and jumped into the car. His energy was pathological. He looked at both of them, critically. 'Let's go.'

They set off in convoy. SERT, heavily armed and disguised in black, tagged behind them in an unmarked car.

'What intelligence do we have on Steve?' asked John Ribot.

Mike grinned. 'Everything we need to know and more. Intelligence analysts grabbed everything – his electricity bill for the past ten years, checked for criminal records, domestic violence, street checks, weapon licences, phone records...'

'And?'

'*Nada.* He's clean.'

'And you believe that?'

'Not a chance.'

John drove smoothly, weaving in and out of the heavy Christmas traffic in Maroochydore, onto the Sunshine Motorway north towards Noosa.

'I must warn you, he'll put up a struggle,' said Mike.

John smiled. 'At least you hope so. I know you, Mike, you're itching for a fight.'

'With this monster, yes. You have your firearms and tasers?'

'Check.'

'Don't hesitate to taser him if he resists arrest. Or use your firearms if he has a weapon.'

'Seriously?' John stared at Mike. Mad Mike. He had quite a reputation as a maverick, used crime to catch crime. His methods were unconventional to say the least. He gave Adam a quick glance and both men had the same thought: what had they got themselves into here? But Mike always got his man.

'What?' said Mike, seeing their incredulous looks.

'You know you're with Mad Mike when he starts talking about going in shooting from the hip. Shelby just told us in the briefing that we were to bring him in without any resort to unnecessary force.'

'Bring him in alive,' added Adam.

Mike raised his eyebrows. 'Shelby knows shit about this arsehole. He cannot be allowed to escape. He's a desperate serial killer who thought nothing of hacking open women, slicing them up for body parts, and then disposing of them. If he were cornered, he might go savage, so we cannot show any weakness, or mercy. Minimal force, my arse.'

'Still, she urges caution,' repeated John, softly. 'She wanted to have him arrested, pay the penalty in court, and then spend a lifetime in jail. Isn't that what we all want?'

'Calm down, John, we'll go by the book. This time.' Mike grinned. 'Shelby's been pen-pushing for too long, doesn't understand police justice, this primeval gut feeling of when to act, when to go for the jugular... that's why we're cops. We need justice, yes, but wild justice, because if he gets to court, his namby-pamby lawyers will find a loophole and get him off and he'll be roaming the streets looking for his next victim.'

'I hear you didn't go by procedure with this case from the very beginning.'

'Fuck procedure,' said Mike. 'Procedure means he walks. If I had followed procedure, we would have arrested him and found nothing, no earring. I would not have been able to get to the truth using procedure.' He mimicked his superior. 'I'm warning you, Mike, don't bring back a corpse.'

'And what did you say to that?'

'I said don't underestimate him, Shelby. He acts the nice husband, the sweet man, who wouldn't hurt a fly, that's his trick. His wife is still not sure about him even with all the hard evidence. But I know what lingers in the heart of men. I know.' He beat his chest. 'If I were him, I'd be prepared for this. He's a military man, and he probably has a trick up his sleeve so be prepared. Be prepared for dirty tricks. Ambush.'

They turned off the motorway at Murdering Creek Road and cruised down the overgrown acreage suburb, slowed down when they reached the road. 'Slow, slow, let's park here. There's the house.'

SERT came onto the radio, confirming they were in place too behind the property.

Mike acknowledged. 'Wait in the bushes, in case he bolts.' And to John and Adam: 'Shoot to kill. He can't get away.'

John looked at his partner. Now they knew Mike was truly unhinged. You could not lawfully shoot a suspect just for decamping from you. And the suspect hadn't even been arrested or charged with anything yet, nor had he been found committing any murder. 'What if he has another victim locked up somewhere?'

Mike shook his head. 'He doesn't keep his victims locked up. He takes what he wants from them, and then dumps them in storm drains over the edge of cliffs, like fly-tipping. They're disposable items, and he's a product of our consumer society.'

'Sure.'

'Think of him like a wild animal, a dingo who snatches babies and mauls them to death for the pleasure of it. When cornered, he may bare his teeth and attack.'

'Gotcha.'

John stared into the driveway, but the house was not visible from the road. Lake Weyba gleamed silver at the far end of the road, and the green patch on their right was the nature reserve through the middle of which Murdering Creek itself ran.

Adam pointed to the road sign. 'Good address for a serial killer to live, don't you think? Murdering Creek.'

Mike looked around at the dense, overgrown foliage. 'Plenty of cover.'

Rainbow lorikeets screeched in the trees.

'Beautiful place,' remarked John. 'What does he do for a living to own such a beautiful property?'

'He's a building contractor. The new airport extension?

That's him. The new mall at Sippy Downs? Atwell Construction.'

'He makes enough money to indulge his little hobby.'

Mike checked his phone: 5.55. 'Now I've scouted the area, know the house. Up there, there's a back entrance, his man cave at the end of the property abuts an access road where the rubbish collectors and tradesmen come. He parks his ute out here too. Comes in the main entrance then tinkers around in his man cave. We have one vehicle already in place in that alley. SERT?'

'SERT is standing by. ETA of suspect?'

'ETA three minutes.'

'Eighteen hundred hours. BCI have confirmed it. 'Shh. I can hear a car.'

They strained to listen. The suburb was so quiet they could hear the whoosh of the motorway four kilometres away against the backdrop of the ocean's roar.

He held up his mobile phone. 'I've planned this day to the tee. Don't someone fuck it up. SERT? Don't make a move until I tell you. This baby's mine.'

SERT's reply was swift. 'You're the only person likely to fuck this up, Summers.'

'Too many times they get away. Not this time, not this time, okay?' He looked at John. 'That is why we wanted Carrie out of it. In case there's resistance, and the man decides to shoot his way out.'

'Why do you think that he might shoot his way out?' asked Adam. 'He has no history of using or possessing a firearm. He never used a firearm in any of his killing sprees, it was always knives, garottes...'

Mike grimaced. 'Those were his torture instruments of pleasure, but when he's cornered, I'm sure he must have thought of his own self-defence. If you had actually read the report, you'd see his military service and history and his ability with firearms. Never heard of illegal firearms, John? Never underestimate a serial killer, much less any killer. Especially one with a military background. He always has a counter plan. Final checks?'

'Is your mobile on silent?'

The SERT van at the back of the house was hidden behind a large plumeria hedge, and theirs was parked behind a row of lilly-pillies so that the suspect would notice nothing out of the ordinary when he returned home. They waited.

The car engine noise grew louder and at six o'clock on the dot, they watched Steve Atwell's ute appear at the turn-off, drive to the entrance, stop while he reached out the driver's window to retrieve his mail from the mailbox at the gate, and then go up the long driveway and disappear behind the foliage where the house was.

John managed to get a glimpse of the alleged killer, an innocuous man in a suit, whistling to himself. Clean-shaven. Short hair. Driving a shiny new Holden Colorado ute.

'So that's what a serial killer looks like,' he whispered. 'So blandly normal.'

'Yup.'

The plan was to nab him as he got out his car, before he could get to the house. They climbed out of the car, ready to intercept. But Mike held them back.

'Okay, now.'

When they turned the corner, the ute was parked further down, right next to a side entrance, and the suspect had already hopped out and gone into the house.

'Shit,' muttered John. 'Wasn't he supposed to go in the front entrance, and we get him before he even gets to the door?'

Mike's mobile phone lit up. A message from SERT.

He's in the fucking house. We saw him go in.

We're onto it, Mike texted back.

'We're fucking idiots,' whispered John. 'Now he has the advantage. Who knows what the hell he has in there?'

Mike was unperturbed. 'It's all part of the plan. My plan.'

'What?'

But John was worried. The suspect could easily start a siege situation. He might have his weapons there and have access to them. It looked as if Mike had deliberately let the suspect go inside.

'Let's wait for SERT to surround the house.'

Mike shook his head. *Hold off, SERT*, he texted. *We got this.* He motioned for the others to keep under cover and walk up the drive to the house. John stared at the grand Queenslander, double storey, a glittering pool at the front.

They walked into the open, climbed the steps to the front door. Mike knocked. He had one hand on his concealed weapon in his jacket holster.

John stood to the side, not knowing what to expect. The house would provide the suspect with cover and they had none. A very dangerous situation. But Mike was grinning. He enjoyed this, had planned it this way. He was itching for a gunfight. *Shit.* There was even the risk of the suspect shooting them through the front door. That's how Summers liked it – the more the risk the better. Mad Mike. *Fuck!*

No answer. Mike tightened his grip on his pistol. John nervously reached for his too. 'We saw him come in.'

'Hello,' Mike called louder, knocking again. 'Atwell?'

Nodded to John. 'A trap?' he mouthed.

He turned the door handle, and it swung open. They looked at each other. 'Cover me,' whispered Mike. He whisked out his weapon. John followed suit, stood by the dark entrance.

'We don't have a warrant to enter the house,' John whispered. 'Just to make an arrest.'

'Fuck the warrant. If we need one, we'll get it later. After we arrest the fucker.'

Mike aimed his weapon into the corridor. John winced. By aiming his weapon into the dark hallway, Mike would be likely to shoot an innocent occupant. But that wouldn't worry Summers. John and Adam held their weapons down and to the side as per procedure. John could see nothing. Why were all these old Queenslanders so dark inside? The stained-glass windows were small and let through hardly any light. A large chandelier hung from the middle of the ceiling. The kitchen light was on further down the corridor.

Mike took measured steps through and John followed. He was holding a torch under the Glock pistol. John followed, holding onto his belt. Summers called out, 'Clear' and they moved into the next room.

'Police. It's the police. Atwell, where are you? If you hear us, respond loudly with a yes. Respond now, Steve Atwell. It's the police.'

The living room and open-plan kitchen was deserted. On the kitchen counter was Carrie's note, written as Mike had instructed. He picked it up, nodded in approval. They surveyed the living area. Mike whispered, 'She said he has an office in the corner of the house.' He followed the corridor past a bathroom, poked his weapon in, but the bathroom was empty. John reached in and pulled back the shower curtain, in case the suspect was lurking here, but it was also empty.

Mike had found the office and pushed open the door. 'Atwell, Police. We have a warrant to come in and search your house. Please respond. Please show yourself. Hands up in the air and no sudden moves. Atwell, are you there?'

The office was deserted too. John followed Mike in and opened the cupboard which was stuffed with boxes and clothes.

'Fuck.' Mike pointed at the empty desk. A printer lay

unplugged, and a mouse and screen but no hard drive. 'She said he had a computer full of incriminating evidence. But it's gone. He must be onto us.'

John watched in amazement as Mike kick-searched the bedrooms, toilets, laundry room. He followed cautiously. There was no sign of their suspect in the house. But he gripped his pistol tight. He was fully ready to have the mad killer leap out from behind a door, attack him. He would shoot, Mike was right, at the slightest opportunity. Where the hell was he? They had seen him walk into the house a moment ago.

He checked the walk-in closet, laundry closet. Nothing. He found Adam in the main bedroom holding a photo of a smiling couple, Steve and Carrie, in happier days. 'He looks like a decent bloke.'

'They all do,' said Mike. His phone lit up and he read the message. 'SERT says the garage light is on.'

'Can you see him?'

Garage is empty, came back the reply.

'Hold off.'

John wiped the sweat from his brow. This was madness.

'He'll be in the man cave, apparently there is a secret place behind the garage. Carrie told me about it.' Mike led the way out of the kitchen door down the path through the wild, unkempt acreage. John and Adam followed.

'Doesn't he ever mow his lawn?' Mike said.

John did not give a fuck about the long grass – he was looking for a shotgun pointing out of a window.

At the garage, Mike indicated the extension at the back, a windowless brick room. The door was open. John and Adam positioned themselves on either side, and Mike knocked on the open door. It was dark inside.

'Police. Police here. Steven Atwell? Steven Atwell. It's the police.'

A shuffle, then the suspect himself emerged from the shadows, startled, in his work clothes, but without the tie, top button undone, a beer bottle in his hand. He was breathless. 'What the...? How did you get in?' Then he saw the Glock pistol and the two detectives flanking Summers, also with weapons at his chest. 'W-whoa. What is this?'

Mike held up his police identification and Steve squinted at it. 'Detective Sergeant Mike Summers from Maroochydore CIB.'

Steve did not look surprised. He was either hiding it well or was truly dissociative and was keeping his killer self well hidden, even from himself. He looked truly bewildered. John kept his eye on the man's hands. He looked unarmed, calm, but you could never tell.

Mike spoke in a casual voice. 'Mind if we step outside and chat for a few minutes?'

Clever, thought John, he didn't want to confront him here, in his own territory. John peered into the dark room. It smelled evil, a scent he could not quite identify, maybe some chlorine-based antiseptic. This was where the accused's wife had found the lock of blonde hair, belonging no doubt to one of his conquests. What other trophies were hidden here, he wondered? He shuddered.

'First, though,' said John, as he saw Mike was not going to do it, 'we need you to consent to a pat-down search. And please hand over your mobile, keys and wallet.'

'Sure.' Atwell raised his arms and John frisked him. No mobile, no keys, no wallet. Most importantly, no concealed weapon.

Then Mike directed him outside. SERT agents appeared from behind a bush, weapons aimed at the suspect.

'It's okay, guys, we got this.' Mike waved them away, and then turned to Atwell, who still had his hands raised in the air, but was, strangely enough, not at all flustered. Most normal suspects would be shitting their pants by now.

Mike lowered his weapon. 'I am Detective Sergeant Mike Summers, and these are my esteemed partners Detective Senior Constable John Ribot, and Detective Senior Constable Adam Lucas.'

Mike indicated that the others could put their weapons away.

'What is this about?' Steve lowered his hands but kept them in sight.

Mike folded his arms. 'Please state your name and address.'

'Steve Atwell, of 29 Clarendon Road, Peregian Beach.'

'I thought this was Lake Weyba?'

'Well no, actually. Technically, this suburb is Peregian Beach, I know it's a long way from the beach, so most people call it Lake Weyba.'

Unreal, thought John. *He's bumbling along casually, as if he hasn't got three detectives surrounding him and a bunch of SERT guys in the bushes. He must be guilty and covering well, or really stupid.*

Steve stared at Mike. 'You're the detective I saw on TV. The murder case, right?'

'No shit, Sherlock.' Mike nodded. 'Mr Atwell, you are under arrest for the murder of Mary Stevens.'

Steve stood back. 'What the fuck? You can't be serious?'

'Okay, you're going to play it innocent, then? Much better. Much better.'

Steve shook his head. 'You're serious. What makes you think I have anything to do with her murder?'

'Place your hands behind your back.'

He did so and John slipped the cuffs on him.

'Would you mind telling me what this is all about? You can't just arrest someone without a reason, and you don't just hand-cuff innocent people.'

'Take it easy, Atwell,' said John. 'A court of law will decide your innocence or guilt.'

'What are you accusing me of, exactly?'

'I will inform you that you do not have to say anything, answer any questions or make any statement as anything you say will be recorded and may later be used in court as evidence.' He indicated the body camera he was wearing. 'Do you under-stand that you do not have to say anything?'

'Yes.'

'Do you understand that anything you say will be recorded?'

'That seems obvious too.'

'Smart-arse, eh? Do you understand that anything you say may later be used in evidence?'

'Yes, I do. But you're saying I have something to do with the murder of that poor young woman? On what grounds?'

'We'll interview you at the station. There is a proper proce-dure here. We're following procedure. We have evidence—'

'Fuck.' Steve pointed his chin at Mike. 'It's the fucking earring, isn't it? My wife discussed going to the cops about it, but I thought it was too far-fetched. You don't seriously think...?'

'We do seriously think, you shithouse,' said Mike. 'Now get your arse moving.'

John nudged him to walk towards the driveway. Steve kept his ground. Stood still. 'I'm not a criminal. I have rights. You can't just come in here... I need to talk to someone. A lawyer. I need to talk to a lawyer. Don't I get one phone call?'

John looked into the man's eyes. He looked wild. Incredu-lous. A good actor. 'At the police station, Mr Atwell, you can have your phone call. Prior to the interview.'

'Can I at least call my wife? She'll be worried.'

Mike and John exchanged looks. Steve saw their unease. 'What?'

'Your wife–' began Mike. Adam stayed him. Cautioned with his eyes.

'What about my wife?'

Mike sighed. 'Your wife can't help you.'

'What do you mean?'

'Mike...' cautioned John. Now he saw the maverick at work. Fuck. Mike had been told explicitly not to bring up the wife, in fact, they were protecting her, and here was Mike using her as bait. He sighed. He gave Mike the evil eye.

Mike nodded to John. 'Let me tell the poor bugger. Steve, it was your wife who gave evidence against you. She turned you in.'

Now Steve looked panicky. 'Carrie? I don't believe you. What is this? Some sort of set-up?'

Shit. John shook his head, clutched his weapon. He could see Mike was enjoying this. This is what gave him his kicks. *So much for fucking procedure.* Then he realised what Mike was doing. He was trying to provoke this man. Into what? Attacking them? He had another agenda here. What was he trying to do?

Steve stiffened and John had to hold him, pull his hand-cuffed hands behind his back, in case he tried to bolt. But the man looked truly shocked. 'What? She knows about this? That's ridiculous. Carrie? She's visiting her mother – she... would have told me... You sure you have the right person?'

Mike shook his head. 'Sorry, mate, but we asked her to keep away this evening. In case there was trouble.'

'She knew about this?'

''Fraid so.'

He looked bewildered, then wild, and tugged to test John's grip, motioned as if he was going to run for it. But he was in cuffs and John was holding his arm tight.

Steve turned to John. He could tell who the softies were. 'I have to call her... Please.'

John gripped the man's arm tight. 'You will need to accompany us to the station now, Mr Atwell.'

'On what grounds?'

'You have been arrested under the PPRA for the offence of murder,' said Mike. 'You will be detained for up to eight hours for interview and investigation. We want to question you about the murder of Cindy Liptrot as well as the death of Julienne Van Tonder, your wife's therapist.'

'Her therapist? She's dead? What the fuck? When did this happen?'

'You should know.'

'What? How would I know anything about that?'

John rolled his eyes. This was totally not police procedure. But Mike was enjoying his moment here. John gave him a pained look. Mike's tactic was provocation. A game he was playing, and that was how he did so well, but flouting police procedure was not a wise thing to do. It could come back and bite him. He was antagonising the suspect. Baiting him. He had been told categorically not to mention the wife, or the therapist. On the first count, the wife was in a safe house precisely because of fear of reprisal and retaliation, and on the second count, there was no proof the therapist had been killed by the same person. Hell, her identity hadn't even been released yet to the public.

'Mike, we'd better... get to the station.'

Steve was still incredulous. Or acting incredulous. Or perhaps he was one of those split personalities whose one half had no idea what his other half had been getting up to. 'Is this a joke? Some candid camera moment?'

'No, I'm afraid not.'

'There's a mistake here, really. This can be cleared up, and you'll be in trouble.'

'Is that a threat? Are you threatening a police officer?'

John saw Mike's smile. He was enjoying this provocation, willing the suspect to make one false move. He looked at Mike's face, saw a primeval loathing and predator instinct there. His body was quivering, his trigger finger itching, and he looked like a dog, a beast of prey.

'You killed those beautiful young women, mutilated them, cut off body parts, you sick fuck. Don't act all stupid and innocent now. We know exactly what you did.'

And now John saw why. Mike had seen the victims first-hand, had been on the scene just after the bodies had been discovered, had seen this man's handiwork, the mutilation, naked, drowned victims, their faces still contorted with the agony of their torturer's marks on them. Who wouldn't want to hurt this man who had done such unspeakable things to these women?

And then the suspect, feigning innocence. Almost mocking, as if he knew he could get away with this. So handsome, suave, and arrogant. No wonder Mike was a maverick, wanted to take justice in his own hands. And he would not leave the suspect alone.

'You've engineered some pretty watertight alibis, I hear.'

John nudged Mike. He shouldn't be questioning the bloody suspect outside of the formal interview process. He had requested a lawyer. They should not commence any interview process until the suspect had the opportunity to contact and confer with his lawyer. Mike knew that. Why was he... taunting the bastard?

'Alibis? What are you talking about? I want to speak to a lawyer.'

'You will, at the station.'

'I want to make a phone call now. I have my rights.'

'You've been watching too many American movies, you shit-house. Who do you want to call?'

'Carrie, my wife. She'll be worried sick about me.'

'The person who dobbed you in?'

'I still don't believe it. Carrie would never do that.'

Mike smiled. 'She came to us. She gave a statement against you, she found evidence which we have proved beyond a shadow of a doubt links you to the murder of Mary Stevens, and Cindy Liptrot and Julienne Van Tonder. How does that make you feel, eh? Your own wife betrayed you. She was in fear of her life.'

Steve slumped. 'This is a nightmare. It can't be true. Carrie would never–' He looked up at Mike. 'Is she okay? Is she safe? Where is she?'

Mike laughed. 'That's rich coming from you. Is the therapist safe? Are those teen girls safe? Well, any future victims are now. You can console yourself with that, Mr fucking Atwell.'

'Yes, she's safe,' said John.

Steve looked wildly at him. 'Where is she? You know where she is? Fuck, this is a conspiracy.'

Mike nodded. 'We know where she is. We put her in protection to keep her safe from you. My superior tells me you beat her up. We feared for her life so we put her in a place where you can't find her.'

'What has she been saying about me?'

'She's under police protection in case you try to intimidate her as a witness.'

'Me? Intimidate a witness? She's my wife, for God's sake. You're intimidating me.'

Mike laughed. 'You're a good actor, Mr Atwell. Or do you really believe your act? Anyway, this is enough pleasant conversation, but we're wasting time here. Let's go.'

Steve clutched his heart. Staggered. His face went pale.

'What the fuck?' said Mike.

'Sorry, guys,' he gasped. 'One last request before you take me in. I have to get my medication. If I'm going to be away for any length of time, and it looks like that's the case, I need my pills. You wouldn't like to deal with me if I haven't taken medication, trust me.'

Mike raised his eyebrow. 'What medication?'

'Heart medicine.'

'Seriously?'

'You want a medical emergency on your hands?'

Mike stared at the suspect who did look as if he was about to collapse. He could see Mike did not want complications here. 'Okay, where is it? John will get it.'

'I'll have to go with him. It's locked up, tamper-proof. Needs my fingerprint to unlock the medical safe.'

'For God's sakes, fuck the medication. We're taking you in.'

John nudged Mike. 'I think it might be easier just to get his medication, otherwise we might have to come back. Detective Senior Sergeant Shelby... procedure.'

'Fucking procedure means we treat criminals like kings.' But he sighed. 'We all go. No funny business.'

Steve breathed out. 'Thank you.'

'Stand down, SERT,' called Mike into his phone.

The suspect led the way into the house to the bathroom. John was wary of tricks, but the suspect was handcuffed, calm, and compliant. He indicated the small medical safe on the wall, and the electronic swipe pad to open it. He could not reach it with his hands cuffed. 'And I need to go to the toilet. I need to take a shit.'

'For fuck's sake, man,' said John.

Mike shook his head. 'Uncuff the bastard.'

'What?'

'Uncuff the bastard. I'm not going to wipe his arse for him.'

John reluctantly took off the cuffs, watched as the suspect opened the medical safe and took down a bottle of pills. John kept a lookout for weapons, sharp objects.

Then the suspect dropped his pants, sat on the toilet, strained his face. A foul smell. 'Sorry guys... a runny stomach... something I ate.'

'Christ, close the door.' Mike slammed the door shut. 'Watching a man take a shit is not in my job description.'

They waited outside the door. Adam stared up at the bright chandeliers. 'Kind of creepy, ain't it?'

'He's creepy.'

'So now you know what a serial killer looks like. What you expected?'

John shook his head. 'What was all that shit you were talking?' he whispered. 'You're provoking a suspect?'

Mike banged the door. 'Hurry up, man, we have to go. Wipe your arse and let's get the fuck out of here.'

No answer.

'Atwell?'

Mike pushed open the door. There was no Atwell. He rushed in, pulled back the shower curtain, looked up at the open window. 'Shit.' He peered out. No one. Nothing. Just forest.

Then the roar of a ute starting up and revving down the driveway.

'Jesus. Get out to the front, quick, we gotta stop him.' Mike rushed up the corridor and out of the front door of the house, raised his weapon and aimed for the flash of blue he saw disappearing around the corner of the drive, now shrouded in thick gum trees. He took one shot at the place he estimated the car would be, but the round thudded into the trees.

'Shoot him, you fucking idiots,' he yelled. 'Damn you.'

John nodded. For once, Mike was right. They actually had the lawful right – prima facie – to use deadly force to prevent a suspect who had been arrested for a life-imprisonment offence from escaping. But by the time they had reached the front of the driveway and had their weapons out, the ute was long gone. They heard it roar onto the main road.

'SERT, the suspect has done a runner,' John called into his phone. 'Heading onto Murdering Creek Road towards the Sunshine Motorway.'

Mike pushed John's mobile aside. 'Come, come, we can catch the bugger, he's heading towards Noosa.'

They ran to the hidden vehicle and leaped in, Mike in the driver's seat, and while John got on the police radio and gave them the details for a Be On the Look Out on the suspect, he started the car, revved it and sped off. But did not get far. The car slumped and ground as if it could not get any traction on the dirt. He got onto the tar road, but could not steer, and the vehicle swerved to the side of the road. Something was seriously wrong. 'A flat tyre?' called Adam, leaning over from the back seat. 'It feels awfully low.'

Mike stopped the car, opened the door and peered out. He could not see the tyres, so got out and stood on the road. He kicked the front tyre, ran to the other side of the car and kicked that one too.

'Am I right?'

'Two fucking slashed tyres!' screamed Mike. 'Look, someone has had a go at all of them with a bloody axe or something.'

The other two climbed out, examined the tyres which were torn and deflated.

'I can't believe it.'

The ute was still audible faintly as it revved up the Sunshine Motorway but must be five or more kilometres away already. They could also hear the SERT vehicle revving at maximum speed in pursuit, then reversing.

'What the fuck, SERT?'

The reply came back. 'The exit has been blocked. We had to go around the front.'

'He...? How? I told you he was onto us.'

'How could he have done it?'

'He was waiting for us,' said Mike. 'He knew we were coming. He probably spotted us when he arrived. And when we went up to the house, he doubled back and slashed the tyres. Fuck. Or he had an accomplice.'

'So, he was onto us, playing innocent and surprised.'

'He's military trained. I knew it. I knew it. He removed the evidence. What did I tell you?' said Mike. 'Is there any way we can get this car moving?'

Adam shook his head. 'We'll have to call for more assistance.'

'But first we get comms to put out a BOLO on that ute, get that fucker. Every police car on the Sunshine Coast will be after him after this.'

'No one gets him but me,' said Mike. 'Try and get onto that Polair chopper and we go after him now. He's mine. No one else's, okay? I'm going after this fucker. This bastard's mine.'

'That will take some time, Mike,' said John. 'By that time he'll be gone. SERT will get him.'

Summers got onto the phone interceptor at comms and gave them the details. Soon, John knew, this would be broadcast to all Sunshine Coast units. Comms would also advise the district duty officer and also Shelby and the duty inspector – and then the superintendent, assistant commissioner and the commissioner of police would know too. All hell would break loose. The media would be advised, and the public would be provided with details of the car as well. Summers would have his balls strung up for letting the suspect escape. Maybe John and Adam too.

Why had they gone along with this stupid idea? It was as if Mad Mike wanted the suspect to escape. He stared at Mike. Yes, exactly. He had created this scene, had given the suspect every opportunity, had wanted a drama, and if not a shootout, a high-speed car chase, choppers, media, the whole shebang.

∾

As soon as she was informed, Detective Senior Sergeant Shelby sent out a BOLO to look out for a blue-coloured 2009 Holden Colorado ute, registration number PSE143, being driven by Steven Atwell, a forty-year-old Caucasian male, 189cm tall, slim and fit build, with short brown hair, last seen heading North on the Sunshine Motorway. 'Suspect has escaped custody after being arrested for an offence code 101.'

Then she called Summers. 'So, you need a ride home, I hear?'

'No, we need a vehicle so we can go in pursuit.'

'You will do nothing of the sort. I've taken care of that. Tomorrow morning, I want to see you in my office so I can tear you another arsehole.'

'By tomorrow morning, he'll he long gone.'

'We'll have him in custody tonight. We don't want you shooting up the whole Sunshine Coast.'

Mike fumed. 'Detective Senior Sergeant Shelby, I want that man. He resisted arrest. He's a serial killer on the loose.'

'We'll nab him. I've spoken to comco who have contacted the duty inspector, police communications Brisbane for authority for the Polair helicopter to engage in the search for the suspect and vehicle.'

'I want him myself.'

'You're not going out tonight in pursuit, that clear? You fucked up, Detective Sergeant Summers. At least you didn't kill the suspect.'

'I took one shot at him.'

'Jesus. Just sit tight. We're sending a vehicle to repair your tyres.'

But as soon as he put down the phone, Mike stepped out of the vehicle. 'Come guys, let's see what evidence we can pick up from his house.'

Unlawfully, of course, thought John. He wanted out of here. His job was on the line because of this idiot Summers. 'You heard her, she said we were to stay put.'

But Mike was already heading back for the Queenslander. He turned on as many outside lights he could find and flooded the house with every light he could turn on inside too.

'What's the idea?' said John. 'Don't be stupid, Mike. Let forensics and intel do this when we get a search warrant.'

'Procedure, eh, Johnno?'

They made their way to the man cave and, seeing as it was still open, searched it thoroughly. But found nothing of interest. The box Carrie had told him about labelled 'Souvenirs' was not anywhere. 'He's taken it away,' said Mike. 'But what about those other clues? She said there were photos on the wall. His wife told me about some souvenirs. That's when I knew we had found our man. Anyone who does this is capable of slicing off little girls' ears.'

But there were no 'souvenirs'. He could see blank spaces on the wall where photos had been hanging. 'Damn.' He rummaged through boxes at the back of the room.

'Let's get scenes of crime and scientific section from Brisbane to do this,' said John. 'They'll search this whole place tooth and nail. Bound to be some blood from the dead girls here some-where. We can't do anything.'

'Just give me a minute here, guys. I need to think.'

John shrugged. They left him in the room for a few minutes. What was he doing in there? Tampering with evidence?

'Mike?' John called into the room. 'I can hear the rescue vehicle.'

Outside, a mechanic had arrived with two new tyres and bounced them off the back of his truck. Mike emerged from the man cave, and they walked down to where the mechanic was jacking up the car. They helped him replace the tyres. The mechanic wiped his brow as he packed his things away. 'Wasn't anyone guarding the vehicle? One of you should have been on the alert.'

'Fuck you,' said Mike. 'Should have. Should have. I should have shot the fucking cunt when I first had him, then we wouldn't be in this mess. But procedure always gets in the way.'

43

SAFE HOUSE, VERRIERDALE. TUESDAY
NIGHT

C arrie spent her first night in protective custody on her
own. Wasn't there supposed to be an armed guard at her
door? And though she had called him, there was no response
from Mike either. She had expected him to at least give her an
update and tell her the news, any news, but her phone was
silent. She spent the evening watching the news on television,
where amateur detectives and journalists speculated about the
now three victims of a local serial killer. She was in shock, still
could not believe her therapist was dead, and that each murder
had been linked to her husband.

And then the breaking news interrupted programmes on all
channels.

'The hunt for a man wanted over a suspected series of murders
in the Sunshine Coast area continues through the evening,
with the suspect fleeing in a blue-coloured 2009 Holden
Colorado ute, registration number PSE143. The suspect is a
Steven Atwell, a forty-year-old Caucasian male, 189cm tall, slim
and fit build, with short brown hair, and last seen heading
North on the Sunshine Motorway. The suspect has escaped

custody after being arrested for suspicion of murder. He has been on the run since just before 7pm, when he escaped arrest at his home in Peregian Beach. Do not approach, as he may be dangerous.'

A photo of her husband flashed up on the screen.

'Jesus. No.' The first thing she felt was shame. Everyone would know. Her family and friends would see this. Then fear. *So he had escaped the arrest. He had fled? Why?*

The news story then flashed back to the murder of the young women. 'Is this the Mutilator?'

A profile of Steve Atwell, building contractor, was sketched out in front of the whole world. Damn the media. They had already convicted him.

The third emotion that hit her was guilt. She had done this. She had gone to the police. She had set him up. She called Mike but there was no answer. Of course not, he was in hot pursuit of a suspect, a serial killer, a murderer. She heard the thudding of a helicopter flying over and stared out at the eucalypt forest surrounding her cottage. What could she do now? She paced up and down, holding her phone, waiting for news. Compulsively watched the TV.

Just before midnight, her phone rang, and she jumped to answer it. 'Mike?

'Honey?'

'Steve...?'

His voice was steady, but a little breathless. 'You okay?'

Should she pretend everything was fine? That his name was not splattered all over the news, that every patrol car was out looking for him?

'Where are you?'

'Where are you?' He sounded angry. 'Carrie, they arrested

me. I had to escape. There's been a ghastly mistake. Do you know anything about this?'

The silence was perhaps too long. She hoped he would take it as shock. 'Steve you're all over the news. They're looking for you.'

'Carrie, they said you gave evidence against me. Tell me that's not true.'

Her heart pounded. She wanted to lie, to say she knew nothing about it. Or else to blame her weakness. *The detective made me do it. I didn't want to...* She had to stand firm. She had done the right thing. 'Steve, I was so confused, when they told me what you did, I had to.'

'What did I do, Carrie? What did they tell you? It's all lies.'

'Steve, I can't do this. Go to the police. Give yourself up.'

'Mike Summers? That worm? He put you up to it?'

'Yes,' she said in a quiet voice.

'The bastard.'

She had always folded, Steve was strong-willed and she had always acquiesced. But not now. He was always the stronger personality and her opinions, thoughts, priorities had always withered before his. That is how their relationship worked – she gave. Gave in. Gave all. But not today. 'You're the bastard.'

'Carrie, that cop said you dobbed me in. You called him. How could you?'

'I was doing what was right. Not listening to your lies anymore.'

'Carrie, I'm coming to get you. We need to sort this out once and for all.'

Now she was scared. The TV was on in the other room, still warning the public about a dangerous serial killer on the loose. *Do not approach this man, call triple zero immediately.*

'What is there to sort out? The earring?'

'That bloody earring? You were obsessed with it. About a

supposed affair I was having. Is that what this is all about? You told him about a supposed affair? I have no idea how it got there.'

'I know you're guilty, Steve. Stop lying to me.'

'I'm not lying to you.'

You threatened my therapist with death and then you killed her in a most brutal way. She wanted to say that too. 'Where are you, Steve?'

'He tried to arrest me, that clown we saw on TV. Guns and all, so I did a little escape artist trick. Escaped so-called lawful custody.'

'Why, Steve? Resisted arrest?'

'I wasn't going to let that punk take me down.'

Her heart pounded. 'Where are you?'

'I can take care of myself, Carrie. But where are you, Carrie, is more the question. A safe house, he told me. Where is it?'

'I can't tell you that, Steve.'

'Safe from what? Safe from who? Me? You think I'm... a danger, a threat? Carrie, what bullshit have they being stuffing in your head?'

'Steve, what are you going to do? You can't run from the police. They'll get you. Give yourself up. They'll find you anyway.'

'That's what you think. I have a plan.'

'A plan?'

'But I need you, Carrie, tell me where you are.'

'Steve. Turn yourself in. This is crazy. I have to stay out of it, for your sake.'

'I see, I see.' Then a burst of anger and she heard him hitting the wall or something near him. 'Who are you, Carrie? Who is this person? You went behind my back. Why didn't you talk to me instead of snivelling off to the cops?'

Her fear turned to anger. 'I did talk to you, Steve and you got mad at me. Yelled. Like you're doing now. Steve, you brought it on yourself. You did this to yourself, all those sneaky things behind my back, the lies. You told me you were at the Noosa Sheraton and you weren't, you weren't at the Gold Coast hotel either. And I found all those girls' names on your computer, and blonde hair from a brunette supposed ex-girlfriend.'

A long pause. 'You broke into my computer? What the fuck? And I explained the hair...'

'All lies, Steve. What am I supposed to think when you come home stinking of perfume; condoms, blonde hair in your secret room? Fuck you, Steve. You lied to me, you gaslighted me, and I do, yes, I really do think you had something to do with the murdered girl. And the others.'

'Is this what they told you to say?'

'They didn't tell me to say anything. I have a mind of my own, Steve. I see what I see, and I see through your lies.'

'Carrie... we need to talk. About what really happened. If you really knew... it's not what you think at all.'

'So, tell me about Nora, Molly, Beatrice.'

'What the hell? So, you have been in my private files. Those are confidential.'

'I saw. They will confiscate your computer, they'll find out the truth, then I'll know. That's why I went to him... them, so I could find out the truth.'

'Carrie, you have no idea what you're messing with. You sent those goons after me?'

'They're the police, Steve. And to run away from them proves you're guilty. I went to them because I thought if there was a chance you're innocent, then they could clear your name. But now I know I was a fool.'

'Carrie, you believe me, don't you? You can't possibly think I killed those women...'

She hesitated a little too long.

'Fuck you,' he said. 'You do think that. And the therapist? Is that true?'

'What, Steve?'

'That's she's dead and I am the alleged killer? Is that true? She's really dead?'

'Yes, Steve. A supposed car accident in Yaroomba last night. She drove off the cliff.'

'So why are they blaming me for that? Are they insane?'

'Because she was found mutilated like the other girls. And because you threatened to kill her a few hours before her death.'

'What?'

'No use denying that one. They have evidence.'

'Who?'

'The police. Detective Senior Sergeant Shelby. So that's why you wanted her card. You didn't want to go to therapy; you wanted to silence her. All this deceit, Steve, makes me sick. She tried to tell the police, dialled triple zero, but it was too late. Steve, she managed to tell the police and apparently has a recording of your threats. So, you didn't silence her. Steve, Steve, who are you?'

'Carrie, you better tell me where you are. I'll come and find you. We need to talk. Straighten this whole bloody thing out.'

'Are you threatening me, Steve?'

'No, Carrie, I'm not bloody threatening you. You dobbed me in. You're threatening me. Did you say anything about the therapist to them? You must have, for them to connect her to me too.'

'I told them the truth, Steve.' She swallowed.

Then a long silence.

'I love you, Carrie. I love you.'

She was silent. Normally the reply would come automatically. *I love you too, Steve.* But she held her tongue. She could no longer be that person; the accommodating lie she had lived her whole married life.

'I gotta go, Carrie. Can't stay too long. Don't tell them I called. They've probably put a telephone interception on your phone. I'll call you later. Stay safe.'

'Where are you, Steve, please just hand yourself in.'

'I can't do that.'

He hung up.

～

She trembled as she made tea, staring at the forest. She suddenly felt terrified of Steve. Of what he could do. It was all true, so very real. What was she supposed to do here? Wait for instructions, Mike had said. She made sure the alarm was on, the doors bolted. She dialled Mike's number, but only got his answering machine. 'Call me please, Mike. I need to speak with you. What happened? Are you okay?' She was about to tell him that Steve had called but couldn't do it. Maybe if they had put an intercept on his phone, they'd know anyway. And they'd trace him and find him.

Doubts tore her apart. Even now when he had threatened her. Mike was right to have put her in this safe house. Steve would come after her. Why else would he insist on knowing where she was hiding? Now she had confronted her husband once and for all. She had spoken her truth. And it made her feel sick.

～

Detective Senior Sergeant Shelby stayed up most of the night, watching the progress – or lack of progress – of the search. Her hopes of finding the suspect swiftly shrank as the night wore on. And even though SERT were minutes behind him on the freeway when he bolted, even though the Polair chopper had been luckily in the area and had scoured the coast, and even though roadblocks had been set up, the suspect had simply vanished.

She thought now that he must have had forewarning, and that he had an accomplice. By early morning, the trail had gone completely cold. They had searched all night and found nothing.

The next morning, back at the station, when he finished his entries on the investigation running log and completed the complaint and search warrant for the house they had conducted an emergency search on, Mike, John and Adam sat through Detective Senior Sergeant Shelby's tirade. She glared at them. 'Now you will explain to me how three of my best armed detectives managed to let one unarmed man not only escape from their clutches but sabotage their vehicles under their very noses.' She told them that an axe had been found by the car in the woods and was being examined by forensics. And that the SERT vehicle's exit had been blocked by a large log that had been rolled onto the back road.

'How had he doubled back from the house to slash their tyres when he was being watched?' asked John.

'He had an accomplice,' said Mike. 'He was onto us.'

'He's military trained. Must have had some tip-off. A leak? Maybe his wife?'

'Not her, I swear,' said Mike.

'Where is she at the moment? Is she safe?'

'I organised police protection for her, as you requested,' said Summers. 'She's in a house of safety I organised.'

'I suggest you check up on her regularly.'

'Will do.'

'How is the search going?' asked John. 'We've heard nothing.'

Shelby shook her head. 'The news is not good. Roadblocks north have found no trace of the ute or the escapee anywhere on the roads north. Trouble is, the Sunshine Motorway fizzles out after a few kilometres into a maze-like multitude of suburbs – Noosaville, Noosa Junction, Noosa Heads, Noosa Waters, Sunshine Beach, Tewantin. He could have gone anywhere.'

'We should have gone after him last night. And if he was as cunning as he looked, he would dump the vehicle as soon as he could.'

Detective Senior Sergeant Shelby shook her head. 'No one gets away from us for long.' But she looked weary.

'Even if we find him, he'll get off on some technicality. Like the last lot.'

'Detective Sergeant Summers, now is probably a good time to caution you on protocol. Do you realise that your highly idiosyncratic ways have likely jeopardised this whole investigation – regarding three murder victims already?'

'How so?'

'Any magistrate will dismiss the earring as evidence because you obtained it under questionable means. Unlawfully. And why did I trust you to arrest the man at his house? We could have nabbed him at work, or on his way home. But to listen to you and foolishly let him set up a trap?'

'I'll stay out of it now, I promise,' Mike said.

She raised an eyebrow.

44

SAFE HOUSE, VERRIERDALE. WEDNESDAY, LATE MORNING

C arrie heard the car drive up the long dirt road to the house. She could not help go into an immediate panic. Was it wise to have put her here in a so-called 'safe house' so isolated that there was no possibility of escape? She dialled Mike's number and thankfully this time he answered immediately. 'Mike, there's a car driving up this road...'

'That's me, Carrie, don't worry, but good of you to be vigilant. I'm right there. I can open the gate with my pass, so don't worry, I'll be there in a second.'

She watched him drive in, park, and bound up the steps to the front door as she opened it.

'Thank God,' she said. 'I was getting a little worried at being so... isolated.'

'Are you okay?'

In response she gave him a bear hug. She was shaking.

'Sit down, Carrie, I'm afraid I have some bad news.'

She stood by the bar to mask her nervousness. 'G&T?'

He shook his head. She poured herself one. Swigged it down.

'We went to your home to apprehend him, arrested him, but then he escaped, fled in his ute.'

'I saw it all on TV, Mike. Any news? Have you found him?'

'He sabotaged our vehicle so we couldn't pursue him.'

'He... what? Steve?' She tried to imagine her husband resisting arrest, sabotaging a police car and going on the run, and couldn't. But then she could not imagine him as a military man either. 'Where is he now?'

'We were hoping you could help us with that. He escaped our clutches, but every police officer in the area is looking for him. We're concerned that he may try to contact you.'

'Why?' She downed the G&T. 'I'm safe here, aren't I?'

'Totally safe. But we think he may try to find you.'

She swallowed. But said nothing.

'He hasn't called you yet, has he?'

She bit her lip.

'Because, Carrie, if he does, we can try to find him that way.'

'Yes, of course.'

'Do you know where he might have gone? Any friends he could hide with?'

'He didn't have any friends. Only work colleagues. He's a loner.'

'Give us the names of anyone you think he might contact.'

She looked doubtful. His secretary? 'I don't know anyone he would contact. He had no friends that I know of. Only work colleagues. Maybe contact them. I don't even know where he went when he lived with me.'

Mike reached over and squeezed her hand. 'So sorry about this.'

His phone rang, and when he answered it, his eyes were wide, and he went pale.

'My God.'

'What is it?' mouthed Carrie. 'Is it about Steve? Have they found him? Caught him?'

Mike nodded his head. Spoke into his phone. 'Dead?' She clutched his hand, and he squeezed it. 'I'll be right there. Jesus.' He hung up.

'What is it?'

'Carrie, I'm sorry but more bad news. They found a body...'

She stifled a scream. 'No.'

The scene flashed before her eyes. Suicide. Steve no longer able to live with himself, had taken his life. And Carrie had done it. She had driven him to this. 'Where?'

'South of Mudjimba. Washed up on the shore.'

'Steve?'

He nodded. 'Yes, he has been busy. Victim number four. A young woman's body has washed up on the rocks. I gotta go.'

'Not Steve?' She was so relieved that she did not quite take it in.

He stood. 'If only I'd stopped him. Now he's onto his next victim.' He gave her a hug. 'Be safe, Carrie, okay? Don't let anyone in, call me if there's anything weird, and if he calls, let us know immediately. Try to get some information out of him. Okay? And don't worry, we'll get him.'

'Mike, please don't leave now.'

'I'll send a guard. And I'll be back soon, okay?'

She watched him drive off, lock the gate behind him and then disappear into the lush green of Verrierdale.

She felt desolate. Another victim. Four so far. Had he fled the police and then murdered someone overnight? It wasn't possible.

She locked the door, made sure the alarm was working, and kept the TV on, but the breaking news did not hit until an hour later. ABC and Channels 7 and 9 were all onto it.

She watched with a fascinated dread as the news slowly unfolded.

Detective Senior Sergeant Shelby and Detective Sergeant Summers fronted the media as usual, looking cool, and in control. 'The offender is on the run, so if you see this man, please dial triple zero immediately. Do not approach him: he is desperate, dangerous.'

A photo of her husband was flashed upon the screen. A smiling photo – Steve's Facebook profile image. By now everyone would know. Her family. Her friends. The shame. The pain. She saw messages on her phone from her sister and her mother, but she did not, could not, respond.

'Who was the victim?' asked a reporter.

'A woman similar in age and appearance to the others,' confirmed Mike. 'Blonde, in her late teens or early twenties, and mutilated hideously, but this time in a way that we can identity the killer. As if he wants us to know who he is now.'

He would not elaborate on the details, but the media had their ways and soon the facts were known. Carrie watched in numb horror.

'Apparently,' said the news announcer after the police statement and question time was over, 'a woman's name was carved into the victim's forehead. Not the name of the victim who has now been confirmed as Tara Cruickshank of Yandina, but another name. Was the killer mistaken about who he thought he had killed?'

A couple had found the body while picnicking on the point. A young man told his story: 'We found this body lying face up in the water. And we saw some letters had been carved into her forehead. M.A.N.D.Y. Mandy. We thought, this is the name of the poor murdered woman, so we reported it to the police that a girl called Mandy had been murdered, but we found out that her name is Tara.'

'We have evidence too,' added the journalist, 'that she was mutilated before she died.'

'No!' Carrie could not bear it. She turned off the TV. So, she had been living with a serial killer for ten years and did not know it until now. Not just a serial killer, but a depraved man who carved his ex-girlfriend's name into an innocent girl's forehead. And if these journalists were to be believed, who mutilated his victims while they were still alive. What sort of sick man was he, and how come she had no clue about his sick behaviour for the last ten years?

Face the truth finally, Carrie, she told herself. *He's a revolting, obsessed man.* Why had he married her? Maybe a cover? Or he was trying to live a normal life, but his demons took over? He was so detached and unemotional, such a loner, she should have seen the signs.

The phone rang. She was flooded with gratitude. 'Mike, please–' she began, then saw that the call was from an unknown number.

'Carrie?'

'Steve?'

'Why do you keep thinking I'm Mike? You mean that bastard cop? What's going on? Does he have a trace on your phone?'

She could not answer. Pure panic hit her. She was talking to a serial killer who had obsessed about his ex-girlfriend to the extent that he could carve her initials on a girl he had just raped and murdered.

'I'm coming over, okay. Is there anyone with you?'

'You don't know where I am, Steve.'

'I do. I have traced your phone.'

Her chest tightened. 'Don't come, please. Yes, there are people here, police guards, you can't come here.'

'I need to speak with you, Carrie.'

But then she remembered she had to try to keep him on the

line and get as much information out of him as she could. 'Where are you, Steve?'

'Carrie, I know they are probably tracing this call, but I just wanted to say I'm all right, I love you, and just want to know that you're okay.'

'I'm shocked. I can't take it in, Steve. I don't know you. Who are you?'

'It will all be fine, I'll be fine, so please don't worry. Just don't believe anything they say. I'm coming for you.' And he was gone.

'Steve?'

Detective Senior Sergeant Shelby turned to Mike right after his media interview. 'When are you going to keep your mouth shut? Since when are you the judge? You can't make statements like that to the media. If we ever catch this bastard, then the defence will have a field day.'

Summers shrugged. 'I just want him caught. Public outrage will maybe help find him. Someone is sure to spot him. How did the forensics do, by the way? Did they get any evidence from his house? His computer was gone, but there must have been something in his man cave.'

'Nothing. It was all removed. But we found an earring. No, not the one Carrie brought to us, another one.'

'Another earring?'

'And it looks as if it belongs to one of the other victims. We've sent it for DNA testing so we'll know sooner or later.'

'I told you we had to move on this one, didn't I tell you last night? But no, you won't listen.'

'Detective Sergeant Summers, I'm warning you. A little reminder about insubordination? Incorrect procedure? You're the one who let him go. No more talking to the bloody media. Are you keeping an eye on his wife?'

'Yes, but nothing so far. He's too busy on the rampage, murdering girls as he goes.'

'Just to correct your media rave, Mike, that murder was committed days ago, just because we found the body now...'

'I wanted to press the advantage,' said Mike. 'Show the public the urgency to catch this killer on the loose. How many more will he kill?'

'Get out of here and start doing your job.'

'He's laughing at us now. On his way to his next killing.'

'He can't hide forever. We've never lost a man yet.'

45

SAFE HOUSE, VERRIERDALE. THURSDAY EVENING

Carrie jumped as her phone rang. She checked the number and saw with relief that it was Mike. 'Did he call?'

She hesitated. Then, 'Yes. I tried to keep him on the line, but he said he knew he was being monitored and he hung up before I could get any information out of him.'

'I guess he's using disposable mobile phones too. He's quite the operator, your husband. Did you know he was a military spy, in covert operations?'

'Covert operations? I had no idea of his other life until I went into his studio. I feel so stupid. Mike, I'm scared now.'

'What did he say to you?'

'That he's coming to get me.'

'Shit. Don't worry, Carrie, we're onto it. He can't trace you there. We are organising twenty-four-seven guards for you. And I'm on my way. Don't worry, we'll catch him. And then he will never bother you again. We found more evidence in his man cave that will convict him. And relax, you're in a fortress. I'll be there as soon as I can get out, okay?'

'Thanks, Mike. Why didn't you tell me the latest victim had his ex-girlfriend's name carved into her head?'

'Sorry, Carrie, it is awful, I didn't know at the time. He's a sick man, trying to... I don't know... get revenge on past girlfriends, or something. But it will soon be over. Trust me.'

'Thanks, Mike.'

She combed through her past life with Steve trying to remember if there had been any signs of his double life. Come to think of it, now it was obvious. He was never home, always distant to her, he had always been secretive, never sharing anything of his past – or present – life with her.

The evening was too quiet. Verrierdale, or at least the eighty or so acre property where she was housed, had no traffic, no hustle and bustle, just wind in the pines, cicadas in the distance, the swish of the ocean far away. An idyllic paradise. But she felt trapped. She watched the sun slowly go golden over the horizon of eucalypts, pulled the blinds down in every room, and poured herself another drink.

She could not just sit here. If Steve said he was coming for her, what was she supposed to do? She was a sitting duck. She poked around the back of the cottage, looking for a contingency plan. If he found her, broke through the defences, which was, she realised, quite likely if he had been a military man with covert operational experience, she would need a place to hide, or a back exit.

She put her head in the bedroom closet. Could she hide here? She shone her phone light into the dark space. And did a double take. Behind the hangers at the back of the closet was a door. It was small, wooden, and at ground level, which meant that it must lead outside or to a cellar. Sure enough, when she peered out of the bedroom window, she saw that the cottage was larger than she had thought, and an extension jutted out and underground behind the bedroom. If this was a cellar, it would be somewhere to hide. If it was a back entrance or exit, she could sneak out here if needed and get away in her car.

She tried the door, but it was, of course, locked. She played her flashlight on the walls of the closet and saw a key hanging on a nail. She smiled. Bingo.

She turned the key in the lock, and it opened the door into a dark musty space. Wooden steps leading down into what must be a cellar sent up a stuffy draught of stale air.

She flicked on a light switch on the side of the panel.

Her phone rang. If it was Mike, she would have asked him what the hell was going on here. But it was an unknown number.

'Hello?'

It was Steve. 'Carrie! I'm coming to get you, okay?'

She said nothing.

'I know where you are, Carrie. I traced your phone. Now I'm on my way. If there is an alarm system, please disable it. And for God's sake, don't tell the cops I'm coming.'

He hung up.

Shit.

She called Mike.

'Carrie?'

'Mike, please come quickly. Steve called. He's coming to get me, he said. He says he knows where I am. He traced my call.'

'Stay put. I'll be right over.'

'Mike, I'm scared.'

'I'll be there in fifteen minutes. Don't worry. You're safe. Turn the lights off. Hide under the bed.'

'Okay.'

She turned off the main light in the bedroom and peered into the cellar. She shut the closet door behind her, climbed down the steps and shut the cellar door behind her too. The light was dim, so she used her phone as a flashlight, and took the steps slowly. She felt claustrophobic. The cellar was windowless, and contained, as cellars do, a stash of wine, old crates, and a bench with some knives, and other tools. The place smelled vile, damp and acrid. She grabbed a large carving knife, and clutched it in her hand, just to feel safer. Kept her phone ready.

She sat on a wooden bench. Waited.

She turned off the cellar light, but it was so creepy, she turned it on again. She had to save her phone battery too, so turned off the flashlight. Listened for any sounds of cars, intruders, but heard nothing. The cellar was insulated.

On the bench beside her was a sweater. She played her light into it. And jumped in fright. A McDonald's logo was emblazoned on the front and the words McDonald's University above the logo. She picked it up and held it up to the light. Surely there was not another hoodie like her husband's? She picked up the sleeve. Here was the turmeric stain he had left on it a few months ago, some car oil drips on the back.

This was Steve's sweater.

But what it was doing here she had no idea.

She smelled the sweater. A faint aroma of Steve, yes but then another foreign yet familiar smell.

This was the sweater both Shelby and that hippy witness had said the man who threatened Julienne and had pushed her car over the edge of the cliff was wearing. It had to be evidence. Perhaps this is where the police had gathered evidence of Steve's crimes.

This cellar must be a holding place for evidence. Strange that Mike had not told her they had found the sweater. But here it was.

At the back of the cellar, she spied another room with a small doorway, open. Maybe this was an exit, a getaway escape route if she was trapped. That would be good. If Steve got here, and managed to find her hidey hole, she had to have an exit plan.

But it was not a way out. It was another sealed room. A darker, dingier, low-ceilinged underground part of the cellar that was dank and humid and stank of mould. She shone her phone light into the musty room, found a switch and flooded the room with flickering neon light.

In the centre of the room was a stone table, with long candles with melted wax stuck onto the surface and dripping off like icicles. On the table was an arrangement of objects, in a circle, some hung on candle stands. She pulled back in fright.

These objects looked like blackened, shrivelled pieces of jerky.

On the wall behind, photos. Of dead bodies. Of women tied to chairs. Of bloodied, dismembered corpses.

A part of her brain was still playing that narrative: *it's an evidence room, the police have gathered all this evidence.* Because of the hoodie she had found, she still had it in her mind that this was a room where they kept evidence. Here were all the articles to prove atrocities had been committed. Here were the missing parts of the women murdered. All of them. And more.

But her intuition was telling her something different. She felt like retching. But had to stay calm. This could not be evidence. The police did not have this evidence. What had Mike said? *If we find the ear, we find the killer.*

On the altar, for that is what it looked like, was a dried ear. What looked like lips. And was that piece of what looked like coral a slice of brain? She was shaking too much to take it in. She peered at the photos on the wall. Hideous photos. Each photo was labelled. MARY. TARA. CINDY. JULIENNE.

She stumbled backwards when the truth finally hit her. *It's his house. The murderer's house. Or Steve's secret den. It wasn't in his man cave at home. It was here. But how? Why?*

She wanted out of the room, but something drove her further in. There was more. At the very back of the cellar came a vile stench and she saw a chair, surrounded with what looked like dried bloodstains. Tied rope. A pot with urine, faeces, vomit. A bloodied dress hanging up in the corner. Handcuffs dangling on the back of the chair.

She clutched the knife. Shone her flashlight on the chair. The blood was sticky, not yet fully dry. The cellar was damp, mouldy, and nothing would dry here, but this looked recent. Very recent.

The cellar door banged. The wind? She did not want to be trapped in here. She imagined being unable to get out, the door only able to open from the outside. She turned back, reached the cellar door and was pushed violently back into the small cellar, and fell hard on the floor. A shadow stood above her. A boot kicked at her hand and the knife went flying. Another kick and her mobile phone was spinning on the other side of the room. The person flipped off the light switch and the cellar was plunged into darkness. Then she felt his arm around her neck, his thumbs pressing into her windpipe. Pushing her back into the room and down onto the chair. She felt the handcuffs click onto her wrists.

'Please, Steve?'

'So, you have found out my little secret.' The voice was a hoarse whisper. Didn't sound like Steve at all. A stranger. But he had been a stranger to her all these years.

'You found me. Steve, please let's get out of here. Please.'

'You bitch. Women are all the same. Young. Old. Curiosity killed the cat. Always. It's in your nature to pry. Couldn't leave it alone, could you?'

'Steve? Please speak in your normal voice. Why the–' A blindfold was roughly tied over her face. 'Steve, I can't breathe, please.'

'So, you found my place. You had to look, didn't you, you had to snoop, pry. I told you not to look.'

'You did? You said you were coming to tell me something. This? I knew, Steve. And it's okay. I won't tell.' She was jabbering, in fear for her life. What was she saying? That the only way she could survive this was to offer to be a co-conspirator with him. She had heard of women who procured young girls for their husbands' perverse tastes. Anything but death. Could she talk her way out of this? He was going to kill her, that was certain, unless...

'Steve, I'm your wife. I'm on your side. Whatever you have done, it's okay. I'll stick by you. For better or for worse. Please take off the blindfold. I can't breathe.'

'You know what I'm going to do to you? Maybe it would be better to have the blindfold on. You have this coming to you... But have it your way.'

He yanked off the blindfold. It took her eyes a while to adjust, and in the dim light she saw who this man was.

'Mike?'

He grinned. 'Sorry about the dramatic entry. I wanted you to think it was Steve.'

She cried with relief. 'Mike! You scared me. Why?'

'Because I extracted a confession out of you. You work with Steve. You're on his side?'

'No. Now can you unlock these handcuffs?'

'You just said that you would work with him.'

'No, Mike, please, I was under duress, I thought he was going to kill me. Please, Mike, no games. I'm stunned. Have you seen this? Did you know this was here?'

He did not look surprised at all. Did not say, 'My God, we've found the killer's lair.' In fact, he looked as if he was familiar with the place; pulled up a chair without even looking to see where it was. Flipped on the light switch as if he knew exactly where it was too.

'I told you to stay put in the cottage. You think I can let you go now? Now you've seen this.'

'Mike?'

He slapped her face. And she reeled.

'You bitch.'

The shock woke her up to a new reality. But it took a while to recalibrate. 'This is your house? This is your cellar.'

'My little safe house. Home away from home.'

'It's not a police safe house?'

'I had to keep an eye on you. I didn't send you to a safe house. I sent you to my little den. You see, I have plans for you.'

'Mike, what are you saying?'

'You're a smart girl, you work it out.' He stomped on the phone with his foot. 'No need to call the police now – I'm here.'

'You're...?' She gestured to the altar.

Mike smiled. 'Me.' He pointed all around him. 'My doing. All of it. What – you're shocked?'

'I don't understand. You're the serial killer? How did Steve get involved? Are you both involved?'

'The first girl I took was years ago. It was always easy to dump them in the ocean – leaves no traces. But I needed a cover, a fall guy, and being a good cop, I knew how evidence worked, what detectives looked for at a crime scene, so I began to construct the scenes carefully. I decided to drop off my cargo in a stolen vehicle each time, so no one could trace me. After I needed to dump Mary, I scouted around Noosa and found a ute in a hotel parking lot that had been left unlocked. The back was full of tradie materials, and I saw my chance – I hotwired it late at night, and took it, loaded my cargo, and dumped her in the ocean. Perfect for a drop-off. I returned it in the early morning, and no one even knew I had taken it. Whoever that ute belonged to, if the cops found it, there would be forensic evidence, blood–'

'Steve's ute?'

'Yup. And I found a handy sweater he had left in the front seat, so I took it, and wore it every time I took a girl. So, if there were any witnesses, it would point to him and his ute.'

'The McDonald's University shirt.' She pointed to the main part of the cellar where she had found the sweater.

'Yup.'

'And the earring? Did you plant that too?'

'No, the earring was the problem– quite fortuitous you found it – because I had misplaced it, couldn't figure out where it had gone. It had my prints all over it. I was worried.' He picked up the severed ear off the altar. 'After all, I did this so I could keep the earring as a memento, and to my dismay, when I got home, I had lost the earring. If anyone found it, it would lead straight to me. Then you showed up at the station talking about an earring, I thought, *brilliant, here's my plan. Get the earring back and wipe it clean, blame Steve.*'

'You did that? Not Steve?'

'You gave me the idea to frame him, to set him up. But I had to get the earring from you and make sure I was not traceable first.'

'So, Steve was… is… innocent?'

'He was the perfect patsy and you played right into my hands. Innocent? I don't think so. The bastard was probably having an affair, and this helped my set-up so well. I used a ute like his every time I picked up and dropped off a lady.'

'And Julienne? Did you kill her too? After Steve threatened her?'

He laughed. 'It was me. I made the phone call, pretending to be your husband. She didn't know him, so she had no clue it was not his voice.'

'It was you? And you murdered Julienne?'

'She had an accident.' He picked up a grey coral-looking dome and thrust it in her face. 'She had a very clever mind, that woman.'

She stared. 'You cut out her brain? Why? And those other women?'

He smiled, folded his arms. 'Yes.' Showed her each body part, naming the victims. Ear? Mary Stevens. Clitoris? Cindy Liptrot. Tongue? Tara Cruickshank. Brain? Julienne Van Tonder. And Carrie Atwell? You choose.'

She wanted to scream but threw up instead.

'Disgusting. We have to keep you clean.' He wiped her mouth with a cloth.

'So, Steve had nothing to do with these deaths?'

'Nothing. But all evidence points to him. I even planted Tara's earring in his man cave, so when forensics finds it, he will not stand a chance. He's guilty.'

'Poor Steve. He was telling the truth. Then why did he resist arrest?'

Mike laughed. 'I couldn't have asked for anything better. I did provoke him. I hoped he would do something stupid, and he did. Now the whole goddamn Australian police force is after him, and when he's found, he'll be blamed for the latest gruesome murder, if he is not shot and killed before that can happen. I made sure everyone thinks he's armed and dangerous.'

'What latest gruesome murder?' she said, dry-mouthed.

'His mutilated wife's body will be found washed up on Coolum Beach rocks. Poor woman. Tortured, disfigured while still alive, a revenge killing for dobbing him in. She knew too much. He nabbed her before she could get to the safe house organised for her in Noosa and killed her.'

'You planned this? You put me here instead of a safe house? I thought that was weird. No guards at the door.'

He nodded. 'Meanwhile, the Mutilator sets up shop some-where else, continues his hobby and Steve pays for his crimes.'

'I was so wrong,' she said quietly.

'I wouldn't get teary over poor Steve,' he said. 'From what I hear, he did some interesting things in the war. Cutting off heads, fists? Didn't you tell me that? You see, Carrie, all men are alike, underneath, no matter how they try to hide it from others or deny it to themselves. Testosterone. And an ache to rape, to kill, to penetrate, to fuck, to be strong. Sex is like murder, haven't you figured that out yet, dear Carrie? Thrusting a hard instru-ment into a woman's flesh? Making her scream in pain? That's what men like, do, live for.'

'Not all men.'

'All men.'

'I love Steve.'

'Silly girl. I enjoyed playing with you, but now I want you to learn another lesson, if you want to be a detective, a private investigator, if you want to know what happened to those girls, I'll show you how it felt to be them. What I did to them. You want to know how I cut them up while they were still alive? How I got every ounce of pain out of them? It's quite an art.'

He took up the sharp blade from the table. 'We're going to have such fun.'

'Please...'

'Too long women have been torturing men, teasing them, playing them. Now which body part of yours do you think I should keep? Lips? What is the weapon you use against us men the most?'

She shrank back. 'I don't use weapons. I'm not in a war with men.'

'Come on! The hashtag MeToo movement? You women signed petitions, you hounded men for being men, being natural. Following their God-given impulses. Driven by those cock-teasing actresses. You don't blame a spider for catching a fly, especially if the fly flaunts itself before the spider.'

'I'm not a fly.'

He raised the knife, stood over her and she shrank back, closed her eyes. This was it. Her death. Without warning, he fell heavily on her, and she was covered with warm blood. The screams coming from her mouth were involuntary. 'Get off me!! Get off me!'

When she woke, she could not figure out where she was. She looked up, and Steve's face loomed over her.

'Carrie?'

'Steve?' A gentle hand on her forehead. 'What happened?

'You fainted.'

'Where am I?'

'In a safe house. A real safe house this time.'

'Where?' She was in a bed, propped up by soft pillows, in a room with French windows overlooking a valley. A distant lake sparkled in the sunlight, and beyond that, large dunes and the ocean. 'How did I get here?'

'I rescued you from that hellhole. This is where I've been holing up for the last few days. It belongs to a friend of mine, Simon Papadopoulos.'

'Do I know him? You've never mentioned him.'

'Buddies from the army. We look out for each other.'

'Where's Mike?' She looked out at her surroundings. 'I don't understand. I thought he attacked me. But I felt no pain. I just must have blacked out.'

'You're safe, Carrie. I got him before he could do anything.'

She stared at the room. 'I remember him on top of me, me falling into black. Did I pass out? I thought I was dead.'

'Sorry, I didn't mean for him to fall on top of you when I hit him. I wasn't thinking, but I had to act fast. Thank God the tracking device I installed on your phone still worked. I came as soon as I could, when I figured out what he was up to.'

'You realised that Mike was the serial killer? You knew? How?'

'Not at first. But I tracked him and realised something was not right. I'm sorry – I hit him a little too hard.'

'Is he dead?'

'He's unconscious. He might wake up with a bit of a headache.'

'Where is he?'

'I left him in that cellar, handcuffed to his chair of torture.'

'Steve?' She reached up her hand and he took it.

'You all right?'

'I think so.'

'You said you loved me.'

She frowned. 'You heard that? You were there?'

'I had to creep in slowly, make sure I had the element of surprise. That cellar door creaked so I had to be ever so slow. And I had to record his confession.' He held up his phone. Smiled.

'You have all that recorded? All that nightmare stuff about how he killed those women, and set you up?'

'I couldn't believe my luck that he wanted to brag about how he committed those murders, and how he framed me. I recorded the whole thing. I've already sent the audio file to Detective Senior Sergeant Shelby.'

'Oh Steve, I still can't believe it, that it was Mike, Detective Sergeant Summers in charge of the investigation who committed the crimes. Is it really true, that he killed all those people?'

He nodded. 'And to think he faced the media each time, wrote up all the reports, led the investigation. A perfect cover.'

'And to think I gave him all that information, I gave him Julienne's card, and he... Poor Julienne. I led him to her.'

'Don't blame yourself, Carrie.'

'I do though. I doubted you. I thought you were the killer. He convinced me. Even Julienne thought it was you.'

'You were right to doubt me. Here, I made you some sugary, milky, warm tea. Drink it. Can you sit up?'

'I'm fine.' But she felt dizzy when he propped her up and helped her drink. Her hands were chafed from the handcuffs. 'I don't understand. Why he did he take me right to his house, instead of a safe house?'

'It's not his house. It's some place he bought years ago to play his terrible games. He lives in Coolum in an apartment. I think his plan was to kill you, dump your body and plant evidence in my studio. When I figured what his game was, I put a trace on your phone so I could find out where he hid you. You were supposed to go to a place of safety in Noosa but never arrived. They were already thinking I'd kidnapped you.'

'When did you know about Mike?'

'I knew something was up, but I was not sure until the very end. Until I got into that cellar and found him confessing to you.'

'So now what?'

'I had to call the cops. That Detective Shelby. I must give myself up. They will have to arrest me.'

'But you're innocent.'

'I escaped lawful custody, remember?'

'Why did you run for it, Steve, if you were innocent?'

'I didn't trust that Mike guy from the beginning. He was looking for a chance to bump me off. That's when I figured it out. I was slowly trying to work out what was going on. I had a tail on me. When you found the earring in my ute, I began to be very suspicious. But I couldn't say anything until I had figured it out. Someone was ghosting me, paralleling me.'

'How did you escape? They said they had the house surrounded.'

He grinned. 'Simon and a few military buddies helped me out there. We do each other favours when needed. A little car sabotage and misdirection was all it took. Child's play for someone who learned combat in the streets of Kabul.'

'Steve, will they put you in jail?'

'Only until they figure it all out. They have evidence now. So now we wait.'

She sipped her tea. Watched the clouds gathering outside. 'I guess we're somewhere near Mount Tinbeerwah?'

'You make a good detective,' he said. 'Yup. Simon's place. Has a few escape routes, and hidey-holes. But you're not supposed to know where we are. You can't tell anyone.'

Something was still niggling her. It still did not all add up, none of it. 'Steve, were you having an affair? I mean, I understand now how the earring got into your car. But the perfume, the condoms, Mandy, those names on your computer. I thought...'

Steve shook his head. 'I know what you thought. But I was telling you the truth. No affair.'

'But those girls' names in your computer? And Mandy I discovered was a brunette. You were lying to me.'

'I understand what you must've thought,' he said. 'Yes, she was brunette, still is, but that week she dyed her hair blonde for a theatre production, and that's why she asked me to take a snippet, because it would be the only time she would be blonde. Why didn't you just ask me that?'

'I thought...'

295

'You thought I was lying, and I was covering up something but not that.'

'What then?'

'It's a long story. Are you ready for all that? For my secret life?'

'I was right then. You do have a secret life.'

'But not the secret life you thought I had. I have to keep that life a secret. Just to protect you.'

'But not an affair?'

'No.'

'Not a secret serial killer?' she said. 'I must say, I found that the most impossible thing of all to believe, even when all the evidence pointed towards you. Go on, tell me.'

'I was in the military as you know, years back.'

'It's a no-go area. You never talk about it.'

'Because I wasn't in a combative role. I was special ops. Intelligence. And when I left, unfortunately that sort of thing doesn't stop. I was recruited to continue doing some spying.'

'What kind of spying are you talking about, Steve?'

'Politics. Corruption. Foreign interference.'

'That's vague.'

'It has to be. But just so you know, some of those late evenings and hotel stays were meetings with other intelligence people. And one of them was heavy on the perfume. I hated lying to you, but these meetings couldn't be compromised.'

'And the girls on the computer – Beatrice? Molly? Nora? More ex-girlfriends? Or current ones?'

'They're code names of operations.'

'Then why girls' names?'

'I had to have code names. If anyone did break into my computer, they'd think... porn, or ex-girlfriends. Better than discovering what they really were.'

'Like your password. Mandy.'

'Exactly. Those files were dummy files to tempt anyone who tried to get into my computer. But it was part of the ruse. Some people would love to get their hands on those files and that information. I do have some enemies. That's why I had to clean out the house when I knew they were coming for me. I didn't want cops seeing anything in there.'

She nodded. 'I find this hard to believe.'

He stroked her hair. 'When I found you in the studio, I thought it was some enemy trying to get the files. Sorry – when you went snooping, I thought it was them.'

'And the photos of the severed head? The man with a cut-off hand?'

'So many questions, Carrie. I was a whistle-blower and was exposing some of the atrocities I witnessed in Afghanistan by our troops. I was not a very popular boy because of that.'

'That was evidence of atrocities?'

He nodded. 'Part of a sting operation. I had to embed myself with them to get evidence. Which I got. But not everyone liked me as you can imagine. Also, because of my background I could not help noticing you and Mike were in communication. His number on your phone. Always calling you. I wondered what he was up to. I saw you together at lunch at Coolum, and at the Surf Club in Mooloolaba. You were always phoning him, so I put a trace on your phone.'

'You spied on me? I felt someone was always watching me.'

'It did look very suspicious. Why was he not using proper police procedure? As if he had something to hide. And now we know. He had to get the earring before the other police did.'

Steve's phone rang, and he looked at the screen. 'I better take this call.' He walked out of the room and into the house. She heard his voice echoing through the corridors. 'No, Simon, it won't be compromised...'

Carrie was finding it difficult to adjust to her husband as a spy, involved in covert operations. He had been gaslighting her all this time, yes, but for different reasons. She climbed out of bed, walked unsteadily to the window and breathed in the fresh air blowing in over the valley. On the horizon, black clouds were amassing, rolling in over the ocean. She could smell the rain coming. Two magpies pecked at a green lawn outside the window, and lorikeets screamed as they flew over the house at jet speed. She stared out at the magnificent view of Noosa on her left, the Noosa River mouth directly ahead, and the ninety-mile beach on her right. Below her gleamed waterways and lakes. She could make out Lake Weyba to the right where they lived, though the suburbs were invisible in all that greenery.

Steve was back. He placed his arms on her shoulders. 'Feeling a little better? Take it easy. You're still in shock.'

'What's happened?'

'Shit's about to hit the fan. The police have Mike, and his little man cave full of the evidence of his atrocities. They also received my audio recording. Detective Shelby wants me to hand myself in. They want to arrest me. And they want to know where you are. You're a missing person, since you didn't arrive at the designated safe house... So, we'd better take you home. We can't compromise this location. Simon says he will do that. Is that okay? The police will want to question you, but not until you're recovered.'

'What about you?'

'I'm going to drive to the Maroochydore Police Station and hand myself in. They're waiting for me.'

'Steve, will you be all right?'

'I will. But what about you? Can you do this?'

'I'll be all right.'

'Just don't reveal this location. We have to keep it safe.'

'I can do that.'

'There will be cops at our home, but I told them you need some time to recover.'

She hugged him. 'Steve, I do love you.'

He squeezed her tight. 'I love you too, Carrie. And don't worry. I'll soon be free. All the evidence is there. One last thing I have to say...'

'Any more secrets?'

'No. What this did was make me realise something. I was spending too much time away, enclosed in myself. Neglecting you. I meant that, when I said I wanted to change. I've been a rotten companion, lover, husband, friend.'

'No, you haven't.'

'The nature of my intelligence work is secretive, but it was no excuse for shutting you out. I'm so sorry. I want to make it up to you.'

A vehicle pulled up outside the house. 'That will be Simon,' he said, waving to a red-haired, bearded man in the driver's seat of a Toyota Land Cruiser. 'He'll look after you. Trust me. Trust him. I owe this man my life.'

She squeezed his hand.

'I'm sorry, Carrie, I lied to you about my covert job. I was stupid. Can we start again?'

'I may have to bail you out of jail, but yes.'

He laughed. 'Before Christmas, please, I have some presents I want to give you in person.'

'Me too.'

'As long as they are not earrings!'

'Not earrings.' He gave her a hug. 'It's going to be all right. We'll be all right.'

'Maybe it will be a good Christmas after all.'

THE END